## "Last night you told me you never intended to stay here."

Ellie kept her eyes on the far side of the lake, where a heron stalked in the shallows. "I know I said I'd trust you, Bram, but I don't know what to think. You're like two different people sometimes—sweet and tender one minute, and then harsh and almost frightening other times."

"*Ja*, I know, and I'm sorry." Bram paused, his own eyes on the motionless heron. The bird was nearly invisible in the shadow of the trees, his gray-blue coloring a shadow within a shadow. Living undercover. How did a man stop living a lie?

"I want to stay, Ellie. But I don't know if I'll be able to." He took her hand in his, and she looked at him.

"Even if you stay, we can never be more than friends." Her voice was soft, almost a whisper, her blue eyes reflecting the water.

"Aren't we already more than friends, Ellie?"

## JAN DREXLER

A recent graduate from Homeschool Mom-hood, Jan Drexler devotes her time to the voices in her head who have been clamoring for attention during the past few decades. Instead of declining Latin nouns and reviewing rhetorical devices, her days are now spent at the computer, where she gives her characters free rein.

She lives in the Black Hills of South Dakota with her husband of thirty years, their four adult children, an extremely furry Husky, and Maggie, the cat who thinks she's a dog. If she isn't sitting at her computer living the lives of her characters, she's probably hiking in the Hills or the Badlands, enjoying the spectacular scenery.

# The Prodigal Son Returns

## JAN DREXLER

HARLEQUIN® LOVE INSPIRED® HISTORICAL

Recycling programs
for this product may
not exist in your area.

™ LOVE INSPIRED BOOKS

ISBN-13: 978-0-373-82966-8

THE PRODIGAL SON RETURNS

www.LoveInspiredBooks.com

**Printed in U.S.A.**

He shall cover thee with his feathers,
and under his wings shalt thou trust:
his truth shall be thy shield and buckler.
—*Psalms* 91:4

To the storytellers in my life, especially
my grandmother, Ethel Sherck Tomlonson Rupel,
and my parents, John and Veva Tomlonson.

To my dear husband and children,
who never stop believing in me.

And to the ladies of Seekerville.net. Without you,
I'd still be typing away, alone in my writer cave.

Soli Deo Gloria

# Chapter One

*LaGrange County, Indiana*
*May 1936*

A high-pitched scream forced Bram Lapp's feet into a run even before his mind could identify the source. He raced up the dusty farm lane between a garden and a plain white house at the top of the sloping yard, and when the next scream sounded, ending in a terrified child's voice yelling, *"Ne, ne!"*, adrenaline rushed in, pushing him faster. He knew that sound all too well—a child was in danger, terrified. Grim possibilities flashed through his mind.

Rounding the corner of the barn, Bram's slick leather soles skidded sideways in the gravel. His feet found purchase, and he focused on the little girl crouched in front of him. A chicken flapped at the end of her outstretched arm, but her eyes were on the four draft horses looming over her. He dived toward her, letting his momentum carry him beyond the horses. Grabbing the girl in his arms, he rolled them both past the dinner-plate-size hooves and slid to a halt at the edge of the grassy backyard.

Bram shoved the child off his chest onto the grass, spitting feathers from his mouth, trying to see past the squawking red hen in his face. Where was she hurt? She screamed even louder as he wrenched the protesting chicken out of her hands and tossed it behind him.

Wide brown eyes cut from the horses to his face and then back again, her screams turning to ragged crying. She tried to pull away, but he kept her close with a firm grip on her arm. If she was hurt, or bleeding, the worst thing she could do would be to run and hide somewhere. He'd seen enough of that with kids on the Chicago streets.

He brushed at the feathers caught in her disheveled brown braids. She no longer looked like a copy of the chicken that still scolded him from a distance, but the tears running down her face clenched at his stomach. He turned her to one side and then the other. No blood that he could see. She ignored his touch; her eyes were fixed on the horses behind his shoulder.

The rattle of the harness told him the horses were moving. Her eyes widened even more as she tried to pull out of his grasp, sucking in a deep breath. Before she could let loose with another scream that might panic the horses further, Bram did the only thing he could think of to prevent it. He clapped his hand over the girl's mouth.

"What are you doing?"

The fury in the young woman's voice registered at the same time as the pain in his hand as the little girl sank her teeth into him. He bit back a curse and released her. With a flurry of skirts, a slim Amish woman descended on them from nowhere and snatched the girl up in her arms. Holding the child close, she fixed her blue eyes on Bram, flashing a warning as she watched him scramble to his feet.

He'd rather face the wrong end of a tommy gun than this... *Wildcat* seemed to be the only word for her.

A wildcat who had no business being angry with him.

His answer barked out in *Deitsch* before he thought about it. "I was just saving that girl from being trampled by these horses, that's all. What did you think I was doing?"

Was that a smile that twitched at the corners of her mouth?

"Those horses?"

Bram turned to look at the draft horses and noticed for the first time they were tied to a hitching rail. The near horse flicked a lazy ear at a fly, a movement that did nothing to quell his rising irritation. He spun back to the young woman and the little girl, who stared at him with one finger in her mouth.

"*Ja,* those horses. No matter how docile they seem, she could be hurt playing around them like that. She was screaming so loudly I assumed she *had* been."

The woman caught the edge of her lower lip between her teeth and hitched the little girl around to her hip. The self-righteous soothing of Bram's prickled temper stopped short at her nod.

"*Ja,* you're right. She shouldn't be near the horses at all. She panics like this every time she gets near them, but you didn't know that." She drew a deep breath that shuddered at the end. "*Denki* for helping."

That shaky breath got him. Bram straightened his jacket and dusted off his gabardine trousers to give his eyes something to focus on. Her steady gaze demanded his apology, but he wasn't about to admit he was sorry for saving the girl, was he?

When he looked up, her gaze was still on him, expectant, her blue eyes a sharp contrast to her brown dress. Even standing on a slight rise above him, her *kapp* barely reached the level of his chin, but he was defenseless.

"I'm sorry. I probably scared her as much as the horses did."

This time he was sure her mouth twitched.

"*Ja,* probably."

Then she did smile, lighting up her face in a way that would make those painted girls back in Chicago green with envy. Bram drew a deep breath. Who would have thought he'd find a beauty like this among these Plain people?

"*Memmi,*" the little girl said, "can I go find *Grossmutti?*"

"*Ja,* for sure." The woman set the girl on the grass and watched her run to the back of the house.

*Memmi?* Bram's thoughts did an about-face. She was married, a mother, and he had let himself get distracted by a pretty face, and an Amish one at that. He was here to buy a horse, nothing more.

"Is your husband around? I heard he had a horse for sale."

The woman paused, the smile gone in a shadow. "I think you're looking for my father. You'll find him in the barn."

Bram glanced toward the barn cellar door as she nodded toward it, but by the time he had turned to her again, she was halfway to the house. "*Denki,*" he called after her. She didn't look back.

\* \* \*

Ellie Miller fought the urge to run to the safety of the *Dawdi Haus* with four-year-old Susan, keeping her walk steady until she joined *Mam* at the clothesline behind the big house.

She had forgotten. An *Englischer* gave her a crooked grin, and she had forgotten about Daniel. How could something so innocent make her forget her own husband?

Something about that *Englischer* didn't make sense…

*Ach,* he had spoken *Deitsch.* His suit and hat were *Englisch* for sure, with that bright yellow necktie, but where had he learned to speak *Deitsch?*

And that grin! Her breath caught at the whispery ache that wrapped around her chest. Daniel had smiled at her often, but without a mischievous dimple that winked at her. What was she doing even letting her mind remember that grin? He was just another *Englischer.*

Ellie pulled a shirt from the basket to hang on the line.

*Ja,* just another *Englischer* who spoke *Deitsch* and made her rebellious heart flip when he smiled.

"Who was that man you were talking to? If it was another tramp, there's a piece of pie in the kitchen." *Mam*'s voice drifted to her from the other side of the clothesline, where she was hanging the girls' dresses.

"He wasn't looking for food. He wanted to talk to *Dat.*" Ellie glanced at the barn, glad for *Dat*'s ease when it came to talking to outsiders. "There was something strange about him. He was wearing *Englisch* clothes, but he spoke *Deitsch.*"

*Mam*'s voice was calm, as if she heard *Englischers* speaking their language all the time. "Maybe he has some Amish friends and learned the language from them. Did he want to buy the gelding *Dat* has for sale?"

"What would he want with a horse?"

"I expect an *Englischer* might want a horse once in a while." *Mam* pulled another dress out of the basket at her feet. "When I see them tear along the roads in those automobiles, I wonder why anyone would hurry that fast just to end up in a ditch."

"Lovina's neighbor only did that once."

"Once is enough, isn't it?" *Mam* pulled the loaded clothesline lower to look at Ellie. "A person can be in too much of a hurry at times. When do you have time to pray, or even think?"

"For sure, I'm glad the church decided to keep them verboten. Not only are they noisy, but they smell terrible. Next thing you know, all the *Englisch* will be buying them."

"*Ach,* not until these hard times are over."

Ellie sighed as she pinned one of her brother's shirts on the line. Would these hard times ever be over?

"I like automobiles." Susan's voice was soft, hesitant.

Ellie looked down at her young daughter. Automobiles? What would she say next?

"Why do you say that?" Ellie shook out the next shirt with a snap.

Susan leaned closer to Ellie from where she squatted next to one-year-old Danny in the grass under the clothesline, her brown eyes wide in her heart-shaped face. "Because they aren't horses." Her words were a whisper as she glanced toward the Belgians waiting to be hitched to the manure spreader.

Ellie pushed the clothespins down firmly. When would Susan get over this fear? Daniel's accident had changed everything.

At this thought, Ellie paused, grasping at the line to control the sudden shaking of her hands. Her mind filled again with the horses' grunting whinnies, the stomping hooves, the smell of fear and blood, Daniel trapped against the barn wall and then falling under those huge hooves… Ellie's stomach churned. That day had left an impression in Susan's mind that affected her even now, months later. It still affected all of them.

Ellie shook her head to brush away the memories and shoved the final clothespin onto the last shirt. What was done was done. She might wish things were different, but her husband was dead. That was a truth she faced every day. She refused to succumb to the stifling blanket of grief that pushed at the edge of her mind, tempting her to sink into its seductive folds.

"All done, *Mam.* Do you want me to help take the clothes in this afternoon?"

"*Ne,* don't bother. I'll have the girls tend to it when they get home from school."

"Come, sweeties." Ellie lifted Danny in her arms while Susan hopped on one foot next to her. "Time to get our dinner started."

Ellie crossed the drive to the worn path between the barn and the vegetable garden that led to the *Dawdi Haus.* The house her grandparents had lived in when she was a child had sheltered her little family during the months since Daniel's death. Susan ran ahead of her along the lane, her earlier fright forgotten.

"Plan on eating supper with us tonight," *Mam* called after her. "I'm fixing a chicken casserole, and there's plenty for all."

"*Ja,* for sure," Ellie called back, then turned her attention to Danny, who was squirming to get out of her arms. "Sit still there, young man." She laughed at the determined expression on his face as she followed Susan.

Ellie watched the little girl skipping ahead, but her mind was full of a queer anticipation. It was as if her birthday was coming or the wild freshness of the first warm air of spring, pushing back the dark clouds of winter....

That *Englischer*'s grin, that was what brought this on. It did something to her, and she frowned at this thought. It didn't matter what an *Englischer* did, no matter how blue his eyes were.

That grin held a secret. What was he thinking when he looked at her?

She hitched Danny up as the thought of what might have been going through his head came to her. *Ach,* why did an *Englischer*'s wicked-looking grin give her such a delicious feeling at the memory of it?

*Dat* and the stranger stood on the threshing floor between the open barn doors, where the fresh air and light were plentiful, but Ellie kept her eyes on the edge of the garden as she hurried to follow Susan. If she glanced their way, would she see that dimple flash as he grinned at her again?

She had to stop thinking about him. He would talk to *Dat* and then be gone, and she'd never see him again, for sure.

In the backyard of the *Dawdi Haus,* Ellie paused to pass her hand along a pair of her oldest son's trousers. Dry already. She'd bring in the laundry before fixing the children's dinner. After she put the little ones down for their naps, she could iron in the quiet time before Johnny, her scholar, came home. She smiled, anticipating the quiet hour or so in the shaded house, alone with her thoughts.

Opening the screen door for Susan, Ellie chanced a look at the big white barn behind her. *Ja,* he was still there, talking with *Dat.* She followed Susan into the house, letting the door close behind them with a ringing slam.

Bram glanced at the man next to him. John Stoltzfus was stern, yet quiet and confident. More like the *grossdatti* he barely remembered than the father he had left behind so many years ago. From the clean, ordered barn to the little girl skipping along the lane at the bottom of the ramp, the Stoltzfus farm was a world away from the home he had remembered growing up.

And a world away from Chicago. In the three days since he'd stepped out of his life in the city and walked back into his past, those twelve years had slipped away until even the stench of the West Side was a half-remembered dream. Was he losing his edge already? It was too easy to fall into this simple, Plain life.

Bram's thoughts followed the young woman in the brown dress as she walked past the barn toward the *Dawdi Haus.* When she ran her hand along the boy's trousers on the clothesline, a door opened into a long-forgotten place in his mind. That simple, feminine action spoke of the home he had tried to forget. How many times had he seen his *Mam* do that same thing?

The breeze brought the scent of freshly plowed fields into the barn as the young woman opened the door of the *Dawdi Haus* and then glanced his way, meeting his eyes before disappearing with an echoing slap of the wooden screen door. Why did she live there? And why were there no men's clothes hanging with the laundry?

Movement next to him drew his attention.

"So you're coming home?"

John's unspoken *finally* lingered at the end of the question, hinting at the speculation Bram knew he would be facing as word of his return spread. He could imagine the stir his disappearance had caused, even here in Eden Township.

"*Ja,* I'm coming home." How much information would get him the entrance into this community that he needed without divulging too much? "When I left, I was young and I thought I could always come back, but time got away from me...." Bram sighed and stared across the road at the rich brown corduroy of soil. A flock of blackbirds scattered through the field, picking at exposed seed.

What would his life be like if he had never left? What did he have now, other than lost time and poor choices?

"You left before you joined the church?"

"*Ja,* I was in my *Rumspringa.*" A *Rumspringa* that had never ended. Once he'd left home, Bram had never intended to return.

"What were you looking for out there?"

He glanced back at the older man's expectant face. From what his brother-in-law, Matthew, had said, John was one of the leaders in this district. Bram needed his support if he would ever be accepted into the community, but it wouldn't be easy. The Amish kept tight fences.

"I'm not sure now. Maybe excitement, freedom. I never found it, though." He cast his glance to the side, away from John, as if he was repentant and ashamed. No, he didn't need to do much acting to slip into this role. "I'm ready to come home."

Bram steadied his expression and looked back at the older man's face. He had said it the right way—John Stoltzfus believed him—but Bram didn't know if he'd ever be ready to come home. He wouldn't be here now if it wasn't for Killer Kavanaugh and the contract the gangster had put out on him.

"The *Ordnung* can be hard to live up to." Bram heard a warning note in John's voice.

"Not as hard as the way I've been living." The memory of Chicago's dirty streets clashed against the reality of the fresh spring air outside the big barn door. Yeah, life in Chicago had been dangerous, exciting, risky— and always hard. At least with the *Ordnung,* a man knew where he stood.

"What does your brother think?"

Samuel. Their father's living legacy. His brief stop at the family farm near Shipshewana earlier in the week had let him know what Samuel thought. Where *Dat* had been cruel, Samuel was petty, but that had been the only difference. From the belligerent set of his chin to his bleary eyes, Samuel was *Dat* all over again.

"*Ja,* well, Samuel doesn't believe I'm back to stay."

"You can understand that. You left a long time ago, and much has happened since then."

Twelve years. Yes, a lot had happened, both here and in Chicago. Bram's stomach clenched. He had to make this work....

He forced his voice to remain quiet, in control. "I hope that with time he'll see I mean what I say." But he wouldn't give Samuel the chance. He could go the rest of his life without seeing his brother again.

"With time," John agreed with a nod. He turned to look back into the shaded interior of the barn, where the horse was tied to a post, the subject closed for now. Bram moved his shoulders against the strain that had crept in without his knowing.

"Partner here should be a good horse for you. He's

a little spirited, but he drives well. My daughter Ellie usually chooses him if she's going out, and she won't put up with a horse that won't mind her. She won't take any chances with the children in the buggy."

"Is she the daughter who just went into the *Dawdi Haus?*"

"*Ja.* She and the children have been living there since her husband died."

So the young woman was a widow? Bram tucked that information away as John lifted each of the gelding's hooves for his inspection. The horse twitched his ears but stood quietly during the process. Bram held out a carrot nub John gave him, and the horse took it, eyeing the stranger as he munched the treat.

"I haven't dealt with horses much the last few years, but he seems to take to me."

"He's a good horse."

"Your price sounds fair." Bram pulled his money clip out of his pocket and peeled off a few bills. "Is it all right if I pick him up on Tuesday? I ordered a buggy from Levi Miller's, and it should be ready to pick up that afternoon."

"*Ja,* for sure." John took the money and shook Bram's hand. "I'll be looking for you on Tuesday."

Cool air washed over Ellie as she and the children went into the shaded kitchen. She shifted Danny on her hip, ready to put the heavy load down.

"Can we play with Noah's Ark?" Susan's favorite toy was a new discovery for Danny.

"*Ja,* that will be good. Why don't you set it up in the front room while I change Danny's diaper?"

Ellie took the baby into the bedroom Danny and Susan shared. She used the second bedroom, while

Johnny slept on the sofa in the front room. The little house had seemed like such a refuge when they had moved in, but they were quickly outgrowing it. *Dat* had offered to add on another bedroom, but Ellie was reluctant to take that step. It seemed so permanent.

She would be moving back to Daniel's farm as soon as she was able to support herself and the children. The farm belonged to her now. It was the children's legacy from their father and his dreams for their future. When she was ready to make the move, then she would tell *Mam* and *Dat*. No use crossing that bridge yet.

Once clean and dry, Danny was anxious to get into the front room to play with Susan. Ellie put him down on the floor while she took care of the diaper and watched him make his way into the next room, doing his own one-foot-one-knee scooting crawl.

"*Ne,* Danny!" Hearing Susan's cry, Ellie stepped through the doorway to see Danny plowing his way through his sister's carefully set up animal pairs, making a beeline for the cows.

"Just set them up again, Susan. You know he's not doing it on purpose."

Ellie picked the marauder up and set him down on his bottom next to the pair of black-and-white cows. He took one in each hand and stuck a cow head into his mouth. He looked up at Ellie with contented adoration on his face, drool dripping down his chin. She couldn't help caressing his soft hair.

"I think we'll have to ask *Dawdi* Hezekiah to make another set of cows."

"*Ne, Memmi,* Danny can play with those. I still have the brown ones."

Ellie gave Susan a smile. The little girl forgave

quickly when it came to Danny. Between the two of them, he was nearly spoiled.

Standing up again sent a twinge through Ellie's back, reminding her of how much work she had done already that morning. She leaned back a bit to ease the strain and caught a glimpse of the strawberry field through the window. She stepped closer to the glass, drinking in the sight of the rows of green leaves nestled in the soil.

Rows of green promising the fulfillment of Daniel's dreams for their children—a home, a future. Giving them what he wanted was the least she could do. She owed him that much.

Ellie rubbed her arms, brushing away the sudden chill that brought goose bumps, and stepped away from the window. Susan chattered to Danny as she walked the wooden animals up the ramp and through the door of the ark. How would she know when she had given the children enough to make up for what she had done?

Brushing the thought aside, she crossed the room to the kitchen. "Susan, I'm going to bring the clothes in. Call me if you or Danny need anything, *ja?*"

"*Ja, Memmi.* I will."

Picking up the empty basket from the back porch, Ellie started with Johnny's shirts, dropping the clothespins into the basket as she folded each shirt. When she reached for Susan's blue dress, the stranger stepped up next to her and took the dress from the line, handing it to her as he dropped the pins with the others.

"I thought I'd check on your little girl before I left."

Ellie froze with the dress in her hands. What was he doing? Asking for *Dat* was one thing, but to speak to her in this way?

"She…she's fine. She's just fine." Ellie concentrated on folding the dress and took Johnny's trousers from the *Englischer* as he dropped more clothespins into the basket. The sleeve of his jacket was gray, with threads of yellow that matched his necktie and the handkerchief in his breast pocket. No one dressed that fancy, not even the *Englischers* in town. Who was he?

"I found your *Dat* in the barn, just like you said. The horse will be perfect for me. John said you've driven him quite a bit."

"*Ja,* I take him when I need to run errands or go visiting." Why didn't he just go? What if *Mam* saw an *Englischer* talking with her?

"My name is Bram. Bram Lapp. And you're Ellie, right?"

Ellie glanced at his face. *Ja,* that grin was there, making a dimple show on his cheek. *Ach,* what a mess! How could she get him to leave and still be polite?

"*Ja,* that's right." Her cheeks were flaming hot under his gaze.

"I'm staying with Matthew and Annie Beachey until I find a farm to buy. Annie's my sister."

Ellie stared at him. "Your sister? But you're…" How could he be Annie's brother? She wasn't *Englisch*.

His grin widened. "Has anyone ever told you how beautiful your eyes are?" He turned away and stepped to the next line to start on the many diapers.

Ellie couldn't pull her eyes away from him, her cheeks burning. How forward could one man be? He ignored her as he pulled the pins off the line and bunched the diapers in his hand. When the line was empty, he dropped the diapers into the basket on top of the clothes.

"I'm glad your little girl is all right." He picked up the basket and started toward the house. He wouldn't just walk inside, would he?

"I can take that." Ellie hurried after him and reached

for the basket. He let her grasp the sides as he paused at the porch steps, but he held on until she looked up at him.

"Will I see you again? I'll be around, you know." His dimple deepened, and she pulled the basket out of his hands. Didn't he understand how rude and forward he was being?

"*Denki* for carrying the basket, but *ne,* I don't think you'll be seeing me again."

She left him and went into the house, closing the solid wood door behind her, shutting him out. Leaning her back against the door, Ellie listened. Would he be so bold as to follow her onto the porch?

Setting the basket on the floor, she stepped to the sink and looked out the window. There he was, walking past the barn toward the road, his hat tilted on the back of his head and his hands in his pockets.

Annie Beachey's brother? Ellie squinted her eyes. *Ja,* perhaps if he wore Plain clothes and a straw hat instead of the gray felt one with the yellow band...

*Ne.* She shook her head and turned to pull a loaf out of the bread box. He was just too *Englisch.* For sure, the clothes made him *Englisch* on the outside, but no Amishman would be so bold with a woman! He was *Englisch* through and through.

Ellie looked up from her task of slicing the bread. She could still see him on the road. He had taken off his jacket and slung it over one shoulder, and as she watched, he did a little skip and kicked at a rock on the road, sending it bouncing along in front of him. He ran up to it and kicked it again, sending it into the ditch. Laughter bubbled up in her throat, and she leaned toward the window to keep him in view as he hunted for the rock in the tall grass at the side of the road. And then he was gone.

Straightening the bread on the cutting board, she cut two more slices for Susan and Danny before she realized she was still smiling. *Ach,* what was it about this *Englischer?* What if he had seen her laughing at him?

She shook her head, putting a frown on her face. *Ne,* that wouldn't do at all. *Englischers* and Amish just didn't mix, especially strange, fancy men. No good Amish woman would let *him* near her and her family.

## Chapter Two

Bram kept to the shady south side of the gravel road, letting his pace settle into a steady walk that would eat up the four miles to Matthew's place. It was pure luck his brother-in-law knew about that horse for sale. A week of walking was enough for him. Selling his Studebaker had been a hard sacrifice to make, but it had been a gift from Kavanaugh.

Too risky to keep.

Everything was risky since that night on Chicago's West Side when Elwood Peters had told him his cover was blown.

Bram loosened his tie and unbuttoned his collar to give himself some air. It had been just this hot that April night, but Bram had gone cold with Peters's terse "You've been made."

How had Kavanaugh known he was the source for the feds? He had been with the gangster for nearly all of the twelve years he had been in Chicago, from the time he had hit the streets with hayseed still stuck in his hair. Kavanaugh had taken him in, taught him some street smarts, shown him the ropes during Prohibition. Man, what a green kid he had been back then—but

Kavanaugh liked him, said he had promise. Sure, some of the other guys had been jealous of him, but nobody messed with one of Kavanaugh's boys.

But it was Elwood Peters who had made a man of him. The Prohibition agent had seen his potential and recruited him to be an informant.

Bram shook his head. No, Peters had done more than just recruit him. He had saved his life. Before Peters came along, Bram had been on the same track as the rest of Kavanaugh's boys—just waiting for his chance to take the boss down. Even though he had seen what happened to the guy who made his move and failed, Bram didn't care. What did he have to live for, anyway?

Then he had run into Peters. Over the past ten years, Peters's job had changed from Prohibition agent, to Treasury agent, to the Federal Bureau, and he had taken Bram with him as his eyes on the street. It had worked out well for both of them.

Bram had shared everything with the older man—everything except his past and his real name. Peters knew him as Dutch, the name Kavanaugh had dubbed him with the first time they met. Bram had added a last name—Sutter—and from then on, Bram Lapp had disappeared into the hazy mist of fading years.

Until now.

Peters was sure Kavanaugh had moved his operation to northern Indiana after Bram's information had led to the breakup of his gang in Chicago, but he needed to know where the boss had gone. Bram was supposed to go with Kavanaugh when he left town, but once his cover was blown, he had to change his plans. He'd be dead if Kavanaugh found him, but he couldn't let the gangster escape, either. He'd never be safe until Kavanaugh was out of the way.

Killer Kavanaugh never gave up until he had his revenge.

And then Bram had come up with this new, hare-brained idea. It seemed like such a good idea in Chicago—go undercover as himself, Bram Lapp, the green Amish kid from Indiana.

But he wasn't green anymore. He had seen and done things the Amish kid he had been couldn't imagine. He had the skills to keep himself alive on the Chicago streets, but would those same skills be useful to him here as he hunted for Kavanaugh's new center of operations? They had to be.

Bram whooshed out a breath. Meanwhile, here he was slipping away into the life he had left twelve years ago. It wasn't what he had expected. Not at all. The deeper he went into this cover, the more he was losing the edge he needed to keep him alive. But without the cover, without immersing himself into this community, it would be impossible to fade into the background the way he needed to.

And there was only one way to fade into this background: he needed to look and act the same as every other Amishman around. Any difference would make him stick out like a sore thumb.

The list. He ticked off the items in his mind as he walked. He had bought the buggy and horse. Next would be a place to farm, equipment and workhorses, and church every other Sunday. And clothes. This drape suit that helped him blend in on Chicago's West Side stuck out too much around here. Besides, his jacket was ruined after sliding in the dirt with that little Amish girl.

That little girl was something else. So much like his younger sisters at that age...

Bram took off his felt hat and ran his fingers through

his hair, trying to get the air to his scalp. Why did re-membering his sisters make him think of a wife and a family?

The curve of Ellie Miller's neck eased into his thoughts. He closed his eyes to capture the moment she'd faced him on her back porch. One strand of soft brown hair had escaped from under her *kapp* and fallen softly along the side of her face. She'd have to reach up and tuck it behind her ear. What would it feel like if he did it for her? He saw the smile she would give him as he caressed her cheek....

Bram stopped the direction of his thoughts with a firm shake of his head. He knew a woman like that wouldn't even look at him. Not Bram Lapp. Not with his past. And not with the job he had to do. No, a woman like that wasn't for him. He'd rather take his chances alone.

Wheels crunching through the gravel on the road behind him made Bram sidestep into the cover of some overhanging branches. Buggy wheels and horse's hooves, not a car. He rolled his shoulders as he waited for the buggy to overtake him. He had to stop being so jumpy. No one knew he was here. Even Peters only had a vague idea of the direction he had gone.

"Bram!"

Bram waved as the buggy caught up to him, and his brother-in-law pulled the horse to a halt.

"You'll be wanting a ride." Matthew was a man to get to his point quickly.

*"Ja, denki."*

The back of the buggy held boxes of supplies, and a frantic peeping rose from one as the buggy lurched forward.

"You bought some chicks?"

"*Ja.* I thought the Yoders might have some to trade for a couple bales of hay." Matthew looked at Bram with a grin. "Annie loves getting new chicks."

Bram let this idea settle in his mind. His sister hadn't asked for chicks, as far as he knew. Matthew had gotten them because he thought Annie might like them. Was that how a real husband acted?

"Did you find the Stoltzfus farm?" Matthew asked.

"*Ja.* John had a nice gelding for sale, just as you said. I'll pick him up on Tuesday."

"I knew John would take care of you. He's a good man."

"*Ja,* he is."

A good man. Bram hadn't known too many of those. He slid a glance at Matthew. His little sister had found a good man.

Matthew pointed ahead with the buggy whip. "Looks like the Jackson place is for sale. It might be the kind of place you've been looking for."

He stopped the horse at the end of the lane. The for-sale sign at the roadside looked new, but the graying barn and leaning fence posts were witness to the toll the recent hard times had taken on the English farmers. Forty acres, the sign said, along with the name of the bank that held the foreclosure. A too-familiar sign these past few years.

"The Jackson place? Do you know why they lost the farm?"

"I'm not sure, but I could see it coming. Ralph Jackson was too quick to spend his money as soon as he sold his crops, and then he'd buy the next year's seed on credit. He only owned the place about five years, but it was long enough to work it into the ground."

"It's vacant. Let's look around."

Matthew pulled the buggy into the lane, and they walked to the barn. Bram examined the siding, the beams and the fences. The barn needed a lot of work, but the structure was sound.

"Forty acres is a good size," Matthew said, looking at the land around them. "There's a creek running through the meadow. Good cropland, too, with the right management."

Bram turned to the house. It might be livable with some work, but he had the time. He needed a farm, and this one fit. All he had to do was go to the bank, sign the papers and hand over the cash, and it would be his. Another item checked off his list.

"The bank on the sign—isn't it in Goshen?"

"*Ja.* I won't be using my buggy tomorrow. You could take it into town if you want to talk to them about it."

"I'll go in the morning, first thing."

Then again, maybe not first thing. This might be another opportunity to get John Stoltzfus firmly on his side, and he wasn't one to pass up an opportunity. He could stop by the Stoltzfus farm before he headed into Goshen tomorrow. A little more grease wouldn't hurt, and besides, old John was pretty savvy. He'd have some good pointers on how to get this farm back on its feet.

It wouldn't hurt to get another glimpse of Ellie, either. Even if she wasn't for him, she was sure a beautiful doll, and looking didn't cost a thing.

Ellie's toes churned the loose black soil between the strawberry rows, soil that ran in muddy rivers as she splashed water on each plant. Her practiced steps kept just ahead of the mud, and she tipped the watering can in time to an *Englisch* hymn she had learned in school.

"'I once was lost, but now am found…'" The fourth

row finished, she stopped to ease her aching muscles and looked back at her work.

*Ach,* even with daily watering, the plants were barely alive. This hot, dry spell was unusual for May. One good rain would set the young plants off to a good start, but as Ellie glanced up at the clear blue sky, she knew it wouldn't happen anytime soon. Until then, it was up to her to keep them alive. She started down the next row, humming as she went.

A warm breeze carried her sisters' voices to her and told her the scholars were home. Mandy and Rebecca ran up the lane to the big house, but Johnny trudged behind them, his head down. There must have been trouble at school again. Setting the watering can on the ground, Ellie closed the gate to the field and went to meet him as he walked alone to the *Dawdi Haus.*

"Hello, Johnny." The six-year-old looked up at her when she spoke, his face streaked where one tear had escaped and made a track down his dirty red cheek. *What happened this time?*

"Are you all right?"

*"Ja."* Johnny tipped his head down as he spoke, drawing the word out in his telltale sign that things were far from all right. There was only one way to get him to talk to her, and that was to pretend she didn't notice his attitude.

"Run on into the house and change into your work clothes while I get your snack. *Dawdi's* waiting for you in the barn."

Johnny looked at the barn, then at his feet. His straw hat hid his face from her, but she knew the look he wore. Daniel had always had the same look when he'd tried to hide something from her, and Johnny was so much like his father.

"Johnny, tell me what's wrong."

"*Dawdi* doesn't need me to help. He has Benjamin and Reuben. They always say I'm too little to do anything."

"You may be littler than Benjamin and Reuben, but I remember when they were your age. They worked with *Dawdi* in the barn just like you do."

"But it's different for them. *Dawdi* is their *dat*."

*Ach*, Johnny. What could she do for a boy who missed his own *dat*?

"Let's go into the house and get your snack, then you can go out to the barn. Your *dawdi* likes having you work with him."

Johnny took the first bite from his cookie while Ellie poured a glass of milk for him. Susan came out of the bedroom, her face flushed with sleep, and peered into Johnny's face as she climbed into her chair.

"Johnny's been crying."

"Haven't." Johnny's contradiction was muffled by the sugar cookie in his mouth.

"*Ja*, you have. You cried at school again."

"Susan, that's enough." Ellie could see Johnny's tears threatening to start again, so she pulled out a chair and sat next to him. "Were you dawdling again?"

Johnny took a drink of his milk. "I was looking out the window."

Ellie sighed. Johnny was always looking somewhere else, forgetting whatever the task at hand should be, forgetting his schoolwork, his chores... She did the same thing, letting food burn on the stove while she looked out the window, letting the memories of her past drown the reality of the present.

"You have to pay more attention at school." She forced the words out. It was her duty, even though she would rather just gather him into her lap the way she had when he was Susan's age. She wished she could give him what he really needed, but that was impossible. She couldn't erase the past year, and she couldn't replace his father.

Levi Zook's face chose that moment to intrude, but she turned the memory firmly away. The widower had made it clear he wanted Ellie to be the mother for his children. But with his own brood, Ellie knew he would never be able to fit Johnny into his life the way her son needed him to. If she ever married again, it would have to be to someone who would be able to take Daniel's place in her life and her children's lives...and there was no one who could do that.

Bram Lapp's devilish grin popped into her thoughts. For sure, no *Englischer* could ever take her Daniel's place, either.

Johnny stared at her, his eyes dark and distant, and she knew she had failed him again. When had her little boy turned into this sad, sullen child? She couldn't remember the last time he had laughed, the last time she had seen him join in a game.

He stuffed the rest of the cookie into his mouth and went to the bedroom to change his clothes.

*Ja,* he needed his father. Someone like Daniel, who would give his life to a growing boy, who would teach him, protect him...

"*Memmi,*" Susan said, interrupting her thoughts. "That *Englischer* man that was here? He saved me from the horses."

"*Dawdi*'s horses weren't going to hurt you." Ellie nibbled on a cookie. That same *Englischer* man had been intruding on her own thoughts all afternoon. Only a city man and her daughter would think *Dat*'s gentle draft horses would hurt them. They were too well trained.

"*Ja,* they were. When Henny Penny ran away, that man saved me and her from the horses." Her eyes widened as she rolled her arm in the air. "He catched me and flew to the grass." She took a drink of her milk and then looked at Ellie again. "He's brave, *Memmi.*"

*Ach,* if she could have Susan's confidence. If only she could just forget that Bram Lapp, but the *Englischer*'s grin danced in front of her eyes. He had really thought Susan was in danger from the horses. What kind of man would ruin his fancy clothes for a little girl and her pet chicken?

"It's good to hear the children playing outside in the evening." *Mam* rinsed another plate in the simple, immaculate kitchen of the big house.

"*Ja,* though I think they'll be disappointed when they don't find any lightning bugs." Ellie dried the plate and placed it in the cupboard with the others. In *Mam*'s kitchen, nothing was ever out of place, from the dishes in the cupboard to *Dat*'s Bible and prayer book on the shelf behind his chair.

*Mam* chuckled. "Children always start hunting for them much too early in the year." She scrubbed at a stubborn spot on the casserole dish. "What did you think about what *Dat* was telling us at supper?"

"About Bram Lapp? I don't know."

"It isn't unheard of, what he's doing." *Mam* rinsed the casserole dish and laid it on the drain board.

"Just because it happens doesn't mean that it's right." Ellie was surprised at the anger behind her words. "A person shouldn't flip-flop when it comes to *Gott.*"

"I've seen others come to their senses after a taste

of worldly life." *Mam* swished the water in the dishpan and found a stray spoon.

"Twelve years is a bit more than a taste."

They worked in silence for a few minutes while Ellie wiped off the table, thinking back twelve years. She had been fourteen, just finishing up at school and beginning to notice the boys, wondering which one would be her husband. If she had met Bram then, would he have given her one of his grins? The thought brought a smile to her face.

Bram must be a few years older than her. Since *Dat* had said he had gone to Chicago while in his *Rumspringa,* he would have been around seventeen back then, which would make him twenty-nine now. Amish men usually didn't stay bachelors that long, but she didn't know about the *Englisch.* Maybe their custom was to wait longer before marrying.

"Do you know his mother or any of his sisters?" Ellie straightened the chairs around the big table.

"I knew his mother years ago—we were girls together—but I lost touch with her after she married and moved to the Shipshewana district. I heard she passed on a few years ago, and her husband, too."

"So if he's from Shipshewana, why isn't he settling up there?"

"Maybe he's looking for a wife."

Ellie shot a glance at her mother. For sure, the corners of her mouth were turned up in a sly grin. She sighed. Lately *Mam* thought every unattached man could be a new husband for her, but Ellie hadn't told her that she never intended to marry again.

"We don't know what he's looking for. He could be here to…to…"

"To what?" *Mam's* face was serene, innocent. How

could she not know what the plans of an *Englischer* from Chicago might be? She must have heard the stories about gangsters and speakeasies. There were all kinds of worldly evils in a city like Chicago.

"*Ach,* I don't know."

"Daughter, we need to give the man a chance. *Dat* asked us to treat him as a friend. Surely we can do that much."

"*Ja,* I suppose…"

A friend. *Ja,* he was friendly enough, but could anyone trust an *Englisch* man? An outsider?

# *Chapter Three*

The next morning's sunshine brought a promise of another hot day to come. Why was it that weeds always grew no matter what the weather, while the garden plants wilted in the heat? Ellie's hoe chopped through another clump of crabgrass growing between the rows of beans.

"See? This one is a dandelion."

Ellie glanced at Susan and Danny just in time to see the baby put a yellow flower in his mouth.

"*Ne, ne,* don't eat it!" Susan's voice was full of disgust.

Ellie smiled as she watched Susan rescue the flower from Danny's mouth. What a help she was. Daniel would have loved to see how his little dishwasher was growing.

The sound of buggy wheels in gravel interrupted her thoughts. If visitors were stopping by, *Mam* might need some help.

"Who's that?" Susan asked.

"I'm not sure." Ellie straightened up and shaded her eyes from the morning sun as the buggy stopped at the barn. "It looks like Matthew Beachey's, but that isn't Matthew driving."

The *Englischer,* Bram Lapp, climbed out and headed for the barn.

"*Ach,* it's that man who was here yesterday. He must want to talk to *Dawdi* again."

She went back to her hoeing, but found herself working with only half her mind on the weeds.

Why was he here? He said he wasn't going to pick up the horse until next week. And a buggy? It just didn't fit with what she knew of the *Englisch. Ja,* she remembered, he wasn't really *Englisch,* but if he wasn't, then why was he still wearing *Englisch* clothes? But the *Englisch* didn't drive buggies. When they drove a horse it was with a wagon or cart, not an Amish buggy. And if *Dat* was right and he was trying to become part of the community again, then why was he still wearing *Englisch* clothes?

Ellie gave a vigorous chop with the hoe that took out a dandelion and three bean plants. She was thinking in circles again. She stopped hoeing and sighed. *Dat* had asked them to welcome the man, but Ellie's first reaction was to ignore him, just as she ignored all *Englisch.*

*Ja,* he was friendly and attractive. But so *Englisch.*

She tackled the weeds again.

The *Englisch* were just like these weeds. If you gave them a chance they might choke a person, distract them from the Amish life—the Plain life. She had seen it happen to other people who had opened themselves to their *Englisch* neighbors, but it wasn't going to happen to her family. It didn't matter that this man wanted to become Amish again. The *Englisch* influence was like a dandelion root: you could try to chop it out, but if you left even a little bit, it would grow again and take over. How could a person turn from one to the other?

Ellie moved to the next row. The squash vines were healthier than the beans. Once they grew a little larger, they would cover the ground with their broad leaves, and the weeds would lose their hold. That was what she loved about her life. Peace, order, community—the *Ordnung*—were a protective covering that kept worldliness from taking root. Once she got rid of these few small weeds, the squash vines would grow unhindered through the rest of the summer.

Bram headed to the buggy he had left outside the barn humming "Blue Moon" under his breath. He stopped with a soft whistle. If he wanted to keep on John Stoltzfus's good side, he'd have to forget those songs for a while. In fact, he had a lot of habits from Chicago that would have to go, but that was part of the job.

John had given him some good, sound advice about the farm he wanted to buy. The man really knew his business. He'd answered Bram's questions for almost an hour and never seemed to be in a hurry. The older man's excitement about the prospects the farm held made Bram wish…what? That he wasn't just buying it for a cover? That he could build it into the kind of place he could be proud of?

Bram stopped, resisting the urge to look back at the barn. With someone like John Stoltzfus around, he'd be able to make something of that farm. Who knew— with someone like John, maybe he could even make something of his life.

He pushed the thought away. Too little, too late. With any luck, he'd find Kavanaugh and be taking off before midsummer anyway.

When Bram reached the hitching rail, the two children at the edge of the garden caught his eye. That little girl was the one from yesterday. She was pretty cute when she wasn't screaming her head off. He chuckled as he watched her try to catch a butterfly that danced among the flowers.

His breath caught when he saw the mother. Dressed in brown again today, Ellie had her back to him. He was glad he wasn't one of the weeds she was hoeing. He'd never survive an attack like that. Her movements were brisk, businesslike, but at the same time Bram found himself caught up in the rhythm of her slim form as she worked.

How did she manage, raising her children without a husband? Bram understood the loneliness of living alone, but to add the responsibility of children to that was beyond him.

Bram found himself drawn to her like a butterfly to a flower. He shook his head. No, he couldn't get involved with a woman like that. A woman like that meant home, responsibilities, commitment. A woman like that deserved better than what he could ever give her. A woman like that would be too hard to leave when his job here was over.

But still, he couldn't ignore her. They were going to be part of the same church, the same community. They could at least be friends.

The little girl's laughter carried toward him on the warm breeze, making his decision for him. He had to get to know her somehow.

A man's laugh broke through Ellie's thoughts, and her stomach flipped when she recognized the *Englischer*'s voice behind her. There he was again! That man was as persistent as a dandelion and much more dangerous.

He squatted next to the children at the edge of the garden, smiling as Danny held up a grubby fist full of wilted weeds and babbled at him. Susan, usually the one to hold back, had her hand on his knee, ready to add her part of the story.

Ellie gripped her hoe. She needed to stop this now, before he wormed his way into their lives, but how?

Bram turned to Susan, laying his hand on hers as he said something that made the girl giggle. Ellie's breath caught at the rapt expression on Susan's face. Somehow the man had broken through her shyness. She smiled as Susan laughed again and gave Bram the dandelion she held in her hand.

Ellie gave herself a mental shake. *Ach,* what was she doing? What nerve that man had, going behind her back to push his *Englisch* ways on her children!

Ellie dropped the hoe and hurried to the edge of the garden. She scooped Danny up from the ground and took Susan's hand.

"Come, children, it's time to go into the house."

"You don't need to take them in. Susan was just telling me about her pet chicken." He smiled at her daughter, his hand resting on the girl's shoulder. "She likes animals, doesn't she?"

"As long as they aren't horses."

Bram's dimple flashed, and Ellie started to return his grin before she caught herself. His face was so open and friendly, his blue eyes deep and inviting, his smile intimate as he watched her.

As lovely as a dandelion blossom in spring, she reminded herself. Lovely and insidious, with the ability to turn the whole garden to weeds. With an effort she held her shoulders a little straighter.

"I must take the children in now." She kept her voice controlled and polite, then turned and walked away from him. Her face was burning. She hated to seem so rude, but an *Englischer* was an *Englischer,* and her job was to protect her children, wasn't it?

The back door of the little house was safely closed before she let herself look through the small porch window. The man—Bram—stood where she'd left him, watching. Why did she feel as if she had taken the hoe to one of her squash plants instead of a dandelion?

"I like that man," Susan said. "Can he come back again?"

"We'll see. Let's wash our hands, and then you can play with Danny while I make a pie for supper."

Susan climbed onto her stool and pulled at the small hand pump that brought water to the kitchen sink.

"He's a nice man." She wiggled her fingers under the running stream.

"*Ja,* I guess."

"He isn't afraid of horses." Susan's eyes grew large as she said this. "He told me *Dawdi*'s horse isn't scary, and he'll let me pet it."

"When will this be?"

"Next week. He said he'll come back and I can pet *Dawdi*'s horse."

Ellie dried Danny's hands and set him on the floor.

"Susan, take Danny in the front room and help him find the cows."

Ellie rubbed at the spot between her eyes where a headache was threatening. How had he convinced Susan to look forward to petting a horse?

Movement out by the garden drew her eyes to the

window over the sink. He was leaving. She watched until the buggy left the drive and turned into the road. How dangerous was he? Ellie tucked a loose strand of hair under her *kapp*. Well, he was *Englisch,* wasn't he?

Wasn't he?

She got out a mixing bowl to make piecrust, then dug into the flour canister with more force than she meant to. Flour spilled onto the counter and floor, wasting it. Ellie bit her lip as tears threatened to come.

Why was a simple thing like making a piecrust so hard? Nothing had been right since Daniel died.

Ellie wiped up the spilled flour. She had to keep everything balanced, normal.

What was normal, anyway?

*Just do what needs to be done; keep to the routine.* That was something she could do. It was when something unusual happened that her life tilted.

That *Englischer.* He upset everything.

*Ne,* that was unfair. He was just the little nudge that sent her stack of balanced plates teetering. It wasn't him; it was her own fault.

Ellie crumbled lard into the flour with her fingers and then added an egg and a teaspoon of vinegar.

Her thoughts found their familiar rut and followed it stubbornly. Her pride had urged Daniel to buy the extra land. The extra land that needed more work and new, green-broke horses.

Her pride, her *hochmut,* had caused her to plead with Daniel, to force him to see things her way. She had wanted the larger farm, and she had urged him to buy the new team so he could work more land. If she had just kept to her place, listened to him…but no, she had to keep after him until he agreed to her ideas. If it hadn't been for her nagging, he never would have bought that half-trained team.

The half-trained team that spooked easily. Too easily. A loose piece of harness, a horsefly bite, a playful barn cat… She'd never know what had set them off that day. All she knew was by the time she'd reached the barnyard with Susan, Daniel was already under their hooves, his body broken and bloody.

Her stubbornness had cost her the only man she had ever loved.

She worked the stiff dough with her hands until it was ready to roll. The rolling pin spun as she spread out the crust.

*Ach, ja*, the punishment for her disobedience had been bitter.

But now, wasn't she sorry? Hadn't she prayed for forgiveness? *Gott* had to be pleased. What more could she do? She went to church, wore her *kapp,* followed the *Ordnung…*

The piecrust was a pale full moon. Ellie eased it off the wooden breadboard and laid it on the pie plate.

She must try harder. The *Ordnung,* the church rules, was there to keep her close to *Gott.* She just had to obey them perfectly, and everything would be all right.

No matter how handsome that *Englischer* Bram Lapp happened to be.

She knew what was most important.

The crust eased into the pan. She trimmed the edge with a knife and then crimped the edges with her fingers. Neat. Perfect. And empty.

Bram swayed with the buggy, letting the clip-clop of the horse's hooves set the pace of his thoughts. He'd known moving back to Indiana wouldn't be easy, but he'd never expected to plunge into a pool with no bottom. Nothing was the way he remembered it. The life he knew as a boy on his father's farm held none of the peaceful order he had found here.

From the simple white house nestled behind a riotous hedge of lilacs to the looming white barn, the Stoltzfus farm was the image of his *grossdatti*'s home, a place he thought he had forgotten since the old man's death when he was a young boy. A whisper of memory rattled the long-closed door in his mind, willing it to open, but Bram waved it off. Memories were deceptive, even ones more than twenty years old. They covered the truth, and this truth was that he had a job to do. *Grossdatti* and his young grandson remained behind their door.

But a question snaked its way up Bram's spine. What would *Grossdatti* say if he could see his grandson now? Bram cast a glance down at the dust caked in the perfect break where his gabardine trousers met his matching two-toned wing-tip shoes. Fancy. *Englisch.* Twelve years as one of Kavanaugh's boys had left their mark.

Was it those long-forgotten memories that kept bringing him back to the Stoltzfus farm? He liked the family. John seemed to be on his side, ready with advice, but the older man was almost too trusting. He'd hate to see what the Chicago streets would do to a man like that.

That little girl. Now, she was something, wasn't she? Bram smiled. When she wasn't screaming in terror, she was almost as pretty as her mother.

The smile faded. The mother. Ellie. She was worse than a bear defending her cubs. He had to get past that barbed-wire barricade she threw up every time he tried to talk to her. There was something about him that rubbed her the wrong way. If he figured that out, then maybe she'd be more civil.

Something else he couldn't figure out was why he cared so much.

Bram chirruped at the horse to try to quicken its pace, but it had only one speed. The drive into Goshen was slower than he remembered, and it took even longer when he had to stop for a train at the Big Four Railroad crossing. The people in the cars stared at him as the train rumbled south toward New Paris and Warsaw.

Oh, what he wouldn't give to trade places with them. But it would be no use. The mob would find him, even if he went as far as Mexico. No, it would be better to keep on course. He'd run across Kavanaugh eventually, then Peters and the bureau would do their job. Maybe Mexico would be a good place to think about after that.

The train disappeared around the bend, and Bram urged the horse up and over the tracks, then on into Goshen.

Main Street was still the same as it had been when he was seventeen. He let out a short laugh at the memory. He couldn't believe he had once thought of this place as a big city.

There was something new. He pulled the horse to a stop in the shade at the courthouse square and stared. On the corner of Main and Lincoln, right on the Lincoln Highway, stood a blockhouse. A limestone fortress. A cop behind the thick glass had a view of the entire intersection.

Bram tied the horse to a black iron hitching post and then snagged a man walking by. "Say, friend, can you tell me what's going on? What's that thing?"

The man gave him a narrow look that made Bram aware of how out of place his expensive suit was in a town like Goshen. "That's our new police booth. The state police built it to keep an eye on the traffic through town and to keep gangsters from robbing our banks."

"What makes them think Goshen is their target?" If the state police were working the same angle as the bureau, it sounded like Peters had good reason to think Kavanaugh had come this way.

"You remember back in thirty-three, when Dillinger stole weapons and bulletproof vests from some Indiana police facilities?"

Bram nodded. Oh, yeah, he remembered. Kavanaugh had gloated about that coup for weeks, even though he hadn't been in on the heists.

"Well, one of those police armories is east of here a ways, and the other two are just south of here, along State Road 15."

Bram looked at the street signs. He had just driven into town on State Road 15.

"To get to any of those places from Chicago, the gangsters had to drive right through here, right through this intersection and right past our banks. And then when Dillinger and Pretty Boy Floyd hit the Merchant's Bank in South Bend a couple years ago, we decided we had to do something to protect our town." The man nodded toward the policeman in the booth. "All he has to do is radio headquarters, and this place will be swarming with troopers."

"So does it work?" Could one cop in a blockhouse discourage the plans of a gang intent on robbing one of these banks? One lone cop wouldn't stop the gangs he knew.

"It must." The man gave Bram a sideways look before walking on. "We haven't seen any gangsters around here."

Bram had heard enough. He walked across the street

and found a spot outside a barbershop on Lincoln two doors from the corner, next to the stairway that led down to the ground-floor establishment. His favorite kind of lookout. Have a quick cigarette, watch for a while, make sure he knew the lay of the land before making his move. He shook his head. He was here legitimately; he didn't need to take these precautions. But still he lit his cigarette, bending his head to the match sheltered in his cupped hand. Habit kept him alive. The bank could wait ten minutes.

He watched the quiet town, pulling the smoke into his lungs. Traffic in Goshen's main intersection rose and fell like the waves on North Beach. Businessmen, lawyers and shopping housewives followed the traffic signals with none of the noisy chaos of the Chicago streets.

He threw the cigarette butt on the ground and screwed it into the sidewalk with his toe. Time to talk to the man at the bank. He took a step away from his cover, but slid back again as a Packard drove by on Main, heading south at a slow cruise. Bram watched the driver. No one he recognized, but he'd know that Packard anywhere. It was Kavanaugh's.

But the big question was, what was he doing here? Bram waited, watching the cop in the blockhouse. He was no fool. Even though the Packard was out of Bram's sight, he could tell the cop was following its progress through town.

Bram counted to fifty—enough time for the Packard to make a slow cruise around the block and come back. Would he come back, or was he cruising through on his way to Warsaw or Fort Wayne?

The Packard eased into view again, slowing to a halt at the traffic signal. Bram stepped farther into the shadow of the doorway when he saw Kavanaugh clearly in the backseat of the Packard and Charlie Harris in the shotgun seat. They didn't look his way, but kept their eyes on the blockhouse. The cop inside leaned into his radio microphone just as the signal turned green. The Packard roared north, back toward South Bend.

It looked as if that police booth worked. Bram gave a low whistle. He never would have believed it if he hadn't seen it. Maybe Kavanaugh wouldn't think hitting this place was worthwhile. Maybe they wouldn't be back. Maybe Kavanaugh would keep heading east, and Bram could get out of this backwater and leave the past behind him for good.

Bram looked at the two banks, sitting diagonally across the intersection like two fat, stuffed ducks. Kavanaugh leave these two beauties alone just because of some cop?

Yeah, and maybe there were snowball fights in hell.

## Chapter Four

Bram backed Matthew's team into place early Wednesday morning, watching as they felt their way past the wagon tongue and stopped just as their tails met the singletree. This was a well-trained team, all right. He'd do nicely to look for one as good. That would be another day, though. Today he was looking at equipment at the auction house in Shipshewana.

The farm's price had been lower than he expected, and he had needed to use only about half of his cash reserves. There was plenty left over to buy whatever else he needed to complete his cover.

He climbed into the wagon seat and then steadied the horses as they shifted, eager to be off. Now he had to wait for Matthew. That man spent so much time with his wife—if Bram didn't know better, he'd think they had been married for only a few days instead of nearly a year.

His *Dat* had never spent more time in the house than he needed to. The house and kitchen were *Mam*'s place, and *Dat* stayed in the barn or the fields. Whenever *Dat* was in the house, *Mam* crept around as if she was walking on eggshells, but it didn't do any good. It didn't matter how hard she tried—she could never do anything good enough for *Dat*.

He rubbed his chin as Annie's laughter drifted through the morning air. *Mam* and *Dat* had never acted like these two, that was for sure. He couldn't remember ever hearing *Mam* laugh, or seeing her smile, but Annie brightened up every time Matthew walked in the door.

"Sorry," Matthew said, finally reaching the waiting wagon.

"You're sure Annie will be all right?" Bram laid on the sarcastic tone in his voice, but Matthew didn't seem to notice.

"I think she'll be fine for the day." He picked up the reins, and the horses leaned into the harness with eager steps. "*Mam* is coming over later to help her get ready for tomorrow's sewing frolic." Matthew grinned at Bram. "Annie's really looking forward to it."

Matthew's excitement was so contagious, Bram couldn't help his own smile. He could do with a bit of whatever made his brother-in-law so happy.

"Giddap there, Pete. Come on, Sam."

"You say this auction is big?"

"*Ja,* for sure it is. Every week, too. It's one of the biggest in the state, and people come from all over."

Bram shot a glance at Matthew.

"From all over? *Englischers,* too?"

"*Ja,* some *Englischers,* especially these last few years with the hard times. But mostly Plain folk—Amish, Mennonite, Brethren."

Bram shifted his shoulders. His new Plain clothes felt comfortable, something that surprised him. He rubbed at the right side of his trousers, where he had inserted a pocket holster under the seam last night after Matthew and Annie had gone to bed. His pistol rested there, out of sight but not out of reach. Who knew who could be hiding in a crowd?

As they drew closer to Shipshewana, the traffic got heavier, and by the time they turned onto Van Buren Street, they were part of a line of wagons, buggies and cars headed for the field behind the sale barn. Matthew pulled the horses up at a shady hitching rail at the edge of the field. Auctioneers' voices drifted out of the barn, quickening Bram's heartbeat with their cadence.

"It sounds like things have started already."

"*Ja*, the livestock auction started at six o'clock. The equipment sale starts at nine, so we're in plenty of time."

"Good. I'd like to look things over before the sale starts."

Matthew led the way to a line of plows, cultivators and other farm equipment outside the sale barn. The first thing he needed to do was to plow his fields, then plant. Matthew said he'd loan Bram his team, but time was pressing. This work should have been done a month ago.

"Here's a good-looking plow."

Bram ran his hand over the seat of the sulky plow. The paint wasn't even chipped. The blades had a few scrapes, but the whole thing looked new.

"This one hasn't seen much use, has it?" Matthew walked around to look at the other side. "It'll go for a pretty penny."

That didn't bother Bram. He had enough money for anything up for sale here.

"Good morning, Bram. Matthew."

Bram turned to see John Stoltzfus heading their way. John's familiar face sent a pleasant nudge to Bram's senses, and he smiled. He couldn't remember the last time being recognized didn't send him reaching for his gun.

"Are you looking for a plow, Bram?"

Even though John's voice was friendly, his question merely curious, Bram's nerves arose. He did a quick check of the crowd around them. Everyone seemed to be focused on the auction and farm equipment. He turned his attention to John.

"*Ja.* I'm getting a late start on the farm, and I need everything."

"You're planning on buying all the equipment you need?"

"Well, I need a plow first. I'll start with that."

"It looks like you might have found one," John said, taking a look at the sulky plow. "But don't buy everything at once. You have neighbors, you know. I have a harrow you can use."

"And you can use our planter," Matthew said.

John turned to Bram. "All you need to do is let the church know, and we'll have your whole farm plowed, planted, cultivated and harvested before the day is over."

Matthew and John both laughed at this. Bram wanted to join in, but caution nagged at him.

"Why would you do that? Why would you loan me your equipment?"

"You're one of us, son." John's words came with a puzzled frown. "Have you been gone so long that you've forgotten our way? How we work together?"

Forgotten? This wasn't part of his memory of growing up here.

"No one ever helped my *Dat,* and I don't remember him ever..." His words stopped as he saw the looks on the other men's faces. John and Matthew exchanged glances. Had he said something wrong? Bram gave a scan to the milling farmers around them again.

"Bram, I'm sorry." John glanced at him, then back at

Matthew. "I forgot about your father…" He cleared his throat. "You can count on us to give you a hand anytime. Anything you need."

*Dat* had never had the easy camaraderie with the men in their community that John and Matthew shared, but as a child Bram never knew why. Now he was beginning to figure it out. He swallowed hard as the memories came rushing out of the place where he had shoved them. *Dat*'s stash of moonshine in the barn, the weeks of missed church, the halfhearted repentance that was just enough to keep the ministers from putting *Dat* under the *bann*…

And most of all, *Dat*'s way of always finding something else to do whenever the men gathered together for a work frolic. The Lapps were never part of the community unless it worked into *Dat*'s plans.

He had shoved those memories away and locked the door as he stood on the roadside with his thumb out, heading west. Oh, yes, he remembered the stares, the whispers. This was one of the reasons he'd left.

Matthew put his hand on Bram's arm, and he almost shrugged it off. He wanted to be angry, to shut out their pity, but he stopped himself. That was what *Dat* would have done.

"Let us give you a hand, Bram."

Matthew's face was grim, but there was no pity there, only the determined offer of an alliance.

Bram nodded, trying on the friendship offered. It felt good.

"*Ja,* I'd welcome the help."

"How many quarts of rhubarb juice do you think we'll end up with?" Lovina dumped another pile of cut rhubarb into the bowl.

"Whatever we end up with, you know it won't be enough. *Dat* drinks a cup every day." Ellie eyed the bowl. A few more inches, and it would be full enough to start the first batch of juice. She was glad that even though Lovina lived several miles away she was still willing to help with this chore every year. The two sisters had made the family supply of rhubarb juice for as long as she could remember—ever since they were the same ages as Mandy and Rebecca, for sure.

"The plants at our place aren't growing as well this year. Noah says it's a sign we're in for another bad year."

"And Noah is always right, of course." Ellie looked sideways at Lovina. Even after four years of marriage, that telltale blush crept up her neck at the mention of Noah's name. Lovina still thought her husband was the next thing to perfect.

"*Ja,* of course." Lovina grinned at her, then went back to her cutting. "I do hope he's wrong this time, though. Another year with no rain will be hard."

Ellie's thoughts went to the field of young strawberry plants. There had to be enough rain to keep them alive. She forced her mind in a different direction.

"What does Noah think about the new baby?"

"He's on top of the world with this one. It was a long time to wait after Rachel before we knew this one was coming."

"Not so long. Rachel is only three."

"*Ja.*" Lovina paused.

Ellie glanced over to see a distant look on her sister's face. *Ach,* she should never have mentioned it. Now Lovina was thinking about the one they had lost after Rachel. She always knew what Lovina was thinking, even though they weren't as close as they had been as girls.

Lovina dumped another pile of cut pieces into the bowl. Ellie added her rhubarb and gave the bowl a shake to even it out.

"Looks like it's time to start cooking the first batch."

"*Ja.* I forgot to ask earlier. Do you have enough sugar?"

"*Mam* said to use sorghum. Sugar is too dear." Ellie added water to the big kettle on her stove and then poured in a pint of the thick, sticky syrup.

"Not too sweet, remember."

"*Ja,* I remember. You say that every year."

"If I didn't say it, it wouldn't be right."

Ellie stirred the mixture and smiled at her sister. She was right. They had to do the same things the same way every year. It was tradition. "Do you think Susan and Rachel will make rhubarb juice together when they're grown?"

"That would be sweet, wouldn't it?" Lovina smiled at the thought, then went back to cutting more rhubarb. "How are the strawberries doing?"

Ellie stirred the rhubarb. *Dat* wouldn't let them hear the end of it if she let them scorch. "Truth to tell, I'm awfully worried about them. It's been so dry."

"Do you think they'll last long enough for you to get berries from them next year?"

"I hope so. I can't bear to think what might happen if they don't...."

"What do you mean?"

Ellie looked at Lovina. She could always share everything with her sister, but should she share this problem now?

"Come on, Ellie. I know when you're worried." Lovina gave her a sudden, piercing look. "You spent all of your money on those plants, didn't you?"

Ellie nodded and went back to stirring the rhubarb.

"You're not in danger of losing your farm, are you?"

"*Ach, ne.* As long as the Brennemans continue to pay their rent, I'll be able to keep up on the taxes. It will just delay moving back there. If the plants don't make it, I'll lose the money I spent on them plus next year's income from selling the berries."

"And the year after…"

"I hoped by that time we'd be back home."

Lovina was silent as she sliced rhubarb.

"Ellie, I haven't said anything before…"

Ellie looked at Lovina. "What is it?"

"It's been almost two years…"

"Not yet. It's been only a year."

Lovina's mouth was a firm line as she turned to her. "It's been longer than that. It will be two years in September. You keep talking about moving home as if you think that will make everything the same as it was."

Ellie turned back to the stewing rhubarb. "I just want to give the children what Daniel wanted for them."

"And what is that?"

"You know, we've talked about it before." Ellie turned to Lovina again and gestured with the spoon. "It's what you and Noah have. Daniel never had a home. He was moved around between relatives until he came to Indiana to live with Hezekiah and Miriam. When he bought our farm, he was determined to give his children what he never had."

"Ellie." Lovina's voice was quiet. "You don't have to do it. Things are different now. Daniel is—"

"Daniel is gone. I know." Ellie turned back to the rhubarb. She didn't want Lovina to see the tears that threatened. "But I'm not, and his children aren't. It's up to me to see that his wishes are carried out."

"Have you thought about what he'd want now?"

"What's that?"

"I think he'd want something more important for his children than a farm. Remember, something else he never had was a father. Don't neglect that, Ellie."

Ellie kept her eyes on the pot of rhubarb. She couldn't marry again. How could she bear to risk that again? Besides, her children had a father, didn't they? She'd never let them forget Daniel.

Silence filled the kitchen, along with the sour-sweet fragrance of cooking rhubarb.

"I hear there's a new man in the area." Lovina kept her eyes on her knife as she said this.

"Where did you hear that?"

"*Mam.* Does he have a family?"

"*Ne,* he's single." *Mam* would have told her that, too. She knew what was on Lovina's mind.

"Oh." Lovina put a long lilt on that one word.

Ellie groaned to herself. What else could she talk about?

"Have you met him?" Lovina asked before Ellie could think of anything.

"*Ja,* I have."

"And?"

"And he's very *Englisch.*"

Lovina put her knife down and turned to Ellie. *"Englisch?"*

"Well, he dresses *Englisch. Dat* says he's been living in Chicago."

"Then what is he doing here?"

*Gut,* maybe this *Englischer* in their midst bothered Lovina as much as it did her.

"I don't know, but *Dat* says he wants to be Amish again."

"What does *Dat* think? Is he serious about this?"

"*Ja. Dat* says he is. He came by on Monday and bought Partner, that gelding *Dat* wanted to sell, and he was back again yesterday."

"So what do you think? Is he nice?"

Ellie's thoughts went to his eyes. She had been so rude to him, but those blue eyes had still smiled at her as if he could see right through her. Could he see what she was thinking? She felt her face grow hot. She hoped he couldn't.

"I wouldn't know. I haven't talked to him much."

"Much? Then you have talked to him."

"*Ja,* a little."

"What does *Dat* say?"

"*Dat* likes him. He's asked the family to give him a chance to be part of the community." Ellie moved the pot of rhubarb to a cooler part of the woodstove as it started simmering. "But those *Englisch* clothes are so fancy, and he's much too bold." Ellie turned to Lovina. "You wouldn't want an *Englischer* to spend too much time with Rachel, would you? Wouldn't you be worried about how he might influence her?"

Lovina was silent as she cut the next bunch of rhubarb into one-inch pieces. She dumped them into the bowl, then turned to Ellie.

"I'd trust *Dat.* I know he's never been wrong when it comes to a man's character. Don't you remember how everyone else thought Noah was wild and wouldn't amount to anything?"

Ellie remembered. Lovina's husband had almost left the community during his *Rumspringa,* but had returned to be baptized and then married Lovina.

"*Dat* never stopped having faith in him. Noah has told me that *Dat*'s support was the one thing that gave him the courage to come back home after his *Rum-*

*springa.* Without someone believing in him…" Lovina picked up another bunch of rhubarb to cut. "Without someone believing in him, Noah might never have come home. If *Dat* thinks we should give this new man the same support, then I think we need to do it."

Was Lovina right? Ellie cut her rhubarb in silence. Was Bram the invasive weed that would ruin their lives, or was she wrong?

She gave her head a decisive shake. As long as he wore those fancy clothes, she couldn't trust him, no matter what *Dat* said.

"You got this plow for a good price." Matthew ended his sentence with a grunt as he and Bram lifted the final piece of the dismantled equipment off the back of the wagon and onto Bram's barn floor.

Bram lifted the tailgate and fastened the latch. "*Ja,* it didn't go as high as I thought it would."

Matthew took a wrench out of the toolbox behind the wagon seat and started reassembling the plow. Bram held the axle steady while Matthew replaced the bolts and tightened them.

"I saw Samuel while we were in Shipshewana."

Bram didn't answer Matthew. So what if his brother had been there? There had been no sign of Kavanaugh, and that was what mattered.

Matthew continued in his mild tone, "We could have taken the time to see him."

"It would have been a waste." Bram kept his eyes on the wheel he was adjusting.

"I know you have your differences, but it doesn't seem right to ignore him."

"My brother and I don't have anything in common, that's all."

"Except you do." Matthew was persistent. "You share your family, your parents, your history..."

Bram glanced at his brother-in-law. Did he have any idea what it was like to grow up as a Lapp?

"*Ja,* we share our history, and that's the problem." Bram tightened the last bolt and stood up to admire the plow. It was a beauty. He wiped his hands on a rag and turned to Matthew.

"Our *Dat* was an alcoholic. I didn't like it, but that's how he was, and that's what killed him." And what probably killed *Mam,* too, in the end. Bram rubbed a bit of grease from the side of his finger. "My brother is just like him, and if I never see Samuel again, I'll be happy."

Bram waited for the shock on Matthew's face. Any Amishman would tell you that the attitude he had toward his brother was sinful, but Matthew's face only showed sadness.

"*Ach,* Bram, Annie never told me all of this."

"*Ja,* well, it happened when she was a little girl—and I don't think the girls saw all of it. *Mam* did what she could to protect them."

The silence that followed was as welcome as rain. Bram fastened the barn door and then climbed onto the wagon seat with Matthew for the drive back to their farm.

"How soon do you think you'll be able to move onto this place?" Matthew asked.

"Next week, I hope." Bram was glad to change the subject. "I've been working on the barn, and I'll need to clean out the house before I move in."

"It'll be a good farm when you're done." Matthew slapped the reins over the horses' backs. "You'll be able to count on the church's help with the farmwork, Bram."

"*Ja,* that will be good. I appreciate it." At least he thought he did. He liked to work alone.

Bram glanced sideways at Matthew. What kind of man had his sister married? A good man, for sure, but he was young. Oh, in years he was almost as old as Bram, but he seemed so naive about the world. All these Amishmen did. Compared to the men in Chicago…well, it was a good thing they'd never meet. These poor fellows wouldn't survive on the streets.

Bram rubbed at the grease on his finger. He had survived, but he had been tougher at seventeen than Matthew was in his twenties. Maybe having a father like his wasn't such a bad thing.

"Lovina, you be sure to take some of these cookies home to Noah." *Mam* took another panful of snickerdoodles out of the oven.

Ellie took in a deep breath full of cinnamon and sugar. No matter how old she was, *Mam*'s kitchen would always be home.

"Were the children good for you today?" Ellie couldn't resist taking a cooled cookie from the counter.

"*Ach, ja.* They are always the best when they're with their *grossmutti*. They play so well together." *Mam* slid another cookie sheet into the oven. "Of course, I haven't seen anything of them once the girls got home from school. They're all in the backyard."

"I must be getting home." Lovina found an extra plate and put some cookies on it. "Noah will be waiting for his supper."

"We'll see you at Matthew Beachey's tomorrow?"

"For sure. I wouldn't miss a frolic for anything."

Ellie put down the cookie she was nibbling. "A frolic?"

"*Ja,*" *Mam* said as she put some more cookies on

Lovina's plate. "Remember? We're having a sewing frolic for Annie Beachey. It's their first little one."

*Ach,* how could she forget? The cookie suddenly lost its flavor. She had let this frolic slip her mind, like most occasions that meant facing a crowd of people.

"You're coming, aren't you, Ellie?" Lovina paused, her hand on the door. "It's been a long time since you've been to any of the frolics or get-togethers."

A long time? Only since Daniel's death.

"We'll get her there." *Mam* put her arm around Ellie's shoulders and gave her a quick hug. "We'll see you tomorrow."

Ellie waited until Lovina was out the door before turning to *Mam.* "I don't think I'll go tomorrow."

"Why ever not? And don't try to give me the excuse that Danny's too young. He'll be fine."

"I…" How could she tell *Mam* how it felt to be in a crowd? She had never liked large groups of people, but lately she was more than just uncomfortable. The thought of all the women talking, laughing, staring at her… Church was bad enough.

"I just don't feel like going."

*Mam* gave her a long look. "I know you don't feel like it, but you've waited long enough. I haven't pushed you, but perhaps I should have. You need to do this, Ellie. You need to be with your church family. The longer you put it off, the harder it will be."

*Mam* was right, of course.

"*Ja,* I'll go." Ellie sighed, but with the sigh came a stirring of something she hadn't felt for a long time. She would go. She had always enjoyed her friends before, hadn't she? Perhaps she would even have fun.

## Chapter Five

As soon as the scholars left the next morning, Ellie and *Mam* were off to Matthew Beachey's in the family buggy.

"Who will be there, *Memmi?*" Susan sat on the front bench seat between them, her legs swinging with the buggy's movements.

Ellie hesitated, her throat dry, and *Mam* answered. "Rachel will be there and most of the children from church."

Susan's anxious face mirrored her own, and Ellie gave the little girl's knee a reassuring squeeze. They both shared an intense shyness around groups of people. Should they have stayed home after all?

Matthew Beachey came out of the barn to greet them as *Mam* drove into the yard.

"Good morning." He reached for Brownie's bridle. "I'll take care of the horse for you while you go on into the house."

"*Denki*, Matthew." *Mam* returned the young man's smile. "You're keeping busy away from the hen party, are you?"

Matthew's natural laugh put Ellie at ease. He was

always friendly and ready for fun—no wonder everyone liked him.

When Bram Lapp walked out of the barn behind Matthew, Ellie looked away and straightened Susan's *kapp.* She had forgotten he might be here.

"Good morning, Bram." *Mam*'s voice was friendly as usual, as if seeing Bram Lapp in the Beachey's farmyard was an everyday occurrence.

"Good morning." He answered *Mam,* but when Ellie finished fussing with Susan and glanced his way again, he was looking directly at her. His eyes were dark, unsure. *Ja,* he remembered how rude she had been the last time they'd talked. She looked over to *Mam* for help, but she was deep in conversation with Matthew.

Bram stepped closer and reached out to help Susan down from the buggy. Before Ellie could stop her, Susan jumped into his arms, and he gently lowered her to the ground. He lifted his hands up for Danny, but when Ellie held the baby close as she stepped down on her own, he just reached into the back of the buggy for her sewing bag and handed it to her.

"I hoped you would come to the frolic." Bram stood close to her, Susan's hand in his.

Ellie stared at his clothes—his Plain clothes. His brand-new shirt and plain-cut trousers were exactly like the ones all the men in the district wore, complete with the fabric suspenders and broad-brimmed hat. He didn't look *Englisch* anymore, and he didn't talk *Englisch*.... Her resolve wavered.

How would she answer him? His nearness was forward and unsettling, but she couldn't help wishing for more. What would she do if he gave her that secretive grin again? The thought brought on a flurry of butterfly wings in her stomach.

"I forgot you'd be here." Her face grew hot as soon as the rude words left her mouth. Why couldn't she talk to him like she would Matthew, or anyone else, for that matter? Every time she spoke with him, her tongue seemed to belong to someone else.

Ellie reached for Susan, but he stopped her with a hand on her arm.

"Have I done something wrong? I know we only met a couple days ago, and you don't know me, but I'd like to change that."

His hand warming her skin through the sleeve of her dress prickled her nerves to awareness of just how long it had been since she had felt a man's touch. She should turn away, let his hand slide off her arm, move to a more appropriate distance, but she was frozen in place.

She glanced up at his face. At her look, a smile spread, flashing the dimple in one cheek and encouraging her own mouth to turn up at the corners. She looked down, her face flushing hot again. What was wrong with her? She was acting like a schoolgirl!

Bram seemed to take her hesitation as an encouraging sign and stepped closer. Ellie found herself leaning toward him to catch the familiar scent of hay mingled with shaving soap, and she breathed in deeply.

*Ja,* just like a schoolgirl. What must he think of her?

"I've bought a farm." His voice was low, the words for her alone. "It's the Jackson place, just a couple miles west of your father's farm. Would you like to see it sometime?"

The Jackson farm? Ellie knew that farm—it was an *Englisch* farm. A blast of cold reality shoved away all thoughts of dimples and hay and…soap. The telephone lines strung from the road to the house on that farm were the fatal testimony. Her shoulders drew back as her chin lifted, and his hand fell to his side.

*"Ne, Denki,"* she answered as firmly as she knew how. "I'm already familiar with that farm."

She took Susan's hand as Bram stepped away, her face flushing hotter than ever. She couldn't have been ruder if she had slapped him in the face. How could she be so harsh? But an *Englisch* farm? Resolve straightened her spine with a snap.

"Come, Susan, it's time to go in the house."

Ellie followed *Mam* up the path to the kitchen door, anxious to get away from those intense blue eyes. She struggled to regain her composure before she reached the porch steps. How could one man upset her so?

Bram blinked as Ellie walked away. What happened? One minute her arm was lying warm and sweetly soft under his hand as she leaned toward him while they talked, and then those shutters had slammed tight again.

Matthew stood next to him with a grin on his face, watching him stare toward the house. "I don't think she likes you. What did you do to her?"

Bram frowned as he turned and checked the buckle on the harness. "Nothing. We were just talking."

"She's been widowed for almost two years now."

*"Ja,* that's what her father told me."

"So when will you ask her to go out with you?"

Bram shot a look at his brother-in-law. Matthew's smile hadn't left his face. One thing about married men was that they were usually quick to make sure every other man ended up in the same trap.

"What makes you think I want to go out with her?"

Matthew didn't respond. He just grinned, waiting for Bram's answer.

"All right. I just did. She turned me down flat."

"Oh, I wouldn't worry about that. She'll come around."

Bram took the horse's bridle and started leading him to the hitching rail on the shady side of the barn. "I didn't say I was giving up, did I?"

The problem was he should give up. He should let that prickly woman go her own way. He didn't need her. He didn't want her.

Bram went into the workshop next to the barn and found the broken harness strap Matthew had told him about. He turned the piece over in his hands. It was in good shape other than that one break.

Nothing felt as right as when he worked with harness leather. He loved this peaceful pleasure that came from handling the supple straps and the satisfaction that came with taking something that had been destroyed and making it whole again. Scarred, perhaps, because you could always see the repair, but useful once more and stronger than it had been.

He started in on the harness, first taking his pocket-knife and cutting the frayed edges off the broken ends of the leather. As he worked, children's laughter drifted in through the shop window from the backyard, and he shifted to get a view of the sandbox from his stool at the workbench. Girls' pastel dresses and boys' shirts in the same hues filled the yard. Older ones played a game of Duck, Duck, Goose. He looked for Susan, but she wasn't among them.

How long had it been since he'd heard children playing without traffic noise mingled with their harsh voices?

Almost as long as he had missed the scent of a woman. A real woman, not girls like Babs, with her cloying odor of dying flowers and smoky bourbon. Babs had never looked at him with the cold eyes Ellie Miller used. No, she had been more than willing to press her silken dress against him, batting her heavy black eyelashes.

His eyes narrowed. Babs made sure he knew what she wanted—or what Kavanaugh paid her to provide—and he was glad he had never taken her up on her offer. He had never spent more time with her than an occasional dinner or as a date to one of Kavanaugh's shindigs. Something about the girl had turned his stomach. Not just her—black-haired Cindy before her and Madge before her. Kavanaugh kept his boys supplied with women.

He took a deep breath, dispelling the memory.

Thoughts of Ellie swirled into his mind to take its place. She had leaned toward him, coming within inches of his chest. He could have reached out for her, pressing her slight form against him while he kissed her... but that would have ruined everything. A woman like Ellie would never put up with what the girls in Chicago begged for. He pushed the thought away.

Her arm under his hand had felt alive, firm, capable. Taking another deep breath, he tried to recapture the scent of...what? Just soap and water? Whatever it was, the memory clung to him.

*Keep focused.*

Bram shaved the two ends of the leather strap with his knife, shaping them to overlap each other. If he did find Kavanaugh, the last thing he needed was for someone to get in the way. The last thing he wanted was for someone to get hurt.

Taking the awl from Matthew's tool bench, he drilled

holes through the splices, lining up the shaved ends so they would overlap in a solid, smooth join.

John Stoltzfus was a good man, and he liked Bram. That was a step in the right direction. He should spend more time with him, but that would mean spending more time around Ellie and her children.

Bram rummaged in a jar for a couple rivets and fitted them into the holes.

That Susan—yeah, she was something. The way she looked up at him with those solemn brown eyes as if he was some sort of hero pulled at his heart.

He glanced through the window at the playing children again. Susan had joined the game, her light green dress and white *kapp* mingling with the other pastels. She laughed as she played, her face sweet and innocent.

A steel band twisted in his gut. What kind of hero could he be to a little girl?

He found Matthew's tack hammer hanging on the wall. A sharp rap sealed the first rivet. He shifted to the second rivet but stopped.

If Ellie looked at him the way Susan did, what would he do then?

His world tilted for a brief moment, then righted. He gave his head a shake and then drove the hammer home on the second rivet.

Focus. Play the part. Lie low under his cover until his job was done, then maybe he could...what? Court her?

Forget her. That was what he needed to do. God help him if he let himself fall for the woman.

Ellie took a deep breath as she laid her hand on the knob of the Beacheys' back door, listening to the women's voices on the other side. Facing Bram Lapp would be easier than stepping through this door.

"Ellie, you can do this."

Ellie turned to see *Mam*'s eyes filled with understanding. The soft words gave her strength.

The crowd of chatting women parted to welcome them as the door opened. Susan clung to Ellie's skirts as they stepped in. Ellie wished she had somewhere to hide, but it was too late. *Mam* had already set her pies on the table and was greeting her friends.

Annie Beachey came over to Ellie as she lingered just inside the door.

"Ellie, I'm so glad you could come!"

Ellie smiled in spite of her churning stomach. Who could resist Annie's contagious happiness? Although how she could be so merry when she must be uncomfortable with the growing baby most of the time was beyond her.

Annie took her bonnet to the back bedroom, and Ellie stepped farther into the kitchen. Sally, her younger sister, came over and took Danny from her arms.

"I've missed this little man."

Sally's easy confidence was just the balm Ellie's nerves needed. This might be a fun outing after all.

"Well, if you hadn't married last fall, you could have been cuddling him all winter."

Sally looked up from nuzzling Danny's neck. "*Ach,* sister. Then I wouldn't be looking forward to my own *boppli,* would I?" Sally turned to Susan. "The other children are playing out in the yard with Dorothy Ann."

"She'll join them soon, I'm sure." Ellie patted Susan's back, knowing these few minutes of shyness would soon be over.

Sally leaned closer to Ellie, lowering her voice. "I saw the way Levi Zook kept watching you a week ago at Meeting. I think he's still sweet on you."

Ellie's face grew warm with embarrassment. Did everyone know about his attentions to her? "I've told Levi we're not suited for each other. I don't know why he's so persistent."

"I do," said Lovina as she joined Sally and Ellie. "I heard his sister from Middlebury wants him to send his younger girls to live with her, and he's desperate to find a new wife so he can keep his family together."

"*Ja,* well, I can understand why he wants a new wife, but it's not going to be me." Ellie turned to greet Lovina with a smile. "We'll be sewing for your little one next." She nodded at Lovina's expanding waist.

As Sally and Lovina started chatting about morning-sickness remedies, Ellie stepped back, feeling the wall that had risen between them. She and her sisters had been inseparable as girls, and her marriage hadn't lessened that close bond. Not until the past couple years.

Now that she was a widow, and they had their husbands... She crossed her arms in front of her, hiding her slim form. She could have been expecting another baby, too, if—well, if things had been different.

*Ne,* she had to stop thinking this way. Things were what they were, and it was *Gott*'s will. A faithful, obedient woman accepted *Gott*'s will, didn't she?

And if it was *Gott*'s will that she accept Levi Zook as her new husband? Ellie suppressed a shudder. She still believed two people should love each other if they married, and as kind and faithful as Levi was, she didn't love him.

Ellie followed some of the other women as they moved toward the front room of the house, where Annie had arranged things for the frolic. A table was set up for cutting material, with several lengths of muslin and flannel ready to be cut into the pieces they would sew into gowns and diapers for the new baby. The room was arranged with chairs in a circle for sewing and visiting. Before long, the four women who had taken the job of cutting the material had pieces ready for sewing, and the rest of the women settled in with their needles and thread.

When Susan went off with the other children, Ellie chose a chair near her sisters, where Danny was still happy on Sally's lap. Taking the next available diaper, one of many they would be making today, she started in on the simple hem. Over the hum of conversation, she heard Bram's name mentioned.

"What did you say his name is?" Minnie Garber asked Annie.

"Bram—short for Abram. He's my brother who is staying with us for a time."

What did Annie think of her *Englisch* brother? Ellie hated the thought of one of her brothers jumping the fence, leaving their family and their ways behind. How would she treat them if they had left and then wanted to return?

"I didn't know you had another brother," Minnie went on. That woman was never shy when it came to gossip.

"Bram has been gone for quite a few years—"

"Gone?" Minnie interrupted. The rest of the room quieted as the other women listened to their conversation.

"*Ja.*" Annie stopped and looked around the room of women waiting to hear what she had to say. "He left home twelve years ago but came back recently. He just bought a farm and will be settling here."

"Twelve years?" Minnie's voice was incredulous.

"Where was he all that time? Did he live in Ohio? Pennsylvania?"

"Um, *ne.*"

Ellie's heart went out to Annie. It was obvious that she wasn't interested in gossiping about her brother.

"He was in Chicago," Annie finally said. Her words were met with silence.

"Chicago?" Minnie sounded stunned.

"*Ja,* but he's home now and wants to be part of our community." Annie looked from one face to another. Most of the women stared at the sewing in their hands, but *Mam* smiled at Annie, encouraging her.

Then Minnie voiced what Ellie had been thinking.

"Won't he have trouble giving up his *Englisch* ways after all this time?"

"He's shedding himself of them as quickly as he can." Annie sounded relieved, as if she was happy to give Minnie an acceptable answer. "When I finished his new clothes yesterday, he wouldn't rest until he had put them on."

"And you say he bought a farm?"

"*Ja,* the Jackson place on Emma Road. He spent all Tuesday afternoon and yesterday tearing out the telephone lines. He's planning to move there next week."

One of Minnie's daughters joined in the conversation from the other side of the circle.

"So all he needs now is a buggy and a wife!"

Good-natured laughter followed her comment, and the conversation shifted to the coming wedding of Minnie's third daughter. Ellie concentrated on finishing the hem on the diaper, letting the conversation flow around her.

Bram was turning the Jackson place into an Amish farm? Could she have been so wrong about him? From what Annie said, he did mean to give up all his *Englisch* ways. If that was true, then *Dat* had been right all along.

Could Minnie's daughter have been right, too, that he was looking for a wife?

She pricked her finger with the needle, and the pain brought a start of tears to her eyes.

If he was, he wouldn't have any problems finding one. He was no Levi Zook.

But it for sure wasn't going to be her. No man was going to take her Daniel's place.

## Chapter Six

"It was a robin. I know it was," said Susan. She nodded to emphasize her certainty.

"It wasn't a robin—it was a blackbird." Johnny's retort was tinged with disdain.

"He had red on him."

"It was a red-winged blackbird. Robins have red breasts, not red shoulders."

Ellie touched Johnny's knee to quiet him before the argument gained strength. She should reprimand them, but on Sunday mornings she just wanted quiet.

The buggy swayed in rhythm to Brownie's trotting hooves. It wasn't as crowded now that Reuben was old enough for his own buggy. *Dat* had agreed he could drive it to Welcome Yoder's for church, and now the two boys were ahead of them on the road, Reuben driving at the same sedate pace. Soon he'd be courting, if he wasn't already, and next Benjamin. At least Mandy and Rebecca were still at home.

Ellie listened to her sisters' chatter. She had been the same way with Sally and Lovina once, their three heads together, sharing their secrets, their dreams. Mandy and Rebecca would have the same sweet girlhood memories.

"There's another robin!"

Johnny looked where Susan pointed. "*Ne,* that one's a blue jay. See how big he is? And his blue feathers?"

Susan didn't argue, but kept her eyes on the side of the road.

Ellie's thoughts went back to Mandy and Rebecca. She'd had that same anticipation when she was their age. Riding to church was an adventure, with Lovina giggling about the boys they would see and Sally bouncing with anticipation of seeing her best friend again. She had looked forward to the singing, even the long sermons, and the fellowship. What had changed?

She never had the urge to kick against the restraints of the church that some people talked about. The *Ordnung* was safe. It provided security against the changing world. Even when her friends tried living outside the protective fence of the *Ordnung* during their *Rumspringa,* Ellie never saw the lure. She knew where she belonged.

Bram Lapp had left the community once.... What would it be like to leave her loved ones behind, to take the children somewhere and start fresh where no one knew her? The thought pressed against her heart, stopping her breath. It would be like dying. *Ne,* she could never leave her home, her family.

*Dat* turned south at the corner, and Ellie closed her eyes against the morning sun hitting her face.

She must work through this emptiness somehow. Church for her meant nothing more than a long day with a headache. The children needed tending, and every week it was harder to keep them still during the meeting. The hymns were so long, the prayers drawn out. There had been a time when the singing was her favorite part of a Sunday. Now she just waited for it to be over.

"Is that one a robin?"

"*Ja,* see his red breast?"

Ellie gave herself a mental shake. Her children needed her. A pasted-on smile was better than none, and a kind word to a friend could help lift her spirits. But how many more church Sundays were going to pass before the smile became genuine again?

*Dat* turned the buggy into the driveway of the Yoders' farm, joining a line of other buggies. When they approached the sidewalk leading to the house, Ellie saw the buggy in front of Reuben's stop. Matthew Beachey jumped down, then reached back to help Annie. He walked with her to the lines of people waiting to go into the house while their buggy drove on.

Bram must be driving the buggy. What would she say to him? She had been so rude on Thursday at the work frolic.

Polite. She could be polite and hope he would forgive her rudeness.

Ellie joined the line of women in the front yard. She returned the smiles of several, exchanging the brief hug and brush of the lips on the cheek that was the kiss of peace. The group was quiet other than occasional murmured greetings. The time for visiting and fellowship would come later.

Bram couldn't keep his eyes up front. Church hadn't changed in twelve years. Even here in Eden Township, the sermons were the same High German as in Shipshewana—difficult to follow and meaningless. He tried to listen to the first sermon, but he lost the minister's point and found his mind wandering, just as it had always done. He concentrated on looking alert and interested while all the time his thoughts were elsewhere.

This morning he couldn't keep his mind off Ellie. Glancing her way, he saw the distracted look, the line between her eyes. His years undercover had taught him to read people, and that line was a telltale sign she had a headache. A young boy sat quietly between her and Elizabeth, and Ellie kept Susan busy playing with a handkerchief baby while the littlest boy slept on her lap.

That one strand of Ellie's hair wouldn't stay tucked in her *kapp,* and Bram tried not to stare. The minister's voice droned on, forgotten. Each time he glanced at her, the strand was looser, until it was a curling mist circling her ear. Every movement of her head caused it to droop a little farther. How far would she let it go before she reached up to tuck it in? What would it feel like if he tucked it in for her? Would the soft, silky strand catch on his newly calloused fingers, or would it glide through his hand like smooth water?

She looked up and caught his eyes, holding them for a brief second before she turned to the front again. A red glow started at her neck and traveled up. Bram ducked his head to the floor and smiled. She wasn't immune to him, either.

When *Dat* stood to preach the main sermon of the morning, Ellie shifted Danny's weight to her other arm. He was a heavy load as he slept on her lap.

"*Memmi,* are we almost done?" Susan's whisper carried to the women around them.

Ellie lifted her finger to her lips to remind Susan to be quiet, then leaned down to whisper in her ear, "Almost."

*Dat* stood with his head bowed. His silent prayer

before the sermon was always longer than any other minister's. *Dat* claimed it was to clear his head and discern the Spirit's leading, and maybe it was. All she knew was that it made the sermon last far longer than her back could bear.

Her head pounded. There—Bram was looking at her again. She turned her head to avoid his gaze, but she could still see him out of the corner of her eye. When would this service be over?

"The passage for today's sermon is from Hebrews, the twelfth chapter, the first three verses." *Dat*'s voice broke into her thoughts.

Ellie tuned the familiar verses out. The women on the other side of *Mam* sat with rapt attention, listening to *Dat* as if hearing the reading for the first time.

*Dat's* voice broke through her thoughts as he started in on his sermon.

"We must take Jesus Christ himself as our example, as the apostle Paul exhorts us in Philippians: 'Let this mind be in you, which was also in Christ Jesus.'"

Of course Jesus Christ should be her example. His humility and sinless life had been held up to her as the goal of every Christian ever since she could remember, but with this thought Ellie shifted. It was her pride that had brought her to this place in her life. She could blame no one but herself.

"Jesus Christ didn't dwell on the trials of his present day. He looked forward to the joy that was set before Him—the joy of His eternal place at the right hand of the throne of *Gott*."

Not dwell on her present trials when they dragged her down on every side? What was *Dat* trying to say?

"So lay aside the sin, the weight of your sin, that you

may run the race set before you. Look forward with joy, and trust *Gott* for the reward He has set before you."

This startled Ellie so much that she missed the rest of the sermon. Trust Him? The *Gott* who took her Daniel? And look forward to what with joy? A life alone, seeking to fulfill Daniel's dreams? She rubbed the spot between her eyebrows where the headache was centered. She could see no joy set before her.

Ellie glanced over to the men's side of the room, where Bram was listening to the sermon instead of trying to catch her eye for once. He leaned forward, resting his forearms on his knees as his gaze fastened on *Dat*. What was he learning from this sermon?

Eli Schrock's testimony followed *Dat*'s sermon, reaffirming everything that had been said, and then he added his own final comment. "You young folk, especially, trust *Gott*'s leading in your life. Follow Him as a sheep follows a shepherd, and then you can hope that He will bring you into His glory."

Follow *Gott?* How could she follow *Gott* when His voice was silent?

The congregation standing for the hymn of dismissal startled Ellie. She had been so caught in her own thoughts that she had missed the closing prayer.

The headache pressed down.

She shifted Danny again to stand with the others, but she didn't sing. She couldn't. She leaned her cheek against Danny's soft hair.

*Ach, Gott.* She kissed Danny's head, swallowing back the tears that wanted to fall. *Ach, Gott, help me. I can't bear this any longer.*

All through dinner, Bram watched for Ellie among the other women who were serving, but with no luck.

He finished his ham sandwich and potato salad, then went to wait under an oak tree while the women cleared the tables.

A group of older boys gathered in the front pasture across the farm lane, a few of them with baseball bats. This was one Sunday afternoon tradition he remembered well.

"Bram, it's good to see you today."

He turned to see John Stoltzfus walking toward him. Bram shook his hand.

"*Denki,* it's good to see you, too."

"How are things going?"

"Coming along." Bram nodded. "The farm is nearly ready for me to move onto it. I pick up my buggy on Tuesday afternoon. I'll be over before then to get the gelding."

John waved his hand in the air, dismissing all that Bram had said.

"I mean the rest of your life. You're still getting on well with your brother-in-law?"

Bram glanced over at Matthew as he stood with a group of other men. Matthew's wiry build made him look as if he'd fit in with the cowboys Bram had seen around the stockyards in Chicago better than in this community of Amish farmers.

"*Ja,* I'm glad Annie married such a good man."

"What about your brother? Have you seen him again?"

He wouldn't have anything to do with Samuel if he could help it, but John wouldn't understand any more than Matthew had.

"I'll leave that up to Samuel. He knows where I am if he wants to see me."

A young boy wandered up to John and leaned against

his leg, glancing up at Bram, his brown eyes looking so much like Susan's that Bram placed him right away. It was the boy who had been sitting with Ellie during church.

"Bram, this is my grandson Johnny."

"Hi, Johnny," Bram said. The boy stuck close to his grandfather and eyed Bram doubtfully.

"Johnny..." Bram could hear the gentle rebuke in John's voice.

"Hello." The boy gave his grandfather's leg a quick hug and then wandered to the edge of the pasture to watch the older boys.

"Johnny is Ellie's oldest," John said as he watched the boy walk away. "He misses his father. *Dawdi* here just doesn't fill in that gap very well."

Bram was silent, watching Johnny as he leaned against the pasture fence, his head tilted into one hand. An outsider. Bram swallowed. Yes, he remembered that part of Sunday afternoons, too. A boy with no father to bring him into the game, and no one cared. At least Johnny had his *Dawdi,* even if John didn't think he was enough.

"What happened to his father?" Bram almost bit back the words, but it was too late. What right did he have to ask?

"It was nearly two years ago." John's eyes were on his grandson as he spoke. "I know Johnny remembers that day well. Ellie has said he still has nightmares about it, even though he didn't witness the accident. Daniel—Johnny's father—had a new team of Belgians. They were green broke, and Daniel planned on finishing their training, but he didn't get a chance. Something spooked them while he was harnessing them for work one morning... trapped him against the barn wall."

John paused, but Bram could fill in where he left off.

It was obvious that John still struggled with his own memories of that day.

"Ellie was right there with Susan. They saw it all. Ellie had to get the horses away from Daniel, and somehow she was able to do it. She stayed calm enough to move the horses into the pasture, send Johnny to the neighbor's for help and try to save Daniel. He died that evening."

"What a tragedy," Bram said. It was the only thing he could say. He saw Ellie in his imagination, trying to save her husband, to protect her children.... She hid a steel core under that stubbornness.

"It was a hard time, especially for her. She and the children moved to our place. She couldn't stay on Daniel's farm, and didn't want to after the accident, but our *Dawdi Haus* was empty, so it was the perfect place for her and the two children. Little Danny came to live with us eight months later."

Bram looked at Johnny again. The boy kicked at the fence post as he leaned against the boards. That whole family needed a man who could be a real husband and father to them.

But that man wasn't him—not by a long shot.

Where was Johnny? Ellie paused in the shade of the big maple tree that grew between the drive and the back door of Welcome Yoder's house and searched each group of church members with her eyes. There he was, watching the softball game.

Now that she had found him, what else could she do? Ellie twisted her fingers together at her waist. The children were all occupied, and the afternoon stretched in front of her. *Dat* wouldn't be ready to go home until the ball game was done. At least the headache was easing.

"Ellie!"

Lovina and Annie Beachey had found a bench near the house, and Lovina was waving her over.

"I haven't gotten a chance to visit with you yet today." Lovina grasped Ellie's hand and pulled her down next to her.

Ellie sighed as she took her seat. "It's good to see you, too. How are both of you feeling?"

"Oh, I'm not sure how much longer I'll be able to wait," Annie said. She fanned herself with a handkerchief. "I know the weather isn't hot yet, but I feel like I have a furnace inside me!"

Ellie laughed at the comical face Annie made. "Just be glad you aren't like poor Lovina. She has the whole summer to wait!"

"Oh, but we all know it's worth it," Lovina said. "I would go through this every summer just to hold a wee one in my arms at the end."

Ellie looked away from them as she felt unexpected tears spring to her eyes. What was the matter with her that she couldn't join in a conversation about babies?

She half listened to Lovina and Annie's conversation as she watched the groups of men in the yard. *Dat* was talking with Bram and a couple others, and then Welcome Yoder and Eli Schrock joined the group. It looked as if *Dat* was making sure Bram met them all.

Levi Zook walked over to join them, his ready laugh already carrying to her ears. *Ja*, and he looked in her direction. Ellie turned her gaze away from the men. Poor Levi. She felt for him, bearing the raising of his children alone since his wife died, but not enough to marry him when she felt nothing more than pity.

She waited until she heard him talking with another group, then looked at Bram again. He blended in so well

with the other men she would never call him *Englisch*
now. His *Englisch* haircut was hidden under his hat,
and with his clean-shaven face, he looked like an older
bachelor. He joined in the conversation and even stood
with the same relaxed posture. If she didn't know better, she would think he really was one of them.

"Ellie." Lovina's voice broke into her thoughts.
"Annie wants to know what you think of her brother
Bram."

"I've only just met him. I can't say what I think of
him yet."

"Well, he's talked about visiting with your *Dat* and
being at the farm," Annie said. "And he's mentioned
everyone in the family except you. That's a sure sign
he's been thinking about you."

Ellie felt her face blush. If he thought about her at
all, it for sure wouldn't be romantic thoughts, as rude
as she'd been. But now, watching him in deep conversation with *Dat* and the other men, she couldn't remember why he had upset her so. It didn't look as if he was
trying to bring his *Englisch* ways to the community; in
fact, it looked as if he was trying hard to fit in.

"How soon will he move to his new farm?" Lovina
asked.

"He said he wants to this next week, but I don't want
him to go yet. That old house is barely livable, and we'll
miss having him around when he goes. But he says he
wants to get started on the spring work. It's getting
late as it is."

Someone in the group of men must have told a joke,
because just then they all started laughing. Bram turned
and looked straight at Ellie, the dimple on his right
cheek making him more attractive than ever. He paused
when he saw her looking at him and gave her a smile

that started sliding into his grin. Ellie turned away before it did. How could she let him catch her watching him?

"I'd better go look for Danny," she said, rising from the bench. "It's time for his diaper to be changed."

"Oh, Sally can do that," Lovina said, catching her arm and pulling her back to her seat again. "We want to know what you think of Bram."

"What I think of him? Why would that make a difference?"

"You're both single, about the same age. Who wouldn't think of the two of you together? You don't have to be secretive about it like the younger folk are. And since you won't consider Levi…"

Ellie tried not resent her sister's clumsy matchmaking. Of course people would think of them pairing up, and after watching Bram today, she realized it wasn't as impossible as she had thought at first. But she wasn't getting married again, no matter how hard Lovina pushed. If she only wanted another husband, she could have married Levi Zook months ago. *Ne,* marriage wasn't in her plans, was it?

"We hardly know each other. I don't think we've spoken more than five words to each other," Ellie said firmly. "Don't count your chickens before they're hatched, Lovina."

"I'm not counting chickens, Ellie, just trying to get the hen to lay a few eggs."

Annie burst into laughter at this, and Ellie found herself smiling at her sister's joke.

"I'll think about it."

But it was hopeless. Lovina wouldn't give up that easily.

\* \* \*

"So Thursday will be good for everyone, then?"

The men all nodded their agreement as John went on. "Bram has seed already." He looked at Bram to get an affirmation. "So bring your teams and equipment."

The conversation drifted away from Thursday's plans to the weather, and when Matthew walked up to him, Bram was ready for some action.

"How about joining the softball game? Those young fellows need to have some friendly competition."

"I don't even remember the last time I played."

"It's something you don't forget. Come on."

He followed Matthew to the pasture, where a group of young men were joining together to make a team. They got some ribbing from the boys on the other team, but it was all in fun.

The boys went up to bat first, and Bram went out to left field. He knew it wouldn't be a rough game with everyone wearing their best clothes, but at least it would get him moving.

The first two batters hit lazy pop-ups to center field. The center fielder missed, and the boys made it to their bases. The next batter struck out. Yes, it would be a quiet game.

Bram looked over to the house between batters and saw Ellie still sitting with Annie and another woman on the bench. She looked preoccupied and was no longer looking at him. What was she thinking about?

The next batter hit a pop-up to center field again, but this time it was caught. One more out before they switched sides.

Bram glanced at Johnny. The boy was watching him. There was something about Ellie's children—first the little girl and now this kid. They had a way of looking at him—how could he ever live up to the trust he saw in their eyes? He glanced over at Ellie again, and the warning bells started going off in his head. He shouldn't get involved.

*Just forget it.*

The longing look on Johnny's face decided for him.

"Johnny," he said, walking over to the fence, "do you want to play left field with me?"

The boy's face brightened, then fell again. He looked at the ground.

"I don't know how. Benjamin and Reuben won't let me. They'll say I'm too little."

*Benjamin and Reuben? That's right, Ellie's brothers.* "They'll have to let you if you're my partner."

"Really?" Johnny said, looking at his face for the first time.

"Sure, come on."

Bram lifted Johnny over the fence and showed him where to stand to wait for the ball.

Johnny turned to Bram as the next batter stepped up to the plate.

"That's Reuben. He always hits the ball."

"If he hits it this way, we'll try to catch it."

Johnny nodded in response, and then he stood with his hands on his knees and his eyes on the batter, in imitation of Bram.

Reuben let the first two pitches go past him and then swung at the third. The big softball hit the bat with a muffled *thunk* and flew toward left field.

"Catch it!" Johnny yelled to Bram.

Bram caught the ball on a bounce and passed it to Johnny.

"Throw to second!"

Johnny tossed the ball to the second baseman, who

picked it up as it rolled along the ground toward him, then tagged the runner from first out.

Bram gave the boy a smile and nod. "Good job, son."

The grin on Johnny's face gave him a start. He didn't look anything like the forlorn kid who had been leaning on the fence. John was right; the boy just needed a man's attention, someone closer to his own father's age.

The afternoon wore on, and more boys Johnny's age joined in the game with their fathers and older brothers. There were more than a dozen players on each team, but no one minded. All too soon the afternoon ended, and it was time for the families to make their way home.

"I hope your *mam* isn't too mad that I let your clothes get dusty."

Johnny looked down at the dirt on his knees in surprise. Bram did his best to brush it off with his hand, but the boy's Sunday pants were still stained when he was done.

"Do you think she'll whip me?"

Bram's heart stopped at the thought of someone whipping this kid. The unsought memory of a hot, dusty barn and a horsewhip in his father's hand rose before he could slam the door shut on it again. He couldn't bear to be the cause of Johnny's suffering.

"I'll explain. She'll have to whip me to get to you."

Bram looked into the boy's eyes. They glowed with merriment.

"I'd like to see her try to whip you!"

"Now, Johnny." Bram's head snapped up at the sound of Ellie's voice. "Have I ever whipped anyone?"

Johnny laughed as he caught hold of his mother's hand. When Ellie's mock frown softened into a winsome smile, Bram understood. He was being let in on a family joke. Nestled against Ellie's left hip, even little

Danny drooled a gap-toothed grin. What kind of family was this?

"*Dawdi* has our buggy ready. It's time to go."

Ellie spoke to Johnny, but her eyes were on Bram. Her usual guarded expression had disappeared. She looked more relaxed. Calm. Willing to talk.

"Thank you for including him in the game." Voice soft, she stepped close while Johnny and Susan dashed for the stone drive. Danny reached out to pat Bram's shoulder, and the baby's touch soothed the prickled feelings of old, dredged up by Johnny's teasing words.

"I haven't seen him have so much fun since…" She stopped and caught her lower lip in her teeth. Why did he think about kissing her right then?

"My brothers forget to include him in what they're doing. They still think of him as being Danny or Susan's age, I guess. You made him very happy."

"It was fun for me, too." Bram cast about for something to say to keep the conversation going. He didn't want to break this better mood, this more friendly approach. "He's a fine boy."

Goodbyes were exchanged as families sorted themselves into the waiting buggies. Ellie should join her family, but she still stood next to him.

She finally looked at him. "I need to apologize to you." Her clear blue eyes held his.

"There are no apologies needed."

"*Ja,* there are. I…well, I was mistaken about something. I was wrong to be so rude to you."

Bram pushed further, in spite of the cacophony of warnings in his head.

"Does that mean that you might go riding with me sometime?"

She cast her eyes away from his. "I…I would have to think about it."

"I'll be at your place on Tuesday. I'll ask you then."

The look she gave him was uncertain, wavering. She nodded a goodbye and then headed to her father's waiting buggy.

Bram's heart started to follow, but he stopped it with a frown. Strong and stubborn he could handle. Vulnerable and unsure? A woman like that would grab him and never let go.

# Chapter Seven

"Walkin's for chumps."

Kavanaugh's words echoed in Bram's mind with every step he took toward the Stoltzfus farm on Tuesday morning.

"You're one of my boys now, and my boys have wheels." Then Kavanaugh had given him the Studebaker.

Puffs of dust rose each time his foot landed on the edge of the gravel road. Man, he missed that Studebaker.

But he didn't miss it enough to risk Kavanaugh finding him first. In this game, he needed every advantage he could get, and his biggest advantage was that Kavanaugh had no idea where he was.

A rising blister on his left heel reminded Bram to shorten his stride. He'd bear a thousand blisters before he'd give up that advantage.

When he reached the crossroads, the trees gave way to a view of John's white barn and outbuildings, and Bram's pace quickened. He was only anxious to get his rig so he wouldn't have to walk anymore, right? He hadn't given Ellie Miller a thought all morning.

But he scanned the garden and the yards before heading to the barn. She wasn't anywhere in sight.

Bram found John on the threshing floor, currying the gray gelding he had purchased last week.

"Good morning," Bram called to him.

John nodded his greeting over the horse's back. He gave a final stroke with the currycomb and then picked up a brush.

"He's almost ready for you." The horse stood quietly while John brushed him.

"There's no big hurry. I'm not due to pick up the buggy until midafternoon."

"You'll eat dinner with us, then?"

Bram hesitated, but the invitation wasn't really a question. If he was at the farm during the noon meal, he would be expected to eat with the family. It was the Amish way. Would Ellie and her children eat with her parents, or did they eat at the *Dawdi Haus?*

"I'll be glad to stay."

"It's too bad today is a school day. Johnny will be sorry he missed you. He chattered away about that softball game all the way home on Sunday."

"It was a lot of fun." Bram rubbed the back of his neck. Johnny's trusting face, that gap-toothed grin, had haunted him ever since he watched the Stoltzfus buggy drive away Sunday afternoon. The whole family had wrapped themselves around his heart somehow. "He's a fine boy."

John stopped his brushing and leaned his arms on the horse's back.

"He's been a sad and moody boy. I've been at a loss as to how to make things better for him and haven't been able to reach him. You did, though. I haven't seen that boy so lively since his father died."

Bram didn't know what to say. He had enjoyed the ball game, too, but he hadn't expected to enjoy the kid. Things were getting complicated.

The sound of a dinner bell drifted into the barn.

"Dinner's almost ready." John gave the horse another pat. "He'll be fine here until this afternoon."

As the two men walked to the house, Bram looked toward the *Dawdi Haus*. Still no sign of Ellie. Just as well. He'd be polite, have dinner and be on his way.

After washing up at the bench outside the back door, Bram followed John into the large kitchen. He took a deep breath. The tantalizing odors drew him in. Potatoes, fried chicken… Bram's throat was suddenly tight when he saw Ellie pouring peas into a serving dish. He took a deep breath.

A tug on his trousers pulled his gaze down.

"I helped set the table."

Bram crouched down to Susan's height. Her brown eyes were shining as she smiled at him.

"*Denki,* I'm sure your *memmi* likes the help."

"I put a fork by your plate."

Bram stifled the urge to take her in his arms. He satisfied himself with stroking her hair. Funny. He had never liked children before, but this little girl…

"Susan, come sit down."

Ellie blushed when he caught her eye, and she gave him a brief smile as Elizabeth directed Bram to a seat and the family took their places.

When they bowed their heads for the silent prayer, the ticking clock in the front room was the only sound, propelling him back to his *grossdatti*'s table. He could almost hear *Grossdatti*'s voice reading from the *Christenpflicht,* the book of prayers, after the meal. What would his life have been like if the old man hadn't died when Bram was so young?

As the prayer ended with a soft "amen" from John, he looked up, directly into Ellie's blue eyes. Her face reddened as she turned away to help Susan choose a piece of chicken.

"What do you have left to do on your farm before you can move in?" John asked as he passed Bram the bowl of potatoes.

"The house isn't livable yet. I thought I might be able to use one room, but then I found a family of skunks living under the floor. They put up a fuss when I tried to get them out of there."

"How did you do it?"

Bram looked around the table. Reuben had asked the question, but everyone was staring at him, including Susan.

"I used a trick I learned from my *grossdatti*." Bram's mind flashed back to the day he had watched the old man trap skunks. He must have been Susan's age.

"I took a box—the right size, of course. It had to be low enough so the skunk couldn't lift its tail." The little girl's eyes got even bigger. "I put a dead fish in it and waited. Sure enough, right about moonrise, here came a mama skunk and her four babies out from under the house and into the box."

"What did you do?" Benjamin asked between bites of potatoes.

"I had an old horse blanket that I threw over that box and wrapped it up tight."

"Didn't they spray you?"

"*Ne.* Remember, the mama skunk couldn't lift her tail."

"What did you do with them?" Susan's voice quavered.

Bram hesitated. Susan's eyes were wide and trustful. He couldn't tell her he had drowned the entire lot.

"I took them out to the woods."

Reuben and Benjamin nodded at each other. *Ne,* he hadn't fooled them.

"What about their *dat?*" Susan asked.

"I caught him the next night and took him out to the woods with his family."

Bram glanced up at Ellie and grinned. The corners of her mouth twitched as she tried to keep herself from smiling. She had enjoyed the skunk story.

"Did I hear they had electricity on the Jackson farm?" John asked.

"I didn't find any electric lines. I don't think the power company has gotten that far yet. There were telephone lines, but I took those down." That had been hard. He could think of a hundred reasons to keep a telephone, but there was still one big one to get rid of the lines. No Amish farmer would have them.

He glanced at Ellie again. She caught his look, her blue eyes smiling. He could drown in those eyes if he wasn't careful.

What had he gotten himself into?

Ellie took as long as she dared washing up after the noon meal. Bram and *Dat* were on the front porch, visiting. How long was he going to stay? How long could she stall? But he was waiting to talk to her, to ask her to come see his farm, to go riding with him.

It was tempting. To have such a nice-looking man look at her the way he did—she hadn't felt that for such a long time. But what if…what if she gave in to him?

Resolve straightened her back like a rod of cold steel. She wouldn't give in to him. Let him be charming, let him be good for Johnny, let him bring a smile to Susan's face. He wasn't going to get to her. She wasn't going to risk that loss again.

When Danny and Susan began fussing in the next room, she couldn't put off taking them home any longer. It was past time for their naps. *Mam* sat with her feet on a stool, taking a much-needed sit-down while she watched the children play in the front room.

"Thank you for dinner, *Mam*." She helped the children put the blocks away.

"It was nothing. You did most of the work." *Mam*'s voice was relaxed, content. She'd take a rest, too, if it kept her as serene as *Mam*.

Susan yawned as they walked along the path to the *Dawdi Haus,* and Danny was already nodding on her shoulder. Ellie kept her face toward her destination. She hated this feeling. She longed to see Bram again, feel his gaze on her and enjoy just being with a man again, but she couldn't let herself give in to that pleasure. What if she enjoyed it too much? What if she got used to it and then…

Why didn't he politely ignore her so they could both go about their business?

After seeing Susan and Danny to their beds, she wandered back to her kitchen to look out the window.

"What are you looking for?" her whispered voice scolded. As if she would be looking for someone.

Ellie gathered her sewing from the front room. She had a bit of handwork to do on Johnny's new pants and hated to sit inside on such a beautiful day. The glider under the tree in the side yard was out of sight of the big house and the barn. She always enjoyed this shady, secluded spot where she could lose herself in her thoughts. No one would know she was there.

She threaded her needle and began to finish up the hem of the trousers. It needed to be good and deep, with plenty of room to let it out as Johnny grew.

"This is a nice place to sit."

Bram's voice came so suddenly that Ellie jumped.

"I didn't mean to startle you. I saw you come around this corner of the house, and I wondered where you had gone."

Ellie didn't answer. His voice was quiet, almost intimate. She slid over on the seat as he sat down beside her. Her mind was whirling—what could she do now? His weight made the glider rock back as he sat and he let it swing forward again. Could she just tell him to leave her alone without sounding too rude?

He pushed the glider back again with one foot. The motion pulled at her mind to relax, to enjoy the feeling of his strong presence.

"That was a good dinner you made."

*"Denki."* She took another stitch.

Bram kept the glider moving. How long would he sit there if she didn't help keep the conversation going? Did she really want him to leave? It was one thing to tell herself she didn't want him around when she was alone in *Mam*'s kitchen, but it was quite another when he was sitting next to her, smiling at her, as he was when she glanced at him.

"Did I hear you say you're going to pick up your new buggy this afternoon?"

*"Ja,* that's right. I'll need to leave in a little while to get there on time, but I wanted to talk to you first."

"Talk to me?" Ellie's sewing slowed, then stopped.

"To ask you to try out my new buggy with me sometime. I'd like to get to know you better."

"I...I don't know...." Ellie could feel her face blushing. She was acting like a girl with her first beau. What was wrong with her? She should just tell him no.

"Why not?" Bram was persistent. "Is it because I'm new? Or because I lived *Englisch* for so long?"

*"Ne."* That wasn't what she meant. "Or *ja,* it was at first, but not now."

"Then you just don't like me."

*"Ach, ne,* it's not that...." Ellie turned to him. How could he think that? Had she gone too far? But he grinned at her with that same cocksure grin, the dimple winking at her. She couldn't help smiling back at him, and then she looked away. What a tease he could be!

Bram turned in the glider so he was sitting sideways, facing her. He put his arm along the back of the seat, his hand brushing her shoulder. Ellie almost sighed with the comfortable pleasure the light touch gave her. It was so tempting to spend time with this man....

"Ellie." Bram's tone was serious now. "I know I shouldn't... I mean, I can't help feeling that...well, there's something about you that I...I think if we spent some time together, we could learn to be friends."

Ellie looked at him. He was teasing again, wasn't he? His eyes held hers. She knew. As she looked into his blue eyes, she knew she could never just be his friend, and as quickly as that thought came, fear followed on its heels.

"I can't." She whispered the words, tears filling her eyes. She couldn't look at him anymore.

"Why not?"

"When I lost Daniel..." Ellie stopped, took a deep breath and let it out to steady herself. "It hurt so much. I can't go through that again." She turned to him, willing him to understand. "Don't ask me to risk that."

Bram looked toward the barn, the muscle in his jaw working. Was he angry?

"I can't promise that you won't be hurt." This time he was the one who whispered. Not angry. He was afraid, too, but of what?

Ellie blinked back the unshed tears. Where had that steel rod of resolve gone? The sensation of this man sitting next to her, encircling her within the shelter of his arms with a bare touch, had banished her determination in a single moment. What would an afternoon or evening with him do?

"I...I can't..."

Bram looked at her, but she turned her face away. She was too close to giving in to risk looking at him. He didn't speak, didn't move.

After a long minute she turned toward him, ready to say that he should leave, but the look on his face arrested her. She had never seen him so open, so vulnerable, so tender. He lifted his hand to her face and touched the strand of hair that always came loose. He let it run through his fingers and then tucked it behind her ear. He leaned closer, his eyes locked on hers.

"You're right." His voice was hoarse, strained. "I know you're right. I can't let you risk this."

Then, abruptly, he was gone, striding toward the barn. He didn't look back.

Ellie's hand shook as she picked up her sewing again, her mind following after Bram as he disappeared around the corner of the house. Her eyes blurred.

The tears that had waited at the edge for so long threatened again, pushing to be released. She hadn't cried when Daniel died, not even through the long months of that winter. She hadn't cried through all the lonely evenings of the spring and summer, or even during Sally's wedding the past fall.

Even when Levi Zook had come courting, even when the temptation of joining their families together had enticed her, she hadn't given in. She had stood firm, holding on to Daniel's dream, keeping the tears walled up.

But now, after this one man showed a hint of tenderness, a crack threatened to burst the dam. Slow, hot tears wet her cheeks as her thoughts raced.

What was it that battered against her defenses? Was it Bram's gentle touch?

She went over their conversation in her mind. It wasn't anything he had said; it was what he did. With his arm around her she had felt sheltered, protected. She hadn't felt so cherished since Daniel had held her last.

The memory of her own helplessness as she had willed Daniel to live, to breathe, to open his eyes assailed her.

"No, no, no!" she whispered to the air, to someone... to *Gott?* "Don't ask me to do that again."

*Dat*'s words during the preaching on Sunday came back to her. What was it he said? Trust *Gott?* A sob rose in her throat at this thought.

She furiously stopped the tears that threatened to overwhelm her again. She needed to think this through. He had hit the center of her whole problem. The layer of cotton fog that lay between her and the sisters and brothers at church, her fear of loving again, the way every day was a hard chore to get through... The trust was gone. *Gott* had betrayed her.

Trusting Him had been so easy once. Joy had been part of her life before, and she longed to have that feeling back. She had done all the right things, lived the right way, but there was more she needed to do.

*Gott* knew she had closed her heart to Him. The tears fell freely again as she considered this. She had closed her heart tightly against the loving Father of her childhood.

*It wasn't my fault.*

The protest rose against a flood of accusations. It *was* her fault. Could she ever be forgiven?

Trust Him. Was it as simple as that?

A phrase from *Mam*'s favorite Psalm echoed in her mind: "He shall cover thee with His feathers, and under His wings shalt thou trust."

Even her? Did He cover her with His feathers? Even though she was the one stubborn chick who must poke her head out from under the shelter?

The words were simple enough. *Gott* could be her refuge, her protection. He would lead her in the right way, if only she could trust Him enough to follow— allow Him to forgive.

Tears streamed down her cheeks as the dam ruptured. She buried her face in the bundle of Johnny's trousers, letting the tears flow. Long minutes passed until the wrenching sobs left her empty of every feeling, drained and exhausted.

She had nowhere else to turn except to hide under His wings. She must trust Him.

Bram struggled to shut the door in his mind. A lesson he had learned in Chicago was to never show your feelings to anyone. Keep thoughts, memories and emotions behind mental doors. That was the only way to survive. But this door refused to shut.

What was his problem? She was just a girl. He had

known plenty of girls before, girls who were a lot prettier than that Plain woman sitting on the other side of the house. Even as he tried to convince himself, he knew that his arguments didn't work. Babs's brittle brightness didn't compare to the gentle womanliness of this one.

She was just a girl! He hammered mercilessly on that imaginary door, willing it to close, shutting away the urge to rush back and crush her in his arms, to kiss her and keep kissing her until she yielded to him and promised to be his.

He stopped short at the barn door. John Stoltzfus would see right through him if he walked into the barn like this.

He took a deep breath, willing the mask to fall across his face. Emotionless, unaffected. He had to get that mental door shut, and quick.

*Stop thinking about her.*

If he wasn't careful, he'd find himself trapped in a marriage he didn't want, slogging through every day following some horse around a field…

*It doesn't have to be like that.*

No, it didn't have to. He saw that in the way John Stoltzfus looked at his wife. Even after all these years, they had something his *mam* and *dat* had never had.

*But that life isn't for you. Stop thinking about her.*

That blasted lock of hair. He rubbed his fingers on his pants to get rid of the silky softness and felt the revolver in his pocket. The unyielding metal stopped him short. Letting his breath out with a whoosh, he felt the door slam shut. Cold, hard reality had done it. If he got too caught up in a girl, it could be the end of him.

Not just him. Cold water ran through his body at this thought. He looked back at the *Dawdi Haus,* sheltered close under the maple trees that filled the yard around it. If the mob had any idea he cared about someone, it would be their first weapon against him. He'd have to keep that door closed and locked, no matter how tempting it was to open.

Ellie pumped water onto a towel and held it to her eyes, glad the tears had finally stopped. The cool water felt good against her hot face. Susan would be getting up from her nap soon, and she didn't want swollen, red eyes to be the first thing she saw.

The ache was gone. Ellie dropped the towel from her face and stared out the kitchen window. The crying had washed away the pain in her chest, arms and throat that had become so normal she barely noticed it. But now it was gone.

She rinsed the towel in fresh water and held it to her face again.

The door of the children's bedroom opened quietly. Ellie put a smile on her face as she turned to greet Susan—a smile that didn't need to be forced. The little girl yawned.

"Did you have a good nap?" Ellie sat down in one of the kitchen chairs and pulled Susan onto her lap.

Susan nodded as she leaned against Ellie. Ellie held her close for a minute, and then she straightened her up so she could rebraid Susan's mussed hair.

"We're going to work in the garden until it's time to make supper." Ellie combed her fine hair with her fingers and then started braiding. "Will you help me?"

"*Ja.* Danny can help, too."

"*Ja,* when he wakes up."

The beans that needed thinning were at the end of the garden closest to the main house. Susan skipped along the path in front of her.

They hadn't gone far when Ellie heard Danny's cry. He hadn't slept long, either.

"Susan, I'm going in to get Danny. I'll be right back."

Susan nodded and stopped at the foot of the ramp leading to the barn to wait. Ellie hurried into the house.

All was quiet as she looked in the door of the bedroom where Danny was sound asleep. He must have had a dream.

As she stepped back out to the porch, she saw Bram leading the big gray gelding down the ramp to the lane. The horse was skittish, prancing sideways and pulling on the halter while Bram talked to him, calming him.

Then she saw Susan. The little girl stood like a statue at the bottom of the ramp, staring at the horse's dancing feet as they came closer and closer. Bram hadn't seen her—couldn't see her as the horse moved sideways, blocking Susan from his sight. The girl didn't move.

With her heart pounding, Ellie ran toward her daughter, but she couldn't move quickly enough. The horse kicked and danced—he would step right over Susan; she would be hit by his hooves.

"Bram!" She screamed his name as she ran. "Stop!"

Thank *Gott* in heaven, he heard her.

Bram halted the horse, calming him with his voice and hands. She saw his face when he noticed Susan just a few feet away. He turned white, then gray. He looked at Ellie, and his eyes reflected her horror of what might have happened.

Ellie reached for Susan, but he held out a hand to stop her.

"Let me." He smiled at her, his face changing in an instant, as if he had slid on a calm mask, and then knelt in front of Susan. The horse shook his head, watching Bram, but stood quietly.

Ellie waited, trying to catch her breath. What was he doing?

"Hello, Susan," he said, his voice quiet and controlled.

Susan's eyes were wide, staring at the horse, and tears ran down her cheeks. At the sound of Bram's voice, she looked at him as he knelt at eye level between her and the horse.

"I just bought this horse from your *dawdi*." Bram went on in the same quiet tone. "Do you want to say hello to him? His name is Partner."

Ellie's instinct was to grab Susan, take her away from the horse. Why torment her like this? But Susan relaxed at Bram's words and even took a step closer to him. He gave her a reassuring smile and picked her up. A rush of warmth flowed through Ellie as she recognized the same step she had taken toward *Gott* just a little while earlier. Susan placed her trust in Bram.

"Partner is so happy to go for a walk with me that he was dancing down the ramp. Did you see him?" Bram's even voice was quiet, inviting.

Susan nodded and leaned against Bram's shoulder, as far from the horse as she could get, but she smiled.

"Do you want to say hello to Partner?"

Susan nodded again.

"Then talk like this." Bram started saying nonsense words in a singsongy voice that made Susan laugh. She imitated him in the same tone of voice.

"Have you ever felt how soft a horse's nose is?"

Susan shook her head, staring at the horse. He was still calm, watching Bram.

"Take your hand like this."

Ellie watched him take Susan's hand and stroke the

horse's nose. She shook her head in disbelief. How did he do that?

Bram turned toward her, and Ellie stepped forward to take Susan from his arms.

*"Denki,"* she said, "Susan has been so frightened of horses ever since—"

"I know," Bram interrupted her. "Your father told me about it."

They stood close together, Susan reaching for Partner while Ellie held her.

"I've been thinking…"

Bram didn't say anything, wasn't even looking at her. He held the horse's head still while Susan patted the whiskery nose.

"I've been thinking that I would like to go riding with you."

Bram shot her a quick look. What was that in his eyes? Fear? *Ne,* longing. Longing that matched her own. He nodded, his Adam's apple bobbing as he swallowed.

"I'd like that, too. How about Sunday afternoon? There's no church that day, right?"

Ellie nodded. "Sunday afternoon will be fine."

Bram gave her a quick smile, but it was a smile that never threatened to slide into his grin. Did he regret asking her? He tucked that stray strand of hair back behind her ear again with a shaky hand.

What had she gotten herself into?

# Chapter Eight

❧

Thursday at noon Ellie ate a quick lunch with *Mam* while *Dat* and the boys were at Bram's farm with the other men. Dishes were done in no time, and Ellie settled the last plate into the cupboard with a quiet clink. She closed the door and turned to survey Mam's kitchen. Were they finished already?

"Doesn't take much to *redd* up after such a small meal, does it?" *Mam* wiped the crumbs from the oil-cloth on the table.

"*Ne,* with *Dat* and the boys away, it was a quiet dinner."

"Why don't you put Susan and Danny down for their naps here, and you can help me finish up my new quilt top."

Susan loved taking her afternoon nap at *Grossmutti*'s house, sleeping in the big upstairs room that Ellie had once shared with her sisters. Danny was already asleep by the time she laid him down on the bed next to Susan. She smiled at her daughter as she pulled the door closed, and Susan responded by putting her own little finger to her lips in a sign that she would be quiet. Susan would be asleep by the time Ellie reached the room off the kitchen that *Mam* used as her sewing room.

*Mam* had most of the blocks already pieced and was arranging them on the sewing table.

"Who is this quilt for?" Ellie asked, picking up one of the blocks. From the colors, it looked as if *Mam* had used leftover scraps from making men's shirts. She had arranged the blocks on her worktable to form the Tumbling Blocks pattern.

"I'm hoping it will be for your brother Reuben."

"A quilt for Reuben? Then he's serious about someone."

*Mam*'s eyes twinkled as she switched blocks around to work out the best order for them.

"You know your brother. He won't tell us for sure, but he's out every Saturday night with someone. And he spends most of Saturday afternoon cleaning his courting buggy."

"It will be fun to have another wedding in the fall."

"*Ach, ja,* it will." *Mam* looked at Ellie. "Maybe two weddings? Wouldn't that be fun?"

"But who else would be getting married? Benjamin is too young...." Suddenly Ellie realized what her mother was hinting at. "Now, *Mam,* don't be getting any ideas."

"Not get any ideas from the look in Levi's eyes when he sees you?"

"I've already told him *ne.* I feel sorry for him, but that's no reason to marry."

"He needs a wife." *Mam* sighed as she switched another block around. "*Dat* and I thought it would make a good match last fall, you and him. Both of you needing someone, and his little ones need a *memmi* for sure."

"*Mam,* we've talked about this already."

"*Ja,* I know." *Mam* waved a quilt block in the air.

"But some time has passed. I thought perhaps you had changed your mind."

"*Ne, Mam.* Nothing has changed." Her mind brought up the image of Bram, the tender look on his face as he had let that stubborn lock of hair glide through his fingers…. Her cheeks grew hot. Something had changed, but not with Levi. Levi had never made her blush.

*Mam* gave up any pretense of working on the quilt and looked directly at Ellie.

"It's time I spoke plain to you, Ellie Miller. You need a husband, and your children need a father. The Bible tells us that young widows should marry, and it's time for you to be thinking about it."

Ellie sat down in one of the small rocking chairs, still holding two of the blocks in her hands, forgotten.

"*Ach, Mam,* I know I should marry again, but I just don't feel ready."

"Daughter, you'll never feel ready."

"But what if…"

"What if you lose him, too?" *Mam* finished the sentence for her quietly. "Is this what has been holding you back? And I'm not just talking about marriage—I've noticed it with the family and with the church family. You're holding yourself at a distance from everyone."

"*Ja.*" Ellie nodded. "I've just come to realize that when Daniel died…" She stopped and wiped away a tear. Tears came every day lately. She took a ragged breath. "When Daniel died, it was like my whole world stopped. I just haven't been able to go on…. I've been so afraid that *Gott* will take someone else—one of the children, or you or *Dat*. If I married again, I'd have to risk losing a husband all over again. I'm just not sure I'm ready to do that—to take that risk."

*Mam* came to sit in the other rocking chair, next to

her. She laid her hand on Ellie's arm. The touch was comforting, warm, familiar.

"*Ja,* I've seen your struggle. But you can trust *Gott.*"

Ellie gave her mother a small smile. "That's just what *Dat* said in his sermon."

"Well, he's usually right."

"*Ja,* he is."

"What about Levi? I've seen him with his children. He's a good father, and he would treat your children as if they were his own."

Ellie nodded, tears threatening again. Levi was a good father, but the look on Susan's face as Bram held her, helping her to overcome her fear of the horse, tightened her throat.

"Don't let your pride stand in the way of *Gott*'s plan for you and your family, Ellie."

*Mam*'s words interrupted her thoughts like a burst soap bubble.

"Pride?"

"Pride is a terrible sin. It can make us think that we know better than *Gott* does. It can make us afraid to trust Him and His plan for our lives."

There was that word again. *Trust.* It should be easy, shouldn't it?

"But how do I know what His plan is?"

*Mam* smiled as she patted Ellie's arm and went back to the worktable.

"Do you remember when you told me you and Daniel had decided to marry?"

Ellie's mind flew back to that long-ago time. Had it really been almost nine years?

"You told me that you knew Daniel was the one for you because you were so happy."

Ellie nodded, unable to trust her voice. That had been such a joyful time, full of bright promise.

"Listen for *Gott,* Ellie, and look for that same feeling of peace. When we are in *Gott*'s will, He gives us peace. Whether Levi is the right one for you or not, *Gott* will lead you to the right decision."

Levi? That decision had already been made. Levi was a nice man and a good father. Someone would love to be his wife, but not her. Marriage to him would mean not only submitting herself to his will, but it would also mean burying Daniel's dreams for his children. Johnny, Susan and Danny would become part of Levi's many children.

And Daniel's legacy would be buried forever.

Bram leaned on the top rail of the pasture fence. It had been a long day, but now ten acres were plowed and planted to corn. It would be a good cash crop to start out. He pulled out his handkerchief and wiped the sweat off his face and neck again.

Matthew joined him at the fence. "We're heading home, Bram."

"I don't know how to thank you."

"*Ach,* don't worry about it. It's what we do."

Was it really as simple as that? Eight men had taken an entire day of work, a day they needed for working on their own places, and had spent it here on his farm. Bram swallowed. A farm that he'd be leaving behind as soon as he found Kavanaugh. With any luck, he'd never even see this corn harvested come November.

Bram thanked each of the men as they left his farm. When he reached Bishop Yoder, the old man took Bram's hand and held it in his own frail ones, but his voice was strong.

"I haven't officially welcomed you back. I hope you're feeling at home here."

"*Ja,* Bishop. The church has made me feel very welcome."

"There's a baptism class starting next week. You're welcome to join it."

Bram's first instinct was to give a pat reply—assure the bishop that he'd be there—but lying to the elderly man didn't come easy.

"I'll have to let you know…."

Bishop nodded, reached up to pat him on the shoulder and then turned to climb onto the seat of the waiting wagon with his two grown sons.

As tired as he was, Bram tried to feel elated over the bishop's words. This meant he was accepted, that they were willing to talk to him about joining the community. But going through baptism and everything that went with it? He was already misleading the church by making them think he was settling here permanently. Bram shifted his shoulders. Lying to that kind old man didn't feel right.

Bram joined John as he stood looking over the newly planted fields. He could hear Benjamin and Reuben hammering in the barn. They had volunteered to repair the box stall and manger so it would be usable.

"A lot of work got done today," John said, his voice tired.

"It sure did. The men really helped out. Getting such a late start as I did, I would never have been able to do this on my own."

"You know you're not alone. When you become part of the community, they help you out." John scraped his boot on the bottom fence rail. "They know you'll return the work when it's needed somewhere else."

Bram rubbed his face, feeling the late-afternoon stubble of his beard. "My *dat*…well, you know what he was like. I don't remember him ever helping out like this."

The sun rode high in the sky, even though suppertime was near. The world he had lived in growing up— that world where his *dat* avoided the other men of the church as much as they avoided him—was far away from this place.

"I saw you talking with Bishop Yoder."

"*Ja.* He invited me to join the membership class."

"That would be a good step, but it isn't something to take lightly."

Bram looked out across the field again, his gut twisting uncomfortably.

"*Ja,* I know. I'm not sure I'm ready yet." Would he ever be ready to join the church? Maybe, if he was able to stay around long enough. For the first time in his life, the thought appealed to him.

"It's better for a man to wait, if there are things in his past that need to be dealt with first."

John's voice was easy, companionable, but his words went straight to Bram's heart, leaving him gasping for air. He had this man figured out, didn't he? He shifted his eyes to John's and then back to the field. Why did he have the feeling John saw right through him?

Bram stood in the center of the drive, between the barn and the house, alone at last. His farm. His fields. His frogs croaking by the stream. It was almost ready for him…ready for a family. He could almost hear children's voices calling from the barn, could almost smell supper cooking on the stove.

Bram stared at the kitchen window of the empty

house. A family? What if he had found someone to marry all those years ago? What if he had never left? Would he have the kind of life Matthew and Annie had?

Probably not. He would have become his *Dat* all over again, just like Samuel, drowning himself in moonshine and anger.

Those years in Chicago weren't wasted. Peters had made something of him—but what? He was good at what he did, and bringing criminals to justice was the right thing to do. So why did his life still feel so empty?

The west-facing window was golden with the reflected setting sun. Dappled shadows played across the surface. If Ellie were there, she'd watch for him through that window. She'd wave and smile; the corners of her mouth would upturn in anticipation of the long summer evening stretching before them.

Ellie. She wasn't in his plans. He had no business getting involved with a woman, especially her. If she was hurt because of him...

He didn't know what he'd do.

And yet, what if she married someone else? Someone who could take care of her, be a father to the children. He shut his eyes at the thought of Johnny's delighted face, Danny's drooling grin, the memory of Susan's shy, sweet smile. So much like her mother.

He rubbed his face with both hands, looking around him. He was still standing in the middle of the barnyard, mooning around like some lovesick teenager. What was happening to him?

The back door of the house stood open. He'd opened both the front and back doors earlier in the day. That skunk smell was fading, but it would need a few more days of airing before the house was livable. He walked through the house to the front bedroom and slid the window closed. The window faced north, and a lilac bush half covered it, throwing the room into shadow. He faced the room, leaning against the windowsill.

Bram buried his face in his hands. The thought of what he should do wrenched his gut. He should keep his distance. Shut every thought of Ellie Miller away. Why did he ever have to meet her? He couldn't marry her. Why had that thought ever entered his head?

But the memory of the few close moments they had shared on her glider the other day came roaring out of the sealed place in his mind. He groaned with the thought of never letting himself be alone with her again. But that was what he should do. He had to forget her. He had to. He could never be just her friend.

If the mob ever found out about her…

He forced his thoughts to obey. Shut the door. Lock Ellie away. *Keep her out of your thoughts.*

He tried to remember Kavanaugh's narrow face, the noise of the city, Babs's platinum bob, to bring something—anything—else to his mind, but the only image that came was a stubborn lock of hair that escaped its confinement under a pure white *kapp*. Ellie again. It would always be Ellie.

He wrenched his thoughts away. Why couldn't he forget her?

With a dash of cold clarity, he knew. God was doing this. Tempting him. Destroying him. What was He doing, meddling in this? It had nothing to do with Him! Bram had spent his entire life ignoring God; why couldn't He do the same?

*Trust Him. Trust Him. Trust Him.*

The memory of John's sermon played like a record needle caught in a groove. John had said that was what he was supposed to do.

Trust God? The way his life was going, he couldn't trust anyone, especially God.

What if he did? What if he trusted God to take care of Ellie, and then He failed?

Did God fail?

What if God trusted him to take care of Ellie, and Bram failed? He'd try his hardest, but he had failed before, and he would do it again. He couldn't bear the thought of being responsible if something happened to Ellie or the children.

*Trust Him.*

Did he dare?


Sunday morning Ellie woke with a dream still haunting the edges of her memory. Daniel. She sat up, trying to clear the lingering remnants of the dream. What time was it?

Amid the predawn clamor of the birds, the dream became clear. She was at a Sunday meeting at the Troyers', and Daniel stood at her shoulder. She had turned toward him—what a joy it was to see his dear face once more—but his expression turned to reproach.

"What about the children?"

He had spoken softly, urgently, and then said it again. "What about the children?"

Then he had turned and walked away from her.

Was he disappointed in her? What had he meant? The children were fine, weren't they? She was trying to keep his memory alive for them.

But Daniel's plans for his family were dropping in the dust with her struggling strawberry patch. They were dying, and she was doing nothing about it. She couldn't let that happen, could she?

Ellie turned on her stomach, burying her face in the

pillow so her crying wouldn't wake the children. Grief and regret pulled long sobs from her throat, cries of anguish that were swallowed by the pillow. She had failed Daniel while he was alive, and she continued to fail him now that he was dead.

Her heart burned.

*"Ach, Gott."* Her voice was a cry of anguish in her head, but only a hoarse whisper escaped into the pillow. *"Ach, Gott,* help me. Why is this so hard?"

Maybe she didn't want to fulfill Daniel's dreams. The thought tore another sob from her throat. How could she think that? She was Daniel's wife. She had promised to work with him in life, and as he lay dying all that long, hot September day, she had promised to continue what they'd started.

What about her own dreams? Had they died with Daniel?

The sobs turned to deep sighs, and Ellie turned to look out the window. Through the top pane above the curtain, she could see the pink-and-yellow streaks of the coming sunrise.

For months she had devoted every thought, every decision to the children, to making sure they received the legacy their father had wanted to give them. Daniel's words from her dream thrummed once more.

Ellie rose from her bed and peered out the window at the lightening world. An uncomfortable shadow in the back of her mind demanded attention. She had to face it. Her dreams? They were for her, not for the children. Stubborn through and through. Would she ever learn her lesson?

What she wanted wasn't what they needed. *Mam* was right, Lovina was right, even Levi Zook was right.

Ellie wiped a hot tear from her cheek. She needed

a husband. Her throat tightened. *Ja,* and the children needed a father, a strong man who could teach them the right way to live through his example.

Across the road, the woodlot stretched to her right. When she was a little girl, she had seen a deer there once, the first one she had ever seen. *Dat* had been as excited as she was, and he had told her how the deer had been hunted for so long that they were very rare, and she was especially blessed to have seen one. *Dat* shared that special memory with her, something that belonged to the two of them.

Her own children had no *dat* to share anything with. Had she been selfish to try to keep Daniel alive for them? Who would they go to when they needed something only a father could give them?

Who would she go to when she needed something only a husband could give her?

Ellie leaned her head against the window frame, turning this question over in her mind. As she watched the birds flit from the trees of the woodlot down to the bit of brackish water in the ditch where the frogs lived, a deer stepped out of the cover of the trees. The doe paused, watching, listening, then took another step and lowered her head to drink. Ellie's breath caught as she watched two fawns follow the doe, mimicking every movement, their long ears flicking at every sound.

She had been doubly blessed by the presence of these beautiful, elusive creatures.

Her eyes filled with tears again as she caught the significance of her thought. *Gott* could also bless her twice by giving her two men to love in her life. Loving another man didn't take anything away from her love for Daniel. How could she have been so blind, thinking that choosing another husband meant she had betrayed Daniel?

The tight band around her throat loosened further, and she took a deep breath, smiling up at the sky, pale yellow in the imminent daybreak.

*"Denki,"* she whispered.

# Chapter Nine

*Mam* helped Susan into the family buggy Sunday afternoon. "Ellie, you're sure you don't want to come with us to Lovina's? I hate for you to miss out on the visit."

"*Ja,* I'm sure. I know you'll have a good time, but I have other plans. Bram will be here soon."

As Ellie handed Danny up to Mandy in the back of the buggy, she saw the look that passed between her parents. Well, let them think what they would, but her plans for this Sunday afternoon were simple. Bram was going to take her to see his farm and get her opinion on what needed to be done in his kitchen. It wasn't as if they were courting!

Once the family buggy was gone, the farm settled into a quiet that Ellie seldom heard. The early-summer sun was hot, and the cows had all sought the shade of the pasture. One pig's grunting echoed through the empty barn, keeping rhythm with the thump and clatter as he rubbed against the wooden planks of the sty.

Ellie wandered to the lilac bushes that surrounded the front porch of the big house, and she buried her face in the blossoms. They were nearly spent, but the scent still lingered. On either side of the front walk, *Mam*'s peony bushes held round pink-and-green buds. Another day or two, and they would burst into bloom.

Sitting on the front step, Ellie was enveloped in the fragrant lilacs growing on either side. She leaned back into the shaded seclusion and pushed aside one of the branches. *Ja,* even after all these years, her very own playhouse still waited between the leggy branches of the bushes. Lovina's had been on the other side of the porch steps, while Sally's had been around the corner.

Was that a cup? Ellie leaned farther into the bush. For sure, there were a cup and a plate, with carefully arranged leaves for food. So Rebecca and Mandy had found the playhouses, too. Had they shared that same thrill of discovery that she and Lovina had the day they found these secret places?

The measured clip-clop of a horse's hooves on the gravel road brought her to her feet. What if Bram found her here? The thought brought heat to her cheeks. They would be alone, hidden from the road by the trees, in the cool shade of the lilac bushes. He was so bold— would he try to kiss her? Did she want him to kiss her? She rubbed her hands on her apron. Friends didn't kiss, and friends didn't think about the feel of his touch on her shoulder.

She hurried to meet him in the lane at the end of the front walk.

"Good afternoon." He smiled as he greeted her, the dimple winking in his cheek. It would be so much easier to be his friend if he didn't have the kind of smile that made her knees feel like jelly.

"Hello, Bram." Ellie climbed into the front seat of the buggy as he brought it to a stop. "It's certainly a nice day for a drive."

Bram reached out a hand to help her, but she ignored it and sat as far from him as possible on the seat to still keep a friendly distance. A sidelong look told her the smile was still there. He truly looked happy to see her. Would she ever figure this man out? The last time they were together, he had hardly looked at her, had hardly talked to her. Men. She had never figured Daniel out, either.

Bram drove the buggy toward the barn and turned around in the circle drive. Partner shook his head with a nicker as Bram guided him back down the drive to the road.

"Sorry, fella. You don't live here anymore."

"He was good friends with Billy, Reuben's goat. You'll have to bring him over sometime to say hello."

Bram looked at her. "You're saying I should bring my horse over here just to say hello to a goat?"

Ellie laughed at the disbelieving look on his face. "If he starts feeling bad, you might try it. It wouldn't be the first time animals missed their friends."

Bram just shook his head and then laughed along with her. "*Ja,* I might just try it sometime."

The laughter started the afternoon out on a friendly note. When Bram reached the end of the drive, he turned right, the opposite direction from his farm.

"I thought we might go down to the lake. The road along there is shady, and it's cooler next to the water."

Bram was right. As soon as they turned onto the county road that led them past Emma Lake, the dappled shade and water-cooled breeze tempered the unusually hot last day of May.

"Look at those kids play." Bram pointed the buggy whip in the direction of some boys laughing and playing in the water. "Kids in Chicago don't have places like this."

"No lakes to swim in?"

"Lake Michigan is close, but for kids on the West Side it might as well be on the moon. On really hot days the fire department will open a hydrant for them to play in the water. With this depression going on, there's nothing for them. No jobs, no money. It's a rough life for a kid."

Ellie tried to picture children with only streets to play in. No trees, no grass—just automobiles and noise. She had to ask him. "Do you miss the city, Bram?"

Bram was silent while he used the buggy whip to shoo deerflies away from Partner's ears. "I did when I first left. There's a certain excitement about the city. Always something going on. Vendors in the streets shouting, the shoe-shine boys trying to make a penny or two, the streetcars clanging by…"

Ellie stole a look at his face. Did he wish he was still there?

He returned her look. His face was serious, but then his smile crept back, filling his eyes with a light she hadn't seen before. "I don't miss it at all."

Bram went back to flicking away the flies.

They turned west for a mile, the overhanging trees still giving them some shelter from the sun. Bram rode without talking, but every few seconds Ellie caught a tune that sounded under his breath. She let herself relax into the rhythm of Partner's hoofbeats, watching the lake as they drove past.

She was on a buggy ride with a man—a man who wasn't her husband. If anyone saw them, there would be talk that they were courting. The look that had passed between her parents told her they were thinking it might be true. There was already speculation about them, just like there had been about Levi in the months after his wife's death. But she and Bram were friends. Nothing more. She knew how to keep her distance.

When they reached Bram's farm, she was surprised at how much it had changed. The run-down place she remembered looked like a true Amish farm now. The house looked almost new with a coat of white paint and the shutters removed. Lilac bushes flanked the front porch, just like at home.

As they drove into the barnyard, Bram motioned to the new boards on the barn that contrasted with the weathered gray of the old siding.

"Next week I'll be painting the barn. Still have a few more boards to replace on the other side." He pulled his horse to a stop at the end of the brick path that led to the back door of the house. "You go on in while I water Partner. Make yourself at home and think about what needs to be done yet."

Ellie let herself in the back door. The back porch had been enclosed at some point, and it held a sink with a pump, handy for washing up after working out in the garden. She opened the door to the kitchen and stepped in.

All of the cabinets were brand-new, and the smell of fresh lumber filled the room. She ran her hand over the wood of the nearest cabinet. Smooth oak planks were joined together with a nearly invisible seam to form the cabinet doors. Bram had taken care with their building.

She turned to take in the rest of the room. As large as *Mam*'s kitchen, it had room for a big family table. Bram had left space for a stove on the wall opposite the sink where the chimney would go up through the center of the house, warming the upstairs bedrooms. Even the wood floor looked as if it had been recently refinished.

This was a kitchen a wife could work in. Ellie ran

her hand along the countertop. Plenty of space for baking, canning, preparing food for her family... *Ja,* any woman would be happy in a kitchen like this.

Ellie turned to the view out the window over the sink. Between the plowed fields and the road was room for a garden, and she could see apple trees in the yard to her right. A big maple tree stood next to the brick walk, with a low branch that was just right for a swing. Wouldn't Susan love a swing like that!

In her imagination Ellie could see her children playing in the yard—Johnny running out to the barn to help with the chores, Susan shooing the chickens into their coop at night, Danny learning to walk in the soft grass...

Bram stepped out of the barn and closed the door behind him, smiling when he saw her watching from the window.

What was she thinking? This was Bram's farm, and she had no right to be imagining her children living here. Her children didn't belong here. Their farm was waiting for them. Daniel's farm, his dream—that was where her children belonged. She owed that to Daniel. It was his legacy to them.

The morning's dream echoed in her mind.

If *Gott* saw fit to bless her with another husband, it surely wouldn't be Bram, would it? Not a man who had spent so much time among the *Englisch,* a man who hadn't even joined the church yet. To marry an unbeliever would weaken her own faith and only confuse the children.

*Ne,* Bram Lapp was not the man for her.

She dried her wet cheeks when she heard Bram open the back door.

* * *

Bram's heart stopped at the sight of Ellie in his kitchen. Like a bolt shot home, it was right.

But it wasn't. Was she wiping away tears?

"Ellie, what's wrong?"

"Nothing." She shook her head and gave him a bright smile. "It's a beautiful kitchen. I haven't looked at the rest."

She glanced toward the door that led to the front room.

"I haven't worked on that part of the house yet." Bram moved to put himself between her and the disaster that was his front room and bedroom. The former owners had left everything from peeling wallpaper to overstuffed, ratty furniture, and he wasn't about to let anyone see his house in that shape.

"What do you think about the kitchen?" He turned her attention back to this room, where every cabinet door had been finished and mounted, every drawer built, every floorboard sanded with thoughts of her. "Does it need anything else?"

"Paint. And a stove and a table."

And her. It needed her. Here. Every day.

Bram drew his palm across the back of his neck. That was just a dream. A pipe dream, but he didn't pull his mind away from the image.

"What color paint should I use?"

Ellie swept her gaze around the kitchen, and Bram couldn't take his eyes off her. Her small, slim form twirled on one foot as she turned.

"Yellow, I think. But not a bright yellow. Soft, like butter."

"*Ja,* yellow would look just right." He took a step closer to her, but she turned away from him. She had been acting as skittish as a barn cat all afternoon. How could he get back to that closeness of last week? Had that one afternoon on her glider scared her as much as it had him?

"I don't know about the stove. What kind should I look for?"

"*Ach,* every woman has her own likes and dislikes."

"I know. What would you choose?"

She gave him a sideways look that made him catch his breath. She looked perfect standing there. Longing was an ache that filled his chest.

"If I were choosing, I'd want one just like my mother's. It's the one I learned to cook on, and I like it." She turned toward him. "But I'm not choosing, Bram. It isn't my home. You need to get a stove you can use."

Bram held her gaze, letting himself indulge in the dream for a few seconds longer. When he had found Kavanaugh and his job was done, he'd be leaving all this, but the sight of Ellie in his kitchen would belong to him forever. A picture to linger over during the lonely nights ahead.

If he could bear to leave it behind...

"I like *Grossmutti* Miriam's cookies."

"What if she didn't make any?"

Johnny loved to tease his sister. Ellie supposed all big brothers acted like that.

"She always has them."

"But what if she didn't make them this time?"

Susan paused, her face clouding as she considered this. "But if she doesn't make them, what would *Dawdi* Hezekiah eat?"

# A SERIES OF HISTORICAL NOVELS!

# GET 2 FREE BOOKS!

## 2 FREE BOOKS

To get your 2 free books, affix this peel-off sticker to the reply card and mail it today!

Plus, receive
## TWO FREE BONUS GIFTS!

*Love Inspired* **HISTORICAL**

**A series of historical love stories that will lift your spirits and warm your soul!**

**W**e'd like to send you two free books to introduce you to the Love Inspired® Historical series. These books are worth over $10, but are yours to keep absolutely FREE! We'll even send you two wonderful surprise gifts. You can't lose!

Each of your **FREE** books is filled with romance, adventure and faith set in various historical periods from biblical times to World War

# GET 2 FREE BOOKS!

## HURRY!
**Return this card today to get 2 FREE Books and 2 FREE Bonus Gifts!**

**YES!** Please send me the **2 FREE Love Inspired® Historical books** and **2 FREE gifts** for which I qualify. I understand that I am under no obligation to purchase anything further, as explained on the back of this card.

PLACE
FREE GIFTS
SEAL HERE

## 102/302 IDL FVU9

FIRST NAME

LAST NAME

ADDRESS

APT.#

CITY

STATE/PROV.

ZIP/POSTAL CODE

▼ DETACH AND MAIL CARD TODAY!

® and ™ are trademarks owned and used by the trademark owner and/or its licensee.
© 2012 HARLEQUIN ENTERPRISES LIMITED. Printed in the U.S.A.

LIH-IV-13

Ellie broke in. "I'm sure the cookies will be waiting for you when we get there."

"Maybe…"

"Johnny, that's enough."

Johnny looked up at her with a grin, his brown eyes shining with fun. Ellie caught her breath. Every month that passed, Johnny looked more like his father, but the change in the past few weeks made her see Daniel in every movement and expression. Ever since Bram had come into their lives….

The children started a game of Twenty Questions to pass the time on the long drive. Danny slept in a make-shift bed on the floor in the back, leaving her free to handle the reins and her mind free to wander. She had started these monthly visits to Daniel's aunt and uncle soon after Danny was born. The older couple grieved as much as she did. When they lost Daniel, and Ellie moved to *Mam* and *Dat*'s, they also lost their daily contact with Daniel's children, the only grandchildren they would ever have.

"There's the creek!" Susan shouted.

Ellie looked past the creek, the landmark the children used to know they had arrived, and saw Miriam and Hezekiah waiting for them in the drive. Their smiling faces told her she should consider bringing the children more than once a month, but when would she fit in another day for this trip? Once a month allowed her to stop by Daniel's farm and collect the rent from the tenants.

"*Ach,* the children!" Miriam held out her arms as the buggy stopped in the drive.

Susan and Johnny jumped out and raced to Miriam, almost knocking over the short, round woman in their enthusiasm. Hezekiah limped over to the buggy to take a sleepy Danny from Ellie.

"Hello, Hezekiah. How are you today?"

"*Ach,* I can't complain." He didn't look at Ellie, but he smiled as he rubbed his beard on Danny's head, making the toddler giggle.

*Ne,* he never complained, but from the way he walked, his arthritis was bad today.

"Good morning, good morning," Miriam called to her over Johnny's head. "Come in. I have coffee ready, and cake."

"And cookies?" Susan was still fearful that Johnny's teasing might come true.

Miriam leaned down and took the little girl's cheeks between her hands. "Of course there are cookies! What would a visit to *Grossmutti* Miriam's be without cookies?"

Hezekiah handed Danny to Miriam as he took Brownie's bridle. Ellie would have taken care of the horse, but the one time she had tried to ease the older man's work, he had shooed her out of his barn with a frown. He would keep working until the arthritis made his joints so stiff he couldn't move. If he could handle things on his own for a few more years, then Johnny would be old enough to help him.

Once Susan and Johnny had helped themselves to a soft sugar cookie from Miriam's cookie tin, they headed out to the barn to see the animals. Miriam put Danny in the high chair she kept waiting in the kitchen and broke up a cookie on the table in front of him.

"It won't be long before this one will be running out to the barn with the others." Miriam patted Danny's arm as if she couldn't get close enough to him.

Ellie remembered *Mam* telling her once that ever since her only daughter had died as an infant, Miriam's arms always seemed to be hungry to hold babies, and it was true. She loved being near the children.

She helped herself to the coffee, pouring two cups, while Miriam cut large pieces of cinnamon-laded coffee cake for them.

"How are your parents?" Miriam asked as she took her seat next to Danny.

"They're doing well." Ellie joined her at the small table. "*Mam* is working on a quilt for Reuben."

"Not Reuben! Already? Who is the girl?"

Ellie smiled. "He hasn't told us yet. He's been very secretive about the whole courtship."

"As he should be. It must be someone from another district. I haven't seen him paying attention to any one girl at our church."

"I don't know. It could be. I know he was sweet on Sarah Yoder at one time, but that was when they were both quite young."

Miriam's face was suddenly serious, and she leaned toward Ellie across the table. "I know I shouldn't say anything. Hezekiah would say it's none of my business, but I have to wonder. Have you ever considered marrying again? I know Levi Zook is ready whenever you are."

The memory of being within the circle of Bram's arms came to Ellie, but she pushed it away.

"I'm too busy with the children to think of marrying again, and there's the farm. We still plan to move back to it when we can. Daniel would want us to."

Miriam stroked Danny's arm. "You're too young to hold on to the past. Don't let yesterday's memories rob you of tomorrow's dreams."

The elderly woman drew a shuddering sigh and took a sip of coffee, then studied the cup carefully as she

spoke. "For many years I prayed to *Gott* to give me another child after we lost our Abigail. I wanted so badly
to give Hezekiah a son." She stopped, caught her bottom lip between her teeth and rubbed her thumb along
the rim of the cup.

Ellie waited for her to go on, blinking back tears.

"I've wished my life away, always looking back to
our poor daughter." Miriam looked up at Ellie. "I have
spent my life grieving, crying for what was lost instead
of looking at the gifts *Gott* has given me. Don't make
the same mistake."

Miriam's eyes were wet as she smiled at Danny. He
grinned at her, squeezing the soft cookie between his
fingers.

"Daniel was the closest we will ever have to a son.
When he came to live with us, I resented him at first.
I had prayed for a baby, not a sixteen-year-old young
man." She turned to Ellie with tears pooling in her eyes.
"But he blessed us with his presence, then with you,
then with the children. *Gott* answered my prayers more
completely than I ever imagined."

She grasped Ellie's hand in her own, her soft, papery skin cool and dry. "Don't make the same mistake,
Ellie. Don't try to bring the past alive again. *Gott* has
other plans for you, better plans than you can imagine."

Ellie smiled back at Miriam, unable to trust her
voice. Wasn't that just what she had been thinking?
That it was time to move on from the past? But to think
*Gott* had better plans for her than Daniel and their family? *Ach,* that couldn't be.

By midafternoon Ellie and the children said goodbye
to Hezekiah and Miriam. The drive to Daniel's farm
was short, just to the end of the mile, then the first farm

on the right. Daniel's land joined Hezekiah's small farm in the middle of the section.

The house needed painting. The paint Daniel had used had faded from the gleaming white, and in places it was peeling. It couldn't be that old, could it? Ellie counted back. It was almost ten years ago that Daniel had bought this land and built the house. He had worked so hard and insisted everything had to be perfect before their wedding.

She could still hear his voice. "This is my family's house, and it will last for generations."

How sad he would be to see his house now. It wasn't just the peeling paint. The lawn was ragged, and the barn door sagged in one spot. Mr. Brenneman wasn't a farmer, although he tried. At least his job in town provided money for them to pay the rent, and they were good tenants, in spite of being *Englisch*.

Ellie saw a rusty black automobile parked near the barn like a dusty beetle as she pulled the buggy up to the hitching post by the back door of the house. Shouldn't Mr. Brenneman be at work on a Monday? Could he be sick? Or was today a holiday for the *Englisch?*

Mrs. Brenneman came to the kitchen door before Ellie got out of the buggy. The young woman looked as if she had been crying, and two children clung to her skirts as she stood on the top step.

"Good afternoon, Mrs. Miller," she said. Something in the *Englisch* woman's voice caused Ellie to stay seated. Something was wrong.

"Good afternoon, Mrs. Brenneman. How are you today?"

The other woman ignored Ellie's question. "We can't pay the rent today. My husband has lost his job."

"When did this happen?"

"Two weeks ago. I wanted to send you word, but James thought he'd be able to find something by the first of the month." Mrs. Brenneman's face was desperate. "Could you let us pay you later? It's only one month. He will surely find work soon, and the crops are already in. I told James we could sell the cow to pay at least some of the rent."

"You can't sell your cow." Ellie refused to think what the delay of the rent would mean to her family, but then, her children weren't in danger of going hungry. "You pay me when you can, Mrs. Brenneman."

The other woman held herself straighter. "We don't take charity, Mrs. Miller."

"And I don't give it, Mrs. Brenneman, but you have your children to think of. You will pay when you can. I know you will."

The other woman's smile trembled. "Thank you for understanding."

"These are hard times for everyone, Mrs. Brenneman. Please send word with the Millers when Mr. Brenneman finds another job."

Ellie turned Brownie toward the road as Mrs. Brenneman went back into the house. Without the rent money, she wouldn't be able to pay the taxes on the farm when they came due next month. If she had only known about this before she bought the strawberry plants! She had counted on the Brennemans paying their rent, and she never thought he would lose his job.

All three children napped on the drive home, giving Ellie plenty of time to think. Too much time. She was thankful the Brennemans wouldn't lose their home again—they had lost one farm to foreclosure already—and besides, it wouldn't help her to turn them out for not paying the rent. At least this way someone was living on the farm.

But where would the money come from for the taxes? The strawberries wouldn't start paying until next year, if they survived that long.

She could ask *Dat* for the money, but she knew what his response would be. He had told her more than once that she should sell the farm and let go of the responsibility. But she couldn't. From the time Daniel had first bought that farm, he had meant it as a legacy for his children. To let the farm go would be letting Daniel's dream die. She couldn't let that happen.

Would the church help her? *Ja,* but Bishop Yoder had already talked to her once about marrying again. The help would most likely come with the condition that she obediently sell her farm and marry Levi Zook or one of the other widowers in the church. She shuddered at the thought of the other two men the bishop had mentioned as possible husbands for her. Both of them were old enough to be her father.

Then there was Bram. He must have money. He had already spent so much on his farm, but where did he get it? He'd come from Chicago with nothing, but he now owned a farm, horse and buggy, and she had seen a brand-new hay rake and a plow in his barn. Most people she knew weren't spending money—they didn't have it. But Bram did. More than enough, it seemed, and he was planning to spend more on a new stove. Was he just going into debt for everything? *Ne,* even she knew banks wouldn't lend money for nothing. So he must have brought it with him from Chicago.

The question circled through her mind: Where did he get his money?

# Chapter Ten

A red sliver of sunrise pierced through the clinging mist of predawn coolness, promising another hot, dry day. Bram glanced at the sky above. The early-morning gray had given way to clear blue in a sweep from east to west. Not a cloud in sight. A good Saturday morning for a barn raising.

Partner's steady trot echoed in the morning stillness as the road led through a stand of sugar maples. The only other noise came from the treetops, where birds chirped and whistled, their predawn singing already done.

Bram settled back in the buggy seat. How long had it been since he had heard a car horn? Did he miss it?

He could come up with a whole list of other things he missed. Smoking. He hadn't had a cigarette since that day in Goshen. An electric refrigerator with cold cuts and cheese for his sandwiches. Telephones. Movies. Music. He missed going to the jazz clubs. That music spoke to his soul.

But staying in Chicago hadn't been an option, not with Kavanaugh's contract out on him. He could have gone west, taken on a new identity, a new job. He could have been enjoying electric fans on hot days instead of sweltering in this breathless humidity.

No, he would never have felt safe, always leery of someone recognizing him when he least expected it.

And he would never have met Ellie. The sound of her name caressed his mind with the soft flutter of wings, opening the doors that contained memories of her. He held each one in turn: standing in his kitchen, talking with her as they rode in his buggy, the light touches she let him give her.

Would she be at today's barn raising? John and the boys would, but would Ellie come?

The dark red shadow hovering at the edge of his mind pulsed. Kavanaugh. Was he still a threat? Bram hadn't seen any sign of him for more than two weeks, even though he had made the rounds through the surrounding towns. His hand slipped down to feel the gun in his pocket. He couldn't let his guard down, not yet.

Another buggy turned onto the road in front of him, and from behind he could hear the sound of a third one. He must be getting close. John had said to go west to County Line Road, then north and follow the buggies. The quiet of the morning was broken.

The barnyard was full of straw hats and black bonnets as families arrived. Bram found a place for his buggy among the others. He tied up Partner, loosened his harness and got his toolbox out of the back. Bram caught the eye of a young boy with a water bucket, and the boy nodded. Partner would be well taken care of by the crew of hostlers too young to help with the carpentry.

He made his way to the spot where the men were gathering.

"Good morning," he said, nodding to several men

he didn't know, and then he joined John and the other men from his church.

"Good morning, Bram," said John. His greeting was seconded by nods from several of the others. "There are coffee and doughnuts over by the house."

"That sounds wonderful," said Matthew as he joined the group. "But at least I had a good breakfast this morning. How is that bachelor cooking these days, Bram? Did you even have breakfast?" He smiled as he shook Bram's hand.

"My toast and coffee were just fine this morning." Bram set his toolbox on the ground. "Both of them black."

The men all laughed. Bram gave them a grin as he headed over to the long tables set up in the yard outside the house.

Plates piled high with fresh doughnuts filled one table, while several women filled coffee cups. Ellie wasn't one of them. Was she even here? How could he ask John without sounding too obvious?

Bram scanned the crowd as he headed back to his toolbox and caught sight of his brother, Samuel, talking with some men from the Shipshewana district. Samuel at a barn raising? This was something new. What was he doing here?

When Samuel looked up, Bram nodded to him, but Samuel turned his back. Well, had he expected anything else?

"Levi Zook is here." Lovina spoke low into Ellie's ear, but every woman in the crowded kitchen heard her.

"Did he bring his children?" *Mam* was across the table from Ellie, where they both worked at rolling out dough.

"*Ja,* all ten of them."

"His Waneta is a big help, isn't she?"

"She and Elias are sixteen years old already. She'll make a *wonderful-gut* wife for some lucky young man in a few years."

Ellie let the talk swirl around her. Levi and his large family took everyone's attention wherever they went. Just as well for him. There were plenty of young women ready to mother his little ones.

She rolled the dough until it filled her half of the table, then picked up the doughnut cutter.

If she had married Levi, her own little ones would be lost in that crowd. Levi's children were older than hers, at least most of them. Her Johnny and his Lavern were together in school, and he had one younger, Susan's age. His little Sam.

*Ja,* her heart went out to those poor motherless children, too, but not so much that she wanted to be part of that family.

The dough on the table filled with empty circles as the cut doughnuts went to the women frying them up. Circle after circle, blending together into an unbroken pattern.

She'd be lost in Levi's family. Daniel would be gone forever.

She gathered up the leftover dough and rerolled it into a smaller round, ready to be cut again.

If she married again... Her thoughts flitted to Bram and then back. She could marry again, and when she did, it would have to be because it was a man, not his children, who loved her and needed her.

"That's the last of the dough." *Mam* emptied the final bowl onto the table and started rolling it out.

"How many have we made?"

"I counted fifteen dozen," said a dark-haired woman at the sink.

Ellie took a deep breath of hot oil and sugar. She loved sweets, but after this morning she for sure wasn't hungry for a doughnut.

She poured herself a cup of coffee and stepped out onto the back porch to get some fresh air. Lovina joined her, carrying plates piled high with delicious-smelling doughnuts ready to take to the serving table.

"Do you know that man over there?" She nodded to a heavyset man helping himself to a handful of doughnuts.

"*Ne,* I don't think I've ever seen him before. Why?"

"He was asking about Bram. He asked me if I knew him and which district we lived in."

"Was he just being friendly?"

"*Ne,* I don't think so. He was very unpleasant."

Ellie's fingers turned cold around her coffee cup. Was Bram in some kind of trouble?

"It's probably someone who knew him from before. It's really none of our concern."

Lovina stared at her and then leaned close, her voice quiet.

"You don't fool me, Ellie Miller. You ignore Levi Zook, a man who's had his eye on you for months, but then you turn all shades of red whenever Bram's name is mentioned. Don't act like you don't care."

Lovina was right. She cared more than she wanted to admit.

"Isaac Sherk has built more barns than anyone else in the area." Matthew moved next to Bram, ready to team up with him. "He'll divide us into crews, and then each crew will work on a section of the barn."

Isaac moved from group to group, assigning work. Bram and the rest of the men from the Eden district were given the west wall, and they headed in that direction. Bram loaded his tool belt with his hammer and chisel and then grabbed a handful of nails from a nearby keg.

"First we put the frame together," Matthew said, "then we raise that up to join the other frames. After that, the rafters are raised, and then we start on the walls and roof."

"How many of these have you been to?"

Matthew grinned. "Only one, and I was a little shaver then, but I remember how it went. Once you've been to a barn raising, you never forget."

Bram looked around at the other teams. There were nearly a hundred men here from the surrounding districts. He looked from face to face. Habit. It was hard to break. Kavanaugh wouldn't be here, not in a million years.

As the groups organized themselves and started pulling the lumber they needed off the pile of waiting saw beams and planks, the sounds of building started. The hum of voices in the cool, moist air was punctuated by the echoing slap of wood hitting wood, the rhythmic sighing of saws and the occasional thwack of a hammer sounding like a car backfiring in the early-morning air. The work progressed as the men warmed up, a shout or two could be heard, and then the hammers started in earnest. Finishing the framing for the walls became a friendly race between teams, and soon there were shouts of triumph as the first wall was raised into place.

Bram kept busy working with his team. As the oldest and most experienced among them, Eli Schrock fell into the lead position for the crew, and Bram watched him carefully. Fitting the big beams together was easy with such an experienced foreman, and their wall was soon up.

When they started hammering the planks onto the frame to enclose the barn, Bram was on more familiar footing. It seemed that most of the men were, because the level of conversation increased and the rhythm of the hammering settled into a steady series of *thwack, thwack, bump* from each man's hammer. Bram was enjoying the repetition when he caught the words of a conversation from the Shipshewana group. It was Samuel's voice.

"*Ja,* you're right about that. I'm just not sure how far we can trust him."

"Does he think he'll just fit in again, after living in Chicago all those years?" This was from the man working next to Samuel.

"I don't see how he can, but I know one thing. He isn't going to waltz in and take what's mine."

"Your old *dat* gave you that farm, not him."

"*Ja,* but he's always had his own way. It would be like him to try to buy me out with that money he brought back from Chicago. Don't you have to wonder where he got all that money?"

Bram looked around the portion of wall he was working on. Samuel had a hammer in his hand, but he wasn't using it. He moved from one man to another a few feet away and started talking to him. A troublemaker, just like he was as a kid. Just like *Dat.* The gossip Samuel was spreading made his stomach grind. All he needed now was for Samuel's rumor to reach the wrong ears. The reward for leading the feds to Kavanaugh's gang had been a hefty one, enough to let him live comfortably for years, but he still had to lie low until his job was finished and Kavanaugh was out of the way for good.

Forget it. Forget him. Bram bent the next two nails under his hammer and gave up. He motioned for Reuben to come over to take his place, then he sat down on a pile of shingles.

Bram let his hands dangle between his knees and stared at the ground. What could he do about Samuel's gossip? The thread of truth in Samuel's words was just enough to hang him, and what if those words got around to Ellie?

"Worn-out, Bram?"

Matthew was next to him, holding out a dipper of water. Bram took it, downed half of it in one gulp and handed it back to Matthew.

"I guess I'm not used to this work yet."

"I volunteered to make a trip into Goshen. The sawmill there has donated another stack of lumber, and I'm going to pick it up. Do you want to go with me? I could use the extra hands."

"*Ja,* for sure." Any excuse to get away from his brother.

Matthew drove the patient horses through the middle of town on Lincoln, past the courthouse square. Bram spotted a policeman still watching the intersection from the police booth. The day he had come into town to buy his farm seemed like a lifetime ago. Had it really only been a few weeks?

Traffic picked up as they neared the industrial district along the canal on the west side of town. After the quiet of the Amish community, the noise of the factories was deafening. Matthew threaded the borrowed team and wagon between parked dray wagons and trucks to the sawmill. They loaded the lumber and were soon heading back through town.

"It's good to get away from those factories," Matthew said as he turned the horses onto Main Street.

"When I first got back from Chicago, I thought I'd go deaf from the silence in the country, but now…"

Bram stopped. He had been letting his gaze move from face to face as they drove by the storefronts when he saw what he had been looking for. Dreading.

Habit paid off.

Bram didn't move, but he let his eyes slide across Kavanaugh's face and ahead to the next corner. He saw Kavanaugh's reaction, though. A flash of puzzled recognition, the faltered step.

*Don't panic.* Bram took a breath, then another, keeping them even and controlled. His mind raced. Did Kavanaugh suspect it was him? He couldn't risk a glance back. Up until now, Kavanaugh had had no idea he was in the area, but if the gangster saw through the disguise… He forced the muscles in his neck to relax. *Just ride.*

His ears roared. He resisted the urge to jump from the slow wagon, to run as fast as he could. Any second now, he'd feel the pluck of Kavanaugh's hand on his sleeve. He'd turn around, look into the gangster's eyes and then who knew what would happen, what Kavanaugh would do. Bram put his hand in his pocket, grasping the comforting butt of his pistol.

Matthew's voice filtered through the roaring in Bram's ears.

"…getting married in the fall. He's already started his beard…"

What was he talking about?

"…says it makes him feel married already. How about you?"

"What?"

"I was talking about my brother. He's starting his beard now. Says he's old enough. What do you think? Should he wait until after the wedding?"

"I guess he could start it now. It'll make a difference in how he looks, won't it?"

*Ja,* that was what he needed. A beard. He needed to work himself into the community even deeper. A man his age without a beard stood out. He'd stop shaving today. He'd blend in so well his own brother wouldn't be able to pick him out of a crowd.

The roaring in his ears eased, and he swallowed. It might be enough. Bram risked a glance back down Main as Matthew turned the team onto Lincoln heading east, out of town. Kavanaugh had turned to follow the wagon, weaving through the other pedestrians to keep it in sight. He was watching Bram, but the puzzled look was still there. He wasn't sure. Yet.

Desperate for some way, any way, to keep Kavanaugh off his track, Bram's mind raced. Would a beard be enough of a disguise? A cold wrench clamped around Bram's gut. What if it wasn't enough? What if, by some freak chance, Kavanaugh found him anyway? He knew too well what the gangster would do to him. To Ellie… to the children.

"Are you all right?" Matthew's voice made him jump. Bram fought for control.

"*Ja,* I'm fine. I just thought I saw someone I knew."

Maybe he should run today. Bram watched the roadside pass by without seeing anything. Leave Indiana, leave Ellie, leave everything. He'd call Peters in the morning, tell him he quit. It was too risky.

Never see Ellie again.

Or stay and risk Kavanaugh using her to get to him. He couldn't bear either one.

Once the wagon crossed the railroad tracks, the sounds of the city faded. Bram risked a look behind them. The road was empty. No Packard followed. Maybe Kavanaugh hadn't recognized him.

Would he even hear the soft purr of the Packard before it was too late?

A wash of cool silk flowed through his mind, giving him the calm he needed.

Bram looked behind him again. Nothing but dusty gravel.

What should he do? The cool-silk feeling flowed again.

Stay, watch, listen. If he stayed, at least he could try to protect Ellie. If he ran, there was no guarantee Kavanaugh would follow. He'd never know if Kavanaugh had recognized him until it was too late.

The cool silk folded around the tight feeling in his gut, loosening it. It was as if someone had been listening to his thoughts and guiding him to the right decision. Whatever it was, it had helped.

*Ja,* he'd stay.


At dinnertime, Ellie volunteered to help with drinks for the workers, even though the job of keeping the men's water glasses filled would let her mingle with them. The thought of seeing Bram made her hands shake, but she had to see him. She couldn't shake off the feeling that something was very wrong.

A sea of muted color swirled through the space between the house and the tables. Hurried snatches of conversation filled the air as the women flew in and out of the house, bringing out the food. Bowls of stewed chicken and noodles, mashed potatoes and jars of chow-chow filled the tables. Sliced loaves of bread sat next to crocks of fresh butter, jars of last year's jam and apple butter. Pies filled another table made of sawhorses and planks, causing the boards to bow precariously in the center.

The whole group of more than two hundred men, women and children fell into silence during the blessing pronounced by Mordecai Miller, bishop of the Forks church, and then the crowd of men lined up at the table and began filling their plates.

Ellie kept the glasses full, nodding to the men she knew as they passed through the line.

"*Ach,* Ellie, this looks *wonderful-gut.*"

Levi Zook smiled at her, his round face red from the morning's work in the sun.

"*Denki,* Levi. I hope you enjoy it."

"Are your children here today?" Levi lingered at the table. Ellie glanced at the row of blue, black and brown shirts waiting for him to move on.

"*Ja,* they're playing with the other children." She moved a cup within reach of the next man in line.

Levi shifted to the side to let the man pass. "You know, I think about you a lot."

*Not here, not now.*

"Levi, I can't talk right now." She tried to keep a pleasant look on her face as she filled another glass with water.

"*Ach,* between your children and mine, there's never a time when we can talk."

Ellie put the pitcher down on the table, ignoring the water sloshing over the sides, and looked straight into Levi's eyes. "We don't have anything to talk about. I told you before—I don't plan to marry again. You need to find someone else."

Levi leaned in close, ignoring the men waiting for him to move on. "You need me as much as I need you, Ellie." His voice was laced with desperation. "Please say you'll consider it."

Suddenly aware of the silence around them, Ellie realized her voice had risen. She and Levi were the center of attention. She turned from Levi to serve the next man in line and looked up into Bram's face. He looked from her to Levi, and his eyes were a stormy gray. How long had he been standing there? Her stomach clenched and unclenched at the thought of the conversation he had just overheard…the conversation everyone had just overheard, she amended as she realized that her brothers and Matthew Beachey were standing right beside him.

She dropped everything and ran—away from the talk, away from the questioning eyes, away from Bram. Blind steps took her to the field where the buggies sat in a row and found *Dat*'s. Climbing into the back, she curled up on the seat. Tears filled her eyes.

How would she ever face him again? How would she ever face any of them again? Not only had she had a conversation with Levi in front of everyone that should have been private, she had drawn attention to herself. Nothing could be more humiliating.

"Ellie?"

*Ach, ne,* it was Bram. Ellie froze. He must have seen her coming this way. Maybe he had missed her scrambling into the back of *Dat*'s buggy.

"Ellie?"

Bram's voice sounded louder, and she heard footsteps in the grass next to the buggy. She curled up tighter, then jumped when Bram's face appeared in the door.

"I thought I saw you go in here. What are you doing?"

Ellie hesitated at the demanding tone of Bram's voice. Was he angry? She cleared her throat.

"I'm fine. I'm just resting for a bit where it's quiet."

"What were you thinking, talking to Levi Zook like that in public? Do you know how many people heard you?"

She nodded, unable to look him in the eye. Ellie waited for him to leave, but he didn't move. It was a mistake to come to the barn raising today. She should have stayed at home, but she had wanted to be with her friends… *Ne,* why try to lie to herself? She had been hoping to see Bram today, but she had for sure made a mess of everything.

"What is he to you, Ellie? Have I been making a fool of myself these past few weeks?"

"*Ach,* Bram, there's nothing going on between Levi and me."

"He seems to think there is."

"That's because he won't take *ne* for an answer."

Bram sighed, his shoulders slumping as he leaned against the buggy door.

"What am I, then?" His voice was nearly a whisper. Did he want her to answer?

How would she answer? What was Bram to her? He raised his eyes to hers, shadowed steel-gray.

Her voice whispered back, "You're no Levi Zook, Bram Lapp."

## Chapter Eleven

Mercifully, Bram left her alone sitting in the back of *Dat*'s buggy. Alone to think about what she had said and done.

Her hands wouldn't stop shaking, even when Ellie clenched her fists, leaning against the buggy wall. She took deep breaths, forcing the threatening tears to stop.

She must face them again, all those people who had heard her outburst, whether she felt like it or not. They would forgive her, of course, but would they ever forget? The longer she stayed hidden in *Dat*'s buggy, the worse it would be.

Ellie smoothed her apron with her hands, bringing back some control. She reached up to tuck any loose hairs under her *kapp* and wiped her cheeks once more. Taking a deep breath, Ellie stepped out of the buggy.

As she rounded the wheels, the heavyset man Lovina had pointed out earlier stepped into her path. He stopped Ellie with a hand on her arm and leaned in close, reeking of unwashed clothing. Why wasn't he working with the other men?

"I'm looking for Bram Lapp. I saw him follow you over here, but then I lost track of him. Where did he go?"

Ellie pulled her arm away from his clumsy fingers. "He went back to work. Why do you want him?"

The man grinned, turning his face into a distorted reflection of Bram's. "I'm his brother. I just wanted to have a chat with him. If you see him, tell him I'm looking for him, all right?"

"*Ja,* I can do that, but you'll find him over at the barn."

Bram's brother winked at her. "*Ne,* I don't need to bother him there. I'll find him. You just give him the message." Ellie started walking away, but the man's voice followed her. "You tell him I want a piece of whatever he has going on, you hear?"

Ellie hurried toward the house, glad to leave Bram's unpleasant brother behind. What could he mean, that he wanted a piece of what Bram was doing? Bram wasn't involved in anything more than getting his farm going, was he?

She stepped into the kitchen, intent on gathering her things and finding her children so they would be ready to leave as soon as *Dat* said it was time. Relief washed over her when she found *Mam* there, sitting at the kitchen table with a whining Danny on her lap. When she was younger, *Mam* would listen to all her sorrows—now it was enough to just sit near her, drawing in her quiet strength.

"*Ach,* Danny, here's your *memmi.*"

At *Mam*'s words Danny turned and lifted his hands to her, and Ellie took her tired boy, letting him bury his face in her shoulder. She sat in an empty chair and settled Danny on her lap. He would be asleep in no time.

Being with *Mam* as she held Danny's small body close comforted her raw nerves. She laid her cheek against Danny's soft head and closed her eyes as she rocked him gently back and forth. If only she could stay like this forever. Forget about Bram, his brother, Levi…everything.

The kitchen was quiet now, or as quiet as it could be during the after-dinner cleanup. Most of the work was being done outside under the shady trees, with women coming into the kitchen now and then to put dishes away. The sounds of the children's games drifted in from the yard.

As Danny's body relaxed into sleep, Ellie opened her eyes and sat straight, adjusting the baby into a position that was comfortable for both of them.

"Do you want to lay him down somewhere?" *Mam* asked, her voice quiet so she wouldn't disturb Danny.

"*Ne,* I'm ready to sit for a while, and I don't want to risk waking him by laying him down in a strange place."

*Mam* nodded. She waited until the kitchen was empty and then said, "I didn't see you at dinner. Did you have a chance to eat?"

Ellie shook her head. "I'm not hungry."

*Mam* gave her a worried look but went on. "The men have been working hard. The new barn is almost done."

"That's *wonderful-gut.*"

If the men were almost done, they could go home soon. Ellie longed for her own kitchen, her own bed. Why had she thought joining the barn raising would be a good idea?

"I saw you talking with Levi earlier."

Did she miss Ellie's humiliating behavior? She must have. "*Ja,* he wanted to visit for a bit."

"He does so well, alone with all those children."

Ellie shifted Danny a little higher on her lap.

"*Mam,* I'm not going to marry Levi Zook."

*Mam* shook her head. Ellie knew that expression on

her face. She wouldn't give up until either she or Levi was married, but she did know when to change the subject.

"I heard some talk about Bram." Ellie nodded, and *Mam* went on. "You know I don't listen to gossip. If what is said has any truth to it, then it should be said openly."

"I don't know if there's any truth to what's being said."

"Have you asked Bram about it?"

"Well, his brother said Bram was involved in something, but I don't know what he meant."

"But what did you hear Bram say?"

A trio of women came into the kitchen just then, laden with clean dishes. With the interruption, Ellie couldn't answer *Mam*'s question. How would she even respond?

Bram swung his hammer in a precise, measured blow. Set the next shingle and set the nail, a swing of the hammer, another nail. Once you learned to shingle a roof, you never forgot. He stopped to straighten his back and wipe the sweat from his forehead.

Below him, women were gathered around a quilting frame that had been set up for the afternoon. He couldn't see Ellie anywhere, but she must still be here. Her brothers were nailing in their shingles on the opposite end of the roof from him.

He returned to his work. It wouldn't do to let those boys get ahead of him. He'd never hear the end of it.

Shingling took concentration and attention, but it was repetitive and allowed his mind to wander. Why hadn't Ellie told him about Levi Zook before? Why did he have to find out about the man's intentions this way?

He hit a nail too hard, and it bent under his hammer. He pulled it out and pocketed it, then put a new one in its place. Precise, measured blows.

He forced himself to concentrate, but the look on Ellie's face as he had left her in the buggy haunted him. She had faith in him, but had she heard the gossip Samuel was spreading? And then there was Kavanaugh. He had to talk to her—he had to warn her.

Warn her about what? To watch for a rat-faced man in a maroon Packard? All he had to go on was that maybe, just maybe Kavanaugh had recognized him and might be looking for him along the back roads of LaGrange County. That wasn't enough for her to take him seriously.

As he reached the peak of the barn roof, Bram took a quick glance at the Stoltzfus boys. They had finished their part of the roof and were filling in the space between him and them. He put his last nail in just as they reached him. "Is that the last?" Bram asked.

"Everything except the rail," said Reuben.

Bram followed the boys down the ladder and watched another crew finish up the ridge. The final nail went in with a cheer, and the men scattered to gather their tools and families.

Trying to keep track of the Stoltzfuses in the milling crowd, Bram lost sight of John and his boys. He made his way toward the house. Ellie must be here somewhere, gathering up her children. Or maybe avoiding him.

"Bram, hold on."

He cringed inwardly at Samuel's call—his brother's call. Did Samuel have anything to say he'd want to hear?

Bram kept his expression calm when Samuel stepped

in front of him, a triumphant grin on his face. He looked as if he was satisfied with his day's work.

"I was surprised to see you here today," Samuel said.

"You shouldn't have been. A barn raising is a time for the whole community to come together." Bram waited. Samuel wanted something, and sooner or later he'd get around to it, but Bram would rather get it done with. He looked past Samuel to where the women were busy gathering up their things and calling their children together. Ellie stepped out of the house carrying Danny.

"I hear you bought yourself a farm."

Bram turned his full attention to Samuel. He was a loose cannon and needed to be dealt with. He could only hope that Ellie wouldn't leave too quickly.

"*Ja,* it's down near Emma. I'm settling there now."

Samuel grinned. "It makes me wonder where you got that kind of money, after being away in Chicago all those years. I've heard the only people in Chicago with money are gangsters."

"I know you've been spreading rumors, Samuel, and there's no truth in them."

"That's not the way I see it. The way I see it, there might be people back in the city willing to pay to find out exactly where your money is. You made a big mistake coming back here."

Bram fought for control, but he knew how to handle a man like Samuel. He drew himself up to his full height, laid his hand on his brother's stocky shoulder and drew him close. He put a pleasant smile on his face, but his words, whispered so only Samuel would hear them, carried the punch he wished he could put into his fist.

"You're the one making the mistake, Samuel. Don't try to threaten me. You don't know anything about any money. As far as you know, I saved up while I was working in Chicago and now I've come back." He leaned closer to Samuel and put one arm around him in a brotherly hug. "I don't need to tell you what might happen if you keep spreading rumors, do I?" he breathed in the other man's ear.

He drew back. Samuel's dismayed face told him his words had carried the right weight. He patted the dirty shirtfront. "I'm glad we had this talk."

Bram pushed past his brother, hoping he hadn't made a mistake leaning into Samuel like that. Hopefully, throwing around a bit of muscle was all he needed to keep him quiet. Even so, he'd have to be careful. Samuel was just the kind of man Kavanaugh loved to use.

Once he reached the back door steps, Ellie was nowhere to be seen.

Standing on the back porch, Bram scanned the crowd, hot with impatience. Samuel had delayed him just long enough. He looked toward the field where the buggies were parked, but in the milling crowd he couldn't tell one family from another.

There, a young woman with a boy walking beside her. He started after them, but before he was even halfway across the yard, he could tell it wasn't her. He shot a glance toward the parked buggies again and swallowed a curse. The Stoltzfus rig was gone.

An endless line of buggies stretched in both directions up and down the road. They were in there somewhere, but he didn't have a chance of catching up with her—not unless he could pull off the impossible.

Partner greeted Bram in his usual way, mouthing the front of his shirt with rubbery lips.

"No time now, boy. We've got to get going."

Bram checked the horse quickly and then reached for the harness. One of the reins was broken. A word from his Chicago past almost made it to his lips at the delay. He couldn't drive Partner with it hanging loose, but how did it get this way?

When he found the two ends, a cold chill ran down his back. They had been cut. This wasn't an accident. He flashed a quick look into the trees of the fencerow. Could Kavanaugh have followed him all the way from Goshen? But the trees weren't hiding anyone—the early-summer growth was too sparse.

He tied the ends so the rein would hold together long enough to get home, slipped the bit into Partner's mouth and tightened the harness buckles. That cut edge was clean. Whoever had done it had used a very sharp knife. Could Samuel have cut the rein? That was the kind of petty crime the brother he knew twelve years ago would have pulled off.

*Ja,* Samuel was the same today as when they were growing up. They had been alike back then, as alike as brothers could be, but he wasn't the same as he had been at seventeen. Seeing Samuel now was like looking into a shadowy mirror…at what he would have become if he hadn't left home.

So what had happened to change him? Life in Chicago, living on the streets? *Ja,* that was part of it. But there was something else. Something had made Samuel's life repulsive to Bram.

Something had given him a new way of looking at what he had been.

That silken coil flowed through him again, and the answer pressed on his mind. God. The same God he had ignored for years was doing something to him…no, for him. Protecting him from being like Samuel, providing Ellie for him. Had that same God brought him back to Indiana and to a new life here?

Would God do that for someone like him?

Bram slowed Partner down to a walk. He'd give Ellie time to settle the children in for the night. But then he had to talk to her.

The sun lowered, turning the whole sky into a deep blue bowl with a fiery red rim to the west. He tilted his head back to find the first star and spied it high in the eastern sky, just above a pale, full moonrise. He let himself relax as he watched more stars reveal themselves one by one, diamonds against deep blue velvet.

*Ja,* he had to talk to her.


Echoes of her footsteps whispered in the quiet house as Ellie walked from room to room, willing her mind to settle so she could sleep.

Johnny's body sprawled on the front room sofa, tangled in his sheets already. She straightened his legs and lifted his arm back onto his makeshift bed from where it dangled over the floor. He didn't wake, but rolled onto his side.

The children had all fallen asleep quickly after a supper of bread and butter. Ellie wished she could join them; she was ready to put this day behind her.

Stepping onto the back porch, she took in the summer night. Every night of her life, as far back as she could remember, she had taken the few moments this ritual required, even in the cold or rain.

The dusky air was warm for June. The sky still held the light of the setting sun, but to the east a full moon hung over the trees. One bright star shone, hanging in the sky above the moon. As Ellie's eyes grew used to the moonlight, she could see more stars dusted across the darkening sky.

An owl swooped out from under the barn's eaves,

the first of several trips back and forth to the nest in the barn loft. Frogs croaked from the bog across the road, the bullfrog's guttural *gunk* contrasting with the peeper's *creak*.

Then a different sound intruded—a horse and buggy on the road. Who would be out this time of night?

The horse slowed as it came closer and turned into the drive by *Dat*'s house. Even in the dusk she could see the pale gray of the horse well enough. It was Bram. Her heart plummeted into her stomach, knowing she must talk to him. She must face him.

He drove past the big house and barn toward the *Dawdi Haus* and pulled Partner to a halt in her yard. When he climbed out of the buggy, he stood watching her. She waited, returning his steady gaze. The silence stretched between them until Bram's feet shifted in the dirt at the bottom of the steps. He leaned on the handrail and looked up at her, his eyes soft in the moonlight.

"Come down here, Ellie. Sit on the step with me."

A warning bell went off in her head. Sitting next to him in the dark would be too close, too intimate.

Any more intimate than feeling his arm encircle her on the glider in her yard?

She sat on the top step, and he joined her in the shadowy dusk.

"I have something important to tell you, but I want you to trust me."

Was he about to tell her what his brother had meant—what was it he had said? He wanted a piece of what Bram had going on. Would she ever be able to trust Bram?

Bram reached for her hand. She let him take it, turn it in his hands, stroke her palm with his finger.

"I need to tell you about…" He stopped, stroked her

palm again. "How can I tell her?" he murmured, as if speaking to himself.

Her mouth was dry, but she had to know the truth.

"Your brother told me he wanted something from you—that you have something going on. Is it something illegal, Bram? Did you come here to hide from the police?"

He looked at her, his face unreadable in the moonlight.

"*Ne,* Ellie. I don't know where Samuel came up with that idea. I'm not hiding from the police."

His hand stroked each of her fingers in turn. She longed to give in to his touch, to lean against his body in the darkness, to feel his strength. She had been fooling herself saying they were just friends. Friends didn't lean this close, mingling their breath, their thoughts.

Bram put an arm around her waist and drew her closer to him. His cheek brushed her cheek, the whiskers scratching against her soft skin. If she turned her face slightly, if she moved at all, his lips would find hers and she would lose herself in his kiss. She didn't move and felt a butterfly-soft kiss on her cheek.

He straightened, putting a few inches between them, but kept her hand covered with his. She should pull it away, disentangle herself from this temptation, but she was too comfortable to move. With one arm around her waist and the other holding her hand, she felt as safe as a nestling bird.

"I need to tell you why I'm here, but for now it needs to be just between the two of us, all right?"

She nodded. A secret? What could he tell her but not *Dat* and the other men?

"I'm not on the run from the police—I'm working with them. Well, with the bureau, at least."

"The bureau?"

"*Ja.* I'm working with the FBI, tracking down a gangster."

A cold chill made Ellie shiver. Gangsters, the FBI, secrets… What kind of man was this?

"Bram, I don't understand. If you're working with the police, why are you here?"

He didn't answer; he stared at her hand caught in his.

"You've been lying to us? Pretending you want to be part of the community, but all the time lying to *Dat,* to your sister…to me?" Her voice dropped to a whisper. How could she even talk about such a thing?

"I…I didn't mean to mislead you." Bram let go of her hand and rubbed his face. "It's gotten out of hand. I meant to just put on a disguise—hide in the community while I tried to find out what Kavanaugh was up to. But it isn't that simple…."

"Lying never is."

"I never planned for this to happen, Ellie." His voice was soft velvet against the night sounds. "I never planned to meet you, your *dat* and *mam,* the children… I never thought I'd find a home."

Ellie's mind spun. Just when she was beginning to trust him, to think he was one of them. "What did you plan?"

"I thought it would take just a few weeks to find Kavanaugh, and then I was going to start over—maybe out west somewhere."

"So you never meant to settle here? What about your farm? What about…" She couldn't ask him. She had no right to ask him what his plans were concerning her. He was just a fancy *Englischer,* and she was Amish. They lived in two different worlds.

"I don't know, Ellie. Everything has changed now."

His body went stiff as a sound drifted toward them from the road. They both turned to watch an automobile, its headlights glaring in the pitch-black of the road under the overhanging trees. It drove slowly, as if the driver was looking for something. The engine roared as the driver picked up speed at the Stoltzfus farm. Ellie heard it continue down the road to the east.

He stood suddenly, putting distance between them.

"I'll watch out for you, Ellie, try to keep you safe. But don't trust anyone, all right? Promise me? I need you to trust me."

He needed her. He needed her to trust him, an *Englischer*. An *Englisch* policeman. His eyes were nearly black in the moonlight, pleading silently with her. This wasn't just any *Englischer*, a stranger. This was Bram. Could she trust him?

From the depths of her soul, it came. Peace.

She did. In spite of her doubts, she trusted him.

She nodded, and he was gone.

The buggy whip popped as Bram urged the horse to a fast trot when they turned onto the road. Ellie held her hand, still warm from his touch, to her cheek as she listened to the fading beat of the horse's hooves in the empty night.

She went back into the dark house and wandered through the kitchen to the front room. She could see up and down the road from her front window, but it was empty.

The room was close. Hot. She opened a window and stood in the fitful air, watching the silver-white moonlight on the strawberry field. A mosquito whined against the cheesecloth screen.

Just...trust him? Do nothing else?

Could she do that?

That elusive peace struggled and was gone, driven away by her nervous fears. He wasn't who she thought he was—a wayward Amishman coming back home. He was an *Englischer,* an outsider, a stranger. How could she have let him into her life? How could she trust him?

How could she love him?

She couldn't love him…she mustn't love him.

*Mam*'s words came back to her. She hadn't said anything about how to trust a man; they had talked about trusting *Gott.*

Panic rose like a frantic butterfly trapped in her closing fingers, but instead of letting the wings beat her into senseless fear again, she tightened her grasp, holding it, examining it.

What was she afraid of? If she trusted *Gott,* what was the worst that could happen?

She could lose Bram. The sweetness of his touch, the soft kiss on her cheek, even his insistence that he trust her all told her they would never be able to be just friends again. Could she bear to take that risk?

What if, in spite of everything, she gave her love to Bram and then… She wiped at the tears that flowed down her cheeks. What if he went through with his plans and she was left alone again? Could she bear that?

The peace she was searching for came back, filling her with a calm that stopped her tears. *Ja,* for Bram she could bear even that.

# *Chapter Twelve*

A scared rabbit, that was what he was.

A few months ago, he would have gone after that Packard. His own car would have followed that rat to his hole and finished this business, and that would have been the end of it. But here he was, stuck in this backward place.

Bram slammed his hand against the side of the buggy in frustration, making Partner jump into a panicked gallop.

"Whoa, boy, it's okay."

The horse settled down, but Bram's nerves still jangled.

He had let himself get into the worst position he could imagine. No car, no backup, no telephone, a woman to worry about…

At the thought of Ellie, he cast a glance backward along the road, where the moonlight stretched its silent way behind him. No lights cast a glow under the overhanging trees, and no motor sound echoed in the still night. Would she be safe?

If anything happened to her…

The rising heat found a focus. Kavanaugh. The man

loved killing, whether he pulled the trigger or ordered one of his men to do the job, and he struck without warning. No open spray of hot bullets from a tommy gun for him. The snake preferred to kill with a der- ringer.

Bram pressed against the lump of the pistol in his pocket. With luck, he could protect himself if Kava- naugh found him, but what about Ellie and the children? What about her parents?

The heat against Kavanaugh was quenched in a dash of ice. Before he'd come, they had been safe. Yeah, sure, the gangsters were in the area, but they never would have thought of searching among these peace- ful farms if it wasn't for him. He was the one who had put them in danger.

Rising irritation hammered against his tactics so far. He had established his cover, but now he needed to use the cover to do more than just hide. Kavanaugh was around, for sure, but it was time for Bram to be on the other side of the table. No more scared rabbit for him. He would become the fox and hunt out that snake.

Should he put a call in to Peters? The FBI agent would love to know he had found Kavanaugh, but then what? All Bram could tell him was that he had seen Kavanaugh in Goshen. Peters wouldn't be able to act on such a slim lead, not when things were so hot in Chicago.

Besides, if he contacted Peters, he'd increase the risk that his location would be known, and it could get out to the wrong people.

Bram shifted on the buggy seat, his skin crawling. Kavanaugh wasn't his only enemy, or his worst. Some- one had tipped off Kavanaugh about the raid in April, and it had to be someone in Peters's office. If he was premature in contacting the Chicago office, he'd have to leave the area quickly and quietly. No goodbyes, no explanations, no contact…not even Ellie.

The scent of her as he had held her close filled his mind, and he shut his eyes against the memory. Why had he dared to kiss her cheek like that? Her sweet face enticed him until he nearly turned the buggy around to get one more look at her. How could he bear to leave her?

He couldn't. The only thing he could do was to start hunting.

Ellie woke with a start in the hot bedroom, the early-morning sun at work already. If she hurried, she might have a chance to water the strawberries before fixing breakfast.

Benjamin was already at her pump, filling a bucket.

"*Denki,* Ben, I slept late this morning." She grabbed a second bucket to fill.

"When I finished my chores early, *Dat* said you might need a hand."

They walked through the gate, each carrying a full bucket of water. Ben had already finished two of the rows, so Ellie started on the third. As she reached each plant, she tipped the bucket to splash water onto it. The ground was dry and dusty, even though she had done this same chore the morning before.

"It's so dry."

"It's bad for your strawberries. Look at this one." Ben stopped watering and knelt down to show Ellie the next plant. "It's hardly grown at all from when you planted it a month ago."

Ellie reached out to lift up the stems of the heat-stressed plant. The seedlings were still green, but the papery leaves and stunted growth told her they were just barely alive.

"If we can just keep them going until it rains..."

"It doesn't look like it will, at least not for the next week."

"Well, it has to rain sometime." Ellie chewed on her lip, remembering the days and weeks without rain two years ago. It couldn't happen again, could it?

"Maybe we're in for another drought. *Dat* said the pond is lower than he's ever seen it."

Ellie shot her brother a glance. He had no idea what a drought would do to her plans. She went back to watering her row. Every farmer knew that weather went in cycles. They had just gone through years of drought, but last year's normal rainfall was the end of that cycle, wasn't it?

"The pond is spring fed—it won't dry up. That will help us, won't it?" There had to be hope somewhere.

"*Ja,* that's what *Dat* said. But it gets low in drought years, just the same."

Low water. But she had a well, and there was another one for the big house and the barn. There would be enough water for them all.

There had to be.

She continued down the row, giving each plant a splash of water.

Ellie straightened for just a minute to ease her back, and her mind flitted ahead to the rest of the day. It was a church Sunday. Would Bram be there?

She tipped the bucket at the next plant.

The thought of seeing him again sent her heart beating fast. Did she even want to see him, after what he told her last night?

*Ja.* When he grinned at her, that secretive grin meant

just for her, it drove all other thoughts out of her head. And then last night when he had kissed her cheek! Ellie stopped with the bucket in midair, remembering that delicious, tender kiss as he had held her close. He made her feel...

Ellie smiled to herself as she finished one row and turned to start the next one. He made her feel like a girl with a beau instead of a widow with three children. Even if he was *Englisch,* even if he was leaving soon, it was a *wonderful-gut* feeling.

"*Ach,* Ellie. What are you smiling about?"

Ben passed her with his bucket, heading back to the pump.

"Today's a meeting Sunday, *ja?*"

"For sure it is. We'd best be hurrying on."

Bram opened the back door of the house quietly, last night's caution still weighing on him. He reached into his pocket to let his hand close around the reassuring grip of the gun while he surveyed the barn and fields. Nothing out of place.

It was early, but he had a harness to mend before church. That cut rein had haunted his dreams. Was it a warning, or was it just Samuel's spiteful way of delaying him?

Bram shifted his shoulders and stepped onto the back porch. He was letting himself get spooked. Caution was one thing, but panic could kill him.

In the quiet of the barn, with Partner's munching the only sound, Bram concentrated on splicing the ends of the harness together. The task of tapering the blunt ends so they would fit together smoothly was so familiar that he did most of the work by touch.

Was this what God was doing to him? His own blunt

edges were being shaped to fit into this community, conforming in a way that he never had during his childhood. God's presence was with him, molding and shaving off the rough edges, taking away his past more cleanly and completely than shutting it up behind a door.

Growing up, he had never felt part of the people, but now God was taking the rough, blunt mess of his life and working it into the community bit by bit, just as he was taking this piece of leather and binding it to the other. Nothing he had ever done gave him the satisfaction that his life here did, even if he did face the frustrations of living without modern conveniences when he needed them. Sometimes conveniences were necessities.

Bram stopped working and looked out the open door of the barn to the quiet lane and the road beyond. If Kavanaugh ever found him, all he had gained would be lost, just as quickly and cleanly as this strap had been cut.

Ellie. Knowing she was close, just a few miles down the road, was like money in the bank. He grimaced at that thought. Not like money, something much more secure, fixed, immovable, like the North Star. No matter where he went or what he did, she would be his center.

Bram tried the strength of the splice, and it held. Time to harness Partner and then get cleaned up for Sunday meeting.

Taking the brush from the wall, he moved into Partner's stall. The horse looked at him, his brown eyes calmly accepting whatever Bram wanted him to do. The horse trusted him.

Ellie's nod last night was her acceptance of him, the one thing he needed. The one thing he craved. She trusted him.

That thought whooshed through him like a north

wind, and with weak knees, he leaned against Partner, the brush dangling from his hand. How could he ever live up to her trust?

There was one big problem, though. He couldn't live up to her trust. He knew that and God knew that, so why had he even asked it of her? All he could do was his best. He prayed it would be enough.

Deacon Beachey's sunny farmyard emptied quickly after families finished the Sunday dinner of cold-cut sandwiches and potato salad. The sweltering heat made activity impossible, and families left early to find some relief in their shaded yards. *Mam* came out of the house with her empty dinner basket hanging from one arm.

"*Dat*'s ready to go home, Ellie. Are you?"

Ellie shifted Danny in her arms. "*Ja,* I'm ready. The children are so hot, and Danny is ready for his nap."

"*Ach,* let me take the sweet boy. I'm sure heat rash is bothering him." *Mam* reached for Danny and then nodded past Ellie. "Besides, I think you might have plans for the rest of the afternoon."

Ellie didn't have to turn around to know Bram was walking toward them; she could see that by the smile on *Mam*'s face. Bram had gotten on her good side when she saw him working so hard at the barn raising yesterday.

"I'll see to the children. They can nap at our house in the downstairs bedroom. It will be cool for them there. You won't need to worry about getting home soon."

"*Mam, ne.* You don't need to…" But *Mam* took Danny to the family buggy, rounding up Johnny and Susan as she went.

"Is she stealing your children?" Bram was smiling as he walked up to her.

"*Ja, Mam* and *Dat* are taking them home. It will be cooler for them there."

"So you're left on your own?"

"I'll be able to get a ride from someone, I'm sure. Lovina and her family are still here."

"You don't need to ask them as long as I'm here."

Bram's eyes dropped as if he had said more than he meant to, and Ellie felt her face heat even more as she remembered the last time they had spoken and how close he had held her. Was he thinking the same thing?

"Will you let me take you home? We can drive around by the lake again. It will be slow, but we're not in a hurry, are we?"

"*Ne,* I'm not in a hurry. It would be a nice drive."

As Bram headed off to get his buggy, a niggling feeling told Ellie he was worried about something, but she had promised to trust him. She let herself watch his shoulders move easily beneath his Sunday coat as he walked. He was a handsome man, pleasant to talk to, and his smiles made her heart flutter. Any woman would be pleased to have his attention. *Ja,* any woman, so why would he think she was special?

"Ellie, do you need a ride home?" Lovina joined her at the edge of the drive with Rachel.

"*Ne, denki.* Bram is taking me."

Noah drove up, and Lovina helped Rachel climb into the buggy, giving Ellie a knowing smile. "Then you'll be busy the rest of the day, *ja?*" Lovina made sure Rachel was settled next to Noah, then stepped closer to Ellie. "Is he taking you somewhere special?"

"*Ne,* just home."

Lovina gave her shoulders a squeeze. "You've been looking too happy lately for this to be just a ride home. I think Bram Lapp is good for you."

"Get yourself on home and take care of your family." Ellie gave Lovina a quick hug before she climbed into Noah's buggy.

What did Lovina mean, Bram was good for her?

Bram's buggy stopped beside her and she looked up at him, smiling as he held the horse quiet so she could climb up to the seat beside him. His dimple winked under his whiskers, making her heart flip as he held out one hand to help her.

*Ja,* Bram was good for her.

Bram kept Partner at a walk. He could smell the lake as they got closer. Emma Lake stretched away to the north from the road, the low water exposing black, silt mud. Lily pads covered the water at this south end, but the rest of the lake was a mirror under the flawless blue sky.

Turning north onto Emma Road, the black silt gave way to a sandy shore separating the lake from the road. Bram pulled Partner over to a spot where someone had placed a bench under a lone tree.

"Do you mind if we stop here for a bit?"

"*Ne.* We can sit in the shade."

Bram helped Ellie settle on the bench near the shore where the overhanging trees made a shady cover.

"This is a great fishing spot."

Ellie didn't answer. She looked out over the quiet lake with that worry line between her eyebrows again.

"Last night…" Bram stopped. He had never felt like this before—as if he was one man torn in two directions. He wished Kavanaugh would just disappear.

"Last night you told me you never intended to stay here." Ellie kept her eyes on the far side of the lake, where a heron stalked in the shallows. "I know I said

I'd trust you, Bram, but I don't know what to think. You're like two different people sometimes—sweet and tender one minute, and then harsh and almost frightening other times."

"*Ja,* I know, and I'm sorry." Bram paused, his own eyes on the motionless heron. The bird was nearly invisible in the shadow of the trees, his gray-blue coloring a shadow within a shadow. Living undercover. How did a man stop living a lie?

"I want to stay, Ellie. But I don't know if I'll be able to." He took her hand in his, and she looked at him.

"Even if you stay, we can never be more than friends." Her voice was soft, almost a whisper, her blue eyes reflecting the water.

"Aren't we already more than friends, Ellie?"

Her face flushed and she turned away again, drawing her hand out of his grasp. "Just because you kissed me once doesn't mean anything. I'm not a woman you should be courting."

Bram picked up a stone from between his feet and threw it into the water. She was right. She wasn't the woman he should be courting, especially now that he knew Kavanaugh was in the neighborhood, but why did she think so?

"You know I can't marry outside the church, Bram."

She said it softly but firmly, as if she had rehearsed the words again and again. He wrestled with the overwhelming desire to prove her wrong, but she was right. He couldn't marry her, at least not now.

"You're going to marry someone else, aren't you?"

Even though she kept her face averted, he could see her eyes filling with tears. "*Ne,* Bram. There's no one else."

"So you plan to remain a widow and raise your children by yourself?" Should he tell her she was crazy for thinking she could do such a thing or admire her for her courage?

"*Ja.* I have to."

"And where will you live? With your parents?"

Ellie swallowed hard. The tears had stopped, leaving her face mottled in the afternoon heat. "I still own Daniel's farm. Our farm. There are tenants there now, but…" Her face paled.

"What's wrong?"

"*Ach,* I try not to think about it, but the tenants haven't paid their rent and I can't pay the taxes."

Who would leave a widow without an income? Bram had a brief flash of what he would do to that faceless man if he ever saw him. "Tell me who they are. I'll get them to pay."

She laid her hand on his arm. "*Ne,* Bram. You can't do anything. Mr. Brenneman lost his job. The family has no money."

The faceless man had a name, a family. Bram's anger disappeared like sand washed away by a wave. "Have you thought of asking John?"

"*Ja, Dat* would help if he could, but he doesn't have that kind of money. And the church would help, but Bishop wants me to marry Levi Zook. He wouldn't say so, but I know he'd expect me to obey his wishes if I took their help."

Levi Zook? The man's round face danced in front of his eyes. Would Ellie consider marrying him? Could he stand by and watch that happen?

"I can help you. When are the taxes due?"

Ellie looked at him, her eyes wide. He'd do anything for her to see her look at him like that again.

"I can't let you do that. It's a lot of money."

"We're friends, aren't we? Can't you let a friend help? You can pay me back after your tenants pay you."

She shifted on the bench. She was considering it, but he knew she had run out of options. Bram prayed she would let him help her. He longed to do so much more than just give her some money.

Ellie turned to face him. "I have to know one thing, Bram. Where did you get your money?"

That wasn't the response he was expecting. "What do you mean?"

"I know you paid cash for your farm. You've spent a lot of money fixing it up, plus buying your buggy, the horse, equipment for the farm... Bram, where did you get that kind of money?"

Bram felt cold in spite of the summer heat. If Ellie was wondering, who else had listened to Samuel's attempt at rabble-rousing yesterday? Would Kavanaugh hear rumors about an Amishman spending cash when no one else had any?

"I earned it working in Chicago. It was a reward for..." For ratting out his friends? *Ne,* for getting murderous scum off the streets. "It was payment for some work I did for the FBI."

Ellie nodded, the line between her eyes relaxing. "All right. I'll let you help me, but only if you don't tell anyone."

That suited Bram perfectly. He'd rather keep any money transactions as quiet as possible.

It wasn't until after he was home and settling Partner in for the night that he remembered he had forgotten to warn her about Kavanaugh.

# Chapter Thirteen

Streaks of lathered sweat covered Partner's flanks by the time Bram turned him into the Stoltzfus family's drive on Thursday afternoon. Today's trip to Goshen, through Middlebury and then to Shipshewana had been exhausting and fruitless. Another day of hunting with no sign of Kavanaugh.

He should go home, but he couldn't pass this close to the Stoltzfus farm without seeing Ellie. Four days had passed since their Sunday drive, four days with thoughts of her crowding every moment. He craved one glimpse, one sure confirmation she was safe.

Tying the horse to the corral fence next to the barn, Bram loosened his harness and made sure he stood in the shade of the tall maple trees. He filled his cupped hands with water in the nearby trough and wet the horse's nose and mouth. Partner was too hot yet to let him drink his fill.

Bram removed his hat and wiped his forehead with a sleeve. The yard was deserted, but that wasn't surprising. In the middle of the afternoon he expected the children to be napping. Ellie and her mother were probably working in the cool house.

The metallic squeak of a pump handle rang through the heavy air, the sound coming from near Ellie's *Dawdi Haus*. Bram turned that direction and then pulled up short at the sight of Ellie and her two brothers carrying buckets of water to the field beyond Ellie's house.

What was she thinking, working like that in this heat?

He met her as she returned to the pump for another trip, and her pale face and bleary gaze told him he hadn't come any too soon. She tried to wave him off as he took the bucket out of her hands, but she let him steer her toward the shaded glider in the side yard.

"The strawberries," Ellie said. Her voice lacked strength, as if she was falling asleep. Bram's stomach clenched, and he hoped he wasn't too late.

Ben and Reuben were at his side.

"We tried to get her to stop," Reuben said, "but she said she'd do the whole field by herself if we didn't help her."

"I can believe it." If he had ever seen a more stubborn woman... "We need a bucket of water and some towels."

While Reuben ran to fill Ellie's abandoned bucket, Bram started to unfasten Ellie's dress at her neckline.

"What are you doing?" Ben reached out to stop him.

"She's suffering from heat exhaustion. We have to keep her from having a heatstroke."

Ben didn't argue; he ran into the house for towels.

"I have to water the plants before they die." Ellie tried to refasten her dress, but her movements were uncoordinated and slow.

"Ellie," Bram said, "we have to cool you off first. You shouldn't have been working out in the heat."

Reuben set the full pail of water next to Bram as he knelt on the ground. "Will she be all right?"

"*Ja,* if we can get her cooled off. Where's John? And your mother?" Bram took the towels Ben brought and plunged them in the cool water.

"They took the girls over to Lovina's. They're making jam, and *Dat* was going to a sale with Noah."

Ben had brought a dipper, and after Bram gave Ellie a drink, they all took turns.

"The children?"

"In the house sleeping."

Bram took one towel, wrung most of the water out of it and draped it over the back of Ellie's neck. Her eyes were closed, and her breathing was rapid. He took another wet towel and began sponging her face. It wasn't enough.

Bram took handfuls of water and poured them over Ellie's feet and lower legs. He wet his towel again and went back to sponging her face, hands and arms.

Ellie caught the towel in one hand and took it from him.

"I can do that, Bram. *Denki.*"

Her face was returning to a normal color. Her eyes looked tired, but the glaze was gone. Bram's stomach unclenched, and he sat back on his heels. He glanced from Ben's flushed face to Reuben's. Ellie wasn't the only one suffering from the heat.

"Do you boys have a swimming hole?"

"*Ja,* but what about Ellie?"

"I'll take care of her. She's out of danger now, but you need to get cooled off, too."

Ben looked at Reuben. After a long minute of indecision, Reuben nodded.

"You're right. We'll take care of your horse before we go."

Bram nodded. "*Denki.*"

* * *

"If I were a different man, I'd throttle you right now." Bram's voice was gentle as he sponged her cheeks with a wet towel.

Ellie didn't answer, but sniffed back threatening tears. He sounded angry with her, but why? She was only taking care of the work that needed to be done.

Bram took the towel off the back of her neck and rinsed it in fresh water before handing it back to her. She held it to her face and neck. The cool cloth felt *wonderful-gut* on her bare skin.

"What were you thinking, working out in that field in this heat?"

"The strawberries. I watered them early this morning, but this afternoon I saw they were dying." She was too weak to stop the tears that fell. "I can't lose those plants."

Bram sat on the glider and offered her another dipper of water. She drank it slowly, the water seeping into her body in cool swallows.

"Those are your strawberries?"

She nodded. "That's why I don't have enough money to pay the taxes on the farm. I used my savings…" Ellie glanced toward the dusty field dotted with shriveled bits of green. "But I'm going to lose them all, aren't I?"

"I'm afraid you've already lost them. It's just too hot. My corn is drying up, too."

Ellie reached a hand to the front of her dress where it hung loose. How did she get this way? She started to refasten it, but Bram stopped her by taking her hand in his.

"Not yet. You haven't cooled down enough."

"But I must look a sight."

When Bram twitched the corner of his mouth into

that secret grin reserved just for her, any resistance she had to him melted away to nothing. *Ja,* she trusted him, and more. Much more.

"You sure do. Are you feeling better?"

"*Ja.* I didn't realize how exhausted I was until I sat down."

Bram still held her hand in his. He reached up with his other hand and tucked some damp hair behind her ear.

"You don't have to worry about the money, remember? I said I had enough."

"But how will I pay you back?"

He squeezed her hand with reassuring pressure. She let the tension drain out of her shoulders.

"You will somehow, but I'm not in a hurry."

Ellie closed her eyes. Bram put his arm around her and pulled her close to him.

Resting in his embrace, Ellie let herself lean into him, giving way to the comforting strength of his presence. Long minutes went by before she thought about moving, but she should.

*Sit up,* she told herself, but instead she opened her eyes to see Bram's face just inches from her own, his expression unreadable, his eyes locked on hers. He bent his head slightly and then paused, his eyes flickering with doubt.

Ellie put her hand up to his cheek, bridging the gap between them. His blue gaze stilled and darkened. He was going to kiss her and she longed to let him, but she couldn't. To kiss him would be a step into a sin she would never be free of.

Forcing herself, she lowered her hand and shifted away from him. A hot breeze played between the two of them on the glider.

\* \* \*

Bram wanted to pursue Ellie as she drew away from him. She had wanted his kiss, but she was right to stop him. With an inward groan, he loosened his hold on her soft, yielding form, his arms already aching with the loss. He kept her as close as he dared with his left arm around her shoulder and closed his right hand around hers. It was small, soft and cool from the wet towel as it lay in his larger one. Relaxed. Trusting. Fragile. A bird in his hand.

His throat tightened as he turned her hand over and stroked her palm with his thumb. What reason had he ever given for her to trust him? How could he ever keep her safe?

He opened his mouth to speak, to warn her about the man he was hunting, but the look on her face stopped him. She was watching their hands together, a small smile turning up the corners of her mouth. A slight breeze had dried a few hanging strands of her hair, and they drifted across her forehead, making her look like a young girl. The worry line that usually strained her features was gone. When had it disappeared?

He couldn't tell her. Not yet. This wasn't the right time to let her know about the violent past that continued to dog his footsteps. Kavanaugh had been close, but even though Bram had spent the past week hunting for him through the neighboring towns, he hadn't seen any sign that the gangster was still around. As long as he kept to his plan, he would be safe.

Bram tightened his hand, enfolding Ellie's in his own. They would both be safe.

"Will we buy ice cream?"

Susan heard her brother. "Ice cream? Will there be ice cream there?"

"Ice cream costs too much money." The disappointed looks on the children's faces pulled at Ellie's heart, but they didn't argue with her. "I think we can buy a treat at the grocery store, though. How about some chocolate to make brownies?"

Johnny and Susan grinned at each other with delight. Trips to town were rare, and even though Daniel would have said the trip was enough of a treat, the chocolate would make it extra special.

"I hear Bram's buggy." Johnny raced out the door to meet him.

"Wait, Susan. You need to wear your *kapp*."

"Just like *Memmi*." Susan smiled up at her, the stiff white *kapp* framing her sweet face as Ellie fit it over her braids.

"*Ja,* just like *Memmi*. Now, you go on out with Johnny. We don't want to keep Bram waiting."

Ellie settled her bonnet over her own *kapp* before picking up Danny. Bram's greeting to the children drifted in through the open window, sending her stomach rolling and heat flooding to her cheeks. Bram was here to take them to LaGrange, to the county tax office.

It was a trip she had been dreading, but Bram had lifted a sore burden from her when he'd offered to loan her the money she needed. She would pay the taxes this morning, and then she didn't need to worry about them for another year. Surely by then Mr. Brenneman would be working again, and she would be able to pay Bram back as well as pay next year's taxes.

Another reason for her light mood filled the field next to the house. At least half of the strawberry plants still survived, in spite of yesterday's heat. Perhaps she would have berries to sell next spring after all.

From Bram's animated conversation with the children as they waited for her in the back of the buggy, it sounded as if he was looking forward to this trip as much as she and the children were. When she stepped out of the house, he came to meet her.

"Good morning." He leaned so close to her she was afraid he was going to start the day with a kiss on her cheek, but he only gave her a grin as he took Danny—that secret grin meant just for her.

"Good morning, Bram. *Denki* for driving us into town."

He helped her into the buggy and then held her hand until she looked at him. "I wouldn't let you go alone. I'm here for you, Ellie." His voice was low, intimate. Her cheeks flushed hot.

Taking Danny from him, she waited as he climbed in on the other side and chirruped to Partner. Her heart fluttered like leaves catching a passing breeze, and she resisted the urge to thread her hand through his elbow as if they were courting. How long had it been since she had felt like this? Bram's strength gave her a security she hadn't known since she was a girl.

Even when Daniel was alive… *Ach,* had she really been the proud, stubborn woman she remembered? She never let him care for her, cherish her. Their lives together could have been even happier if she had learned to be content with what Daniel—and *Gott*—provided for her. She shied away from the thought that perhaps their lives together could have been longer if she hadn't insisted that he expand the farm. How had Daniel ever put up with her? How did *Gott* ever put up with her?

She stole a glance at Bram and caught him watching her, a quiet smile on his face. *Ja,* she could get used to this.

When they arrived in LaGrange, Bram drove Partner

to a hitching rail in the shade on the courthouse square. Their footsteps echoed in the vast entrance of the lime- stone building, cool and dark after the blazing sunshine. Bram found the tax office, and Ellie signed the papers while he handed the money to the clerk.

Bram shepherded them outside again and steered them to a bench on the shady lawn.

"Now I think we need to do some shopping."

"*Ja,* I hoped we could stop at a grocer's."

Bram cleared his throat, watching the children as they played a hopping game on the cement walk. "I was thinking of a dry-goods store."

"I don't need anything there."

"I think you do."

Ellie thought of the few coins in her pocketbook. Some baking soda, flour and the chocolate would use all her money.

"Bram," she said, lowering her voice so the children wouldn't hear, "I only brought enough to buy the gro- ceries I need."

"You need a new dress." His lowered voice matched hers, and he held her gaze with his own.

He was right, of course. The brown one she was wearing had been mended many times, but it would still do. The children's clothes came first when she had money to spend on fabric.

"I don't need a new dress, even if I could afford it."

"Ellie, let me buy you the material. Enough for Susan, too."

Her face flushed hot as she glanced at Susan playing tag with Johnny. The little girl's dress was much too short. Watching her, Ellie knew she had lost the argu- ment, but only part of it.

"I'll let you loan me some money for a new dress for Susan."

"Enough for both of you. And it's not a loan. It's a gift."

Ellie started shaking her head.

"Ellie, please." His eyes were pleading. "I have more than enough money. Let me do this."

A cold thought fluttered in the back of her mind. His money again. She was coming to depend on him too much.

He lifted her hand from her lap and held it entwined in his solid, capable fingers. He leaned close to her, letting Danny pat his short beard.

"Let me take care of you." His whisper was carried off on the breeze, but not before it reached her ears.

Tears stung her eyes as his words destroyed any argument she had left. She nodded without speaking.

Bram glanced in the windows of the empty building next to the dry-goods store as they came back onto the sidewalk. Another closed bank was a common enough sight these days, but this one meant he didn't have to worry about Kavanaugh showing up here. He could relax his guard a bit and enjoy the day.

The stop in the store had been a success. He had persuaded Ellie to choose several pieces of fabric. One was green, perfect for weekdays, and another was a deep blue that matched her eyes. That would be for Sundays. A couple lengths of black and white for aprons and other necessities hadn't been hard to convince her to add in. He had also bought a new straw hat for Johnny and one for himself.

"If I cut carefully," Ellie said, her eyes glowing, "I'm sure I can make some shirts for Johnny and Danny out of the blue. And there is enough of the green to make dresses for both Susan and myself."

Bram had never seen Ellie so animated. If he had known new fabric would make her this happy, he would have made this trip weeks ago.

When they reached the buggy, he checked on Partner while Ellie helped Johnny put the bundles in the back of the rig. He wasn't ready to take them home. Ellie would immerse herself in her work again, and he'd have to make another round of the nearby towns, looking for some sign of Kavanaugh. There must be something he could do to make this day last longer.

Activity at the drugstore caught his eye. *Ja,* a lunch counter would be a *wonderful-gut* treat for Ellie and the children.

He took Danny from Ellie's arms and stopped her before she climbed in the buggy. "Are you ready for lunch?"

"Lunch? I didn't pack anything. I thought I would make dinner at home."

He pointed toward the drugstore and then reached for Susan's hand. "There's a lunch counter over here. Have you ever eaten at one?"

"You mean buy a meal?"

Her voice was incredulous. If she only knew how many hundreds of meals he had eaten at lunch counters just like this one.

"*Ja,* buy a meal. I'm sure the egg-salad sandwiches here are almost as good as yours."

She looked at him with suspicion. "You've never tried one of mine, so how do you know?"

Bram laughed at this. "Let's just go in and eat."

Watching Ellie enjoy the new experience of eating out made everything he had done to earn that money worth it. Johnny and Susan swung their legs as they sat on their stools at the counter eating their hot dogs while Danny ate bits of a grilled cheese that Ellie cut up for him. She had been nervous at first, but she had relaxed at her first bite of a chicken-salad sandwich.

To top off the treat, Bram ordered ice-cream cones. He was sure Johnny's eyes would pop when the clerk handed his to him. Life didn't get much better than this.

The final stop was at the grocer's around the corner from the drugstore. Ellie bought her supplies, and Bram filled a box with groceries for himself, making sure he bought plenty of sugar. Ellie was probably using sorghum in everything she baked, since sugar was expensive. He'd slip the sack into her box later.

Finally, Bram couldn't put it off any longer. Their errands were done, and the tired look on the children's faces told him it was time to go home. As Bram led them to the buggy still tied at the courthouse, he exchanged a glance with Ellie. Was this what a family was supposed to feel like? He would give anything for more days like this one.

Out of habit, he scanned the streets surrounding the square while he boosted the children into the back of the rig. LaGrange was a much smaller town than Goshen, in the next county over. There were a few cars and several buggies, but the county seat wasn't crowded.

Then Bram saw it. A maroon Packard purred up State Road 9 from the south and passed by just half a block away. The fragile buggy was all that stood between Bram and the car, and his stomach plummeted to his feet just the same as if he had been standing exposed on the curb as the car drove slowly by. He gripped the sides of the buggy with cold fingers as he watched

the Packard cruise through the small town, then on to
the north.

"Bram, are you all right?"

The black tunnel of his vision cleared. Ellie was staring at him, and all three children looked at him with
solemn faces. He took a deep breath, forcing his fingers
to release their hold.

"*Ja,* I'm all right. Just thought I saw someone I
knew."

Ellie kept her eyes on him but didn't say anything
more. That worry line had shown up again.

Bram turned Partner toward the south, heading
down Hawpatch Road before turning west, toward the
Stoltzfus farm. His mind raced, matching the pace of
his heart. If he took a roundabout way, there was a
chance they'd be able to get home before Kavanaugh
found them.

He worked the reins in his sweaty hands, trying to
get a better grip. He felt like swearing, but the words
stuck in his throat. He had let his guard down and had
made the fatal error of underestimating Kavanaugh.
Worse yet, Ellie and the children were in danger. He
was trapped by his own stupid mistake.

Glancing behind them at the empty road, Bram adjusted the reins again and took a deep breath, forcing
himself to relax.

He had panicked, and panic was deadly. Kavanaugh,
if it was Kavanaugh, hadn't seen him. He gave himself
a mental shake and checked the road again. He just had
to get Ellie and the children home safely.

Ellie watched Bram as he leaned forward on the
buggy seat, the reins tight in his hands, his jaw set.
What could have gone wrong this time? Ellie cast her

mind back over the morning, but she couldn't think of anything that would have made Bram angry. It had been a fun family outing.

Catching her breath at this thought, she turned her face to the dusty roadside. With Bram beside her, she could pretend they were a complete family. How could she have let him worm his way this far into their lives... into her heart? Bram had been honest with her, letting her know his future plans. He wasn't Amish, in spite of his upbringing. He had turned his back on the Amish once, and he would do it again as soon as his work here was done. He wasn't a man she could count on being there for her children. He wasn't a man to fall in love with.

She turned to check on the children in the back of the buggy. Susan had fallen asleep, lying on the narrow seat. Johnny sat beside her, his new hat on his head, watching the roadside. His face was the picture of little-boy contentment. She had grown used to his sullen expression and downturned eyes, but ever since Bram had taken him into that ball game, Johnny had been a different boy. Bram's attention had brought back the boy she knew before Daniel's accident.

Danny sighed on her lap and turned his sleeping, sweaty face upward. She leaned closer to him to catch his sweet baby scent. Why did they have to grow up?

A sudden thought stopped her. Danny would grow up, and he would never have any memories of his father, only the stories she could tell him. Susan had been so young—did she remember anything about Daniel? And Johnny's memories were already blurred. He told stories of going fishing with his father, or traveling with him, but Ellie knew he had never done those things. Daniel was just a dream to him.

Ellie would never forget her husband, his plans. He had longed to give his children the home he had never known as an orphan, handed off from relative to relative until he ended up with Hezekiah and Miriam. His only goal had been for his children to know a life he had never lived, but now she was the only one left to keep his dreams and his memory alive.

Her mind flitted over the morning. Bram had been so loving and caring, making the children laugh at his jokes and surprising them with ice cream. The memories of Daniel she tried to keep fresh for her children would never bring them the same joy.

Bram turned in the seat and took a long look down the empty road behind them. When he turned back to the front again, his jaw was clenched. Maybe he regretted taking them to town and the time it had taken from his work. Whatever it was, he was acting as if this morning had never happened. Was it something she had done that brought this change?

*"Denki,"* she said. Her voice felt muffled in the hot air.

Bram turned to look at her, his body jerking as if he had forgotten she was there.

*"Denki* for what?" His words were clipped, sharp. Was he angry? She really didn't know him well enough to tell.

*"Denki* for driving us to LaGrange, and for the material…and for lunch…" Her voice faltered. He wasn't listening.

Bram nodded, his eyes hard, and then he turned and chirruped Partner into a faster trot, although the horse was already covered with sweat.

"Bram, I'm not in a hurry to get home."

He looked at her again, then behind them. His face

was a blank, stony mask. He licked his lips and glanced behind them once more.

"*Ja,* you're right." He pulled Partner to a walk but shifted in his seat with a restless kick of his feet against the dashboard.

Would he tell her what was wrong? She had to know if she had done or said something to make him act like this. It had happened before, this abrupt change from tender and attentive to hard and angry.

Trusting *Gott* was one thing; she could rest in His all-powerful care. But trusting a man? Ellie glanced at Bram's face, still hard and closed. He looked back at her, and his eyes softened. Without a word he transferred the reins to one hand and put the other on top of her hands enfolding Danny. He gave them a gentle squeeze while the corners of his mouth turned up in a reassuring smile.

*Ja,* she could trust this man.

## Chapter Fourteen

~

Susan and Danny were both still sleeping when they reached the Stoltzfus farm, and Johnny's head was nodding.

"I'll carry Susan in for you." Bram followed Ellie into the *Dawdi Haus*. She nodded toward the bedroom on the left as she took Danny into the other one. The dim room was cool after the brassy sunshine, and Bram laid the little girl on the bed with the blank-faced doll leaning against the pillow.

Johnny followed them and crawled up on the other side of the bed, his eyes closed already. Bram took the boy's new straw hat off his head and smoothed the brown curls. Johnny's face was flushed but peaceful. No cares troubled him.

Bram swallowed, a stone of regret lodged in his throat. Had he ever been this innocent?

"They'll all sleep for a while after the excitement of the morning," Ellie said as he returned to the kitchen.

"*Ja*, you're right." He stood in the center of the small room that spoke of Ellie everywhere he looked, from a jar of flowers on the table to the neatly folded dish towel draped over the pump handle. The serene order soothed the panic slamming around in his head ever since he had seen that Packard in LaGrange.

Every time he came to the conclusion that it couldn't be Kavanaugh's car, another part of his mind convinced him it was. It was as if the car was following him, haunting him with an unseen presence.

Ellie opened a cabinet door and got out two glasses. "I have some ice down in the cellar. Would you like some mint tea?"

"That sounds *wonderful-gut,* but if I'm going to stay for a while, I have to take care of Partner."

"*Ja.* I'll bring the tea to the glider. It's shady out there."

As Bram unharnessed the horse, his thoughts went to that maroon Packard again. There had been something about it that wasn't quite right, and the answer hovered on the edge of his thoughts. He let Partner take a quick drink of water at the trough by the pump and then tied him to a tree in the side yard, where he could crop the grass along the shady side of the fence.

The sparse rows of strawberries caught Bram's eye. Some of the plants were still holding on, and they had better survive, for Ellie's sake. Her heart was set on making money from those berries, and any other year it would have been a sure thing, a good investment. But the way this summer was turning out, it looked as if she was going to lose everything.

He met Ellie at the glider and took the glass full of ice and green mint tea that she handed him. He breathed in the scent of mint as he took his first swallow. It gushed down his throat, cool and sweet.

"*Ach,* this is good. Where did you get the ice?"

"Years ago my *Grossdatti* built an icehouse. All the neighbors harvest the ice on Emma Lake in the winter, and we store it for them. Ben and Reuben brought a block for me yesterday, and I keep it packed in straw in the cellar."

As Bram kicked at the grass under the glider, setting it in motion, his thoughts went back to that Packard. What could he do if that had been Kavanaugh? He had made the mistake of convincing himself they were safe in LaGrange, but he could never take Ellie's safety for granted. He hated ruining the end of their day together, but he had to warn her about the danger.

"Are you feeling better?"

Ellie's question interrupted his thoughts.

"What do you mean? I feel fine."

"I just thought… I mean, ever since we left LaGrange you've seemed like you were upset about something."

Either she knew him better than most people, or he was losing his touch at controlling his feelings.

"I'm sorry. It's nothing to do with you or the children." He had to tell her. He hated to have her living with the same caution he did, but if Kavanaugh came around, she had to know enough to protect herself from him.

"Ellie, I have to tell you—" He stopped, looking at her profile as she sat quietly, waiting for him to speak. What he had to tell her would ruin that trusting innocence. Wasn't there another way?

Ellie wiped a thumb-wide swath through the condensation on her glass, waiting for Bram to continue.

"When I lived in Chicago, things were pretty rough."

She glanced at him. He sat with his forearms resting on his legs, dangling the cold glass between his knees. She didn't want to hear about his *Englisch* days, but he still belonged to that world.

"What do mean?"

He shrugged his shoulders and sat up, taking a drink of his tea. "You know, the mob, the cops." He looked at her. "I did some things that you wouldn't like."

"Does it matter, what I would approve of?"

He took another swallow, his Adam's apple bobbing as he watched Partner crop the grass along the fence. When he looked back at her, his eyes were dark with regret.

"*Ja,* Ellie, it matters. More than I ever thought it would."

She looked away. *Ja,* it mattered.

"A man in my kind of work makes some enemies, and I made one of the worst kind."

"*Ach,* Bram…" Ellie cast about in her mind for an answer, her heart breaking. "Our way is to love our enemies and to pray for them."

"Not this kind of enemy." Bram's voice was harsh, his eyes focused on his glass. He upended it, draining it, and then turned to her. "I grew up hearing the teaching of the church, with the 'love your enemies' and all that, but I don't think the church fathers dealt with the kind of men I've seen."

"*Ne,* they didn't have gangsters in the old country, but you know the stories of how our ancestors were persecuted and hunted down like criminals, and yet the doctrine of nonresistance stood the test during that time."

"And how many died? Maybe they should have fought back. Maybe sometimes there are things worth fighting for."

"Nothing is worth disobedience to *Gott.*"

"Even the safety of your children?"

Ellie choked down a sob in her throat. She didn't

know how she would act if someone threatened her children, but the church's teaching was clear.

"We are not to resist those who are against us."

Bram put his empty glass down in the grass as he stood, sending the glider rocking. He paced over to Partner and ran his hand along the horse's neck and then abruptly turned back toward her.

"This man I'm looking for is evil, Ellie. He has killed before, and he'll kill again without a thought. He would hurt you and the children only because I care about you. He has to be stopped."

"With force? With violence?"

"He doesn't understand any other way."

Ellie shifted her eyes from his. Were there really such evil men in the world? Men beyond the reach of *Gott* Himself?

Bram knelt in front of her, capturing her hands in his, spilling her tea.

"Ellie, promise me, if you see an *Englisch* stranger hanging around, or if he comes to the farm…" Bram stopped. He wiped one hand across his eyes as if trying to erase a nightmare. "If you see anyone, tell me. Don't talk to him. Don't tell him anything." Bram tightened his grasp on her hands. "Don't…Ellie, don't trust him. This man, his name is Kavanaugh, and he's dangerous. If you see him, send someone to get me—Ben or Reuben. Can you do that?"

Ellie stared into his eyes, seeing her own fear reflected there. What would she do if this stranger came around? If she sent word to Bram, the way he asked, would he use violence against this gangster? On the other hand, if she warned Bram, perhaps he could escape from this man and save himself.

"*Ja,* Bram, I will, but only so you can avoid him. I don't fear for myself, only for you."

Bram reached one hand to that stubborn lock of hair that never stayed put and tucked it behind her ear.

"I'll try my best to keep you safe, Ellie. You have my word on that."

Bram kept Partner at a walk all the way home from the Stoltzfus farm. He had rushed out of LaGrange so fast that he had risked his horse's health. Well, better risk the horse than Ellie and the children.

But then, really, what good would it have done? No matter how fast he pushed Partner, a car could overtake them. His mouth went dry as the scenario played itself out in his mind—he could have lost everything.

That Packard. One elusive detail flicked at the edge of his mind. He closed his eyes, trying to capture a picture of the car in his memory. Chrome. That car in LaGrange didn't have any chrome trim. Bram laughed out loud in his relief. What kind of idiot was he to be jumping at every car he saw?

But just as quickly, the memory of his panic sobered him. It could have been Kavanaugh just as easily as someone else. The gangster was in the area, and Bram was almost certain he had been recognized in Goshen that day with Matthew. As long as he stayed here, he would be haunted by his past.

Should he leave, then? Get back to his original plan and keep moving on? He had known he shouldn't get tangled up with a woman.... Now it wasn't just his safety he needed to worry about. This whole affair could cost both their lives.

In all his years of working and living undercover, living the lie that had become his life, he never thought he would let himself get ensnared like this. But this time was different—this assignment had been screwy from the beginning. Who ever heard of going undercover by being yourself? And now he was in trouble. Big trouble. Not only had he been spotted—maybe—but for the first time in his life, he wanted to stay in this cover.

For the first time in his life, he had something to work for, a life to build. If he was free of Kavanaugh, free of his past, he could turn his farm into something worthwhile, something for a family.

Bram rubbed his palm over his face.

*Ja,* in any other job he would say it was time to get out. But where would he go? Mexico was the only option he could see.

What about Ellie and the children? That morning's trip had given him a glimpse of the family they could be together, but now that vision was slipping away as quickly as a piece of ice melting on a hot afternoon.

He loved her.

He couldn't love her; he wouldn't love her. Loving her would only make her a target for Kavanaugh, and he wouldn't be foolish enough to risk that.

But it was too late.

He loved her.

He felt that now-familiar upsurge of calm, like a cool-silk breeze. God knew he loved her.

But what could he do? If he stayed here, they would all continue to be in danger. Kavanaugh was too close. If he had recognized Bram in Goshen that day, he wouldn't give up until he found him. There was nowhere he could hide.

If he left…

If he left, he would be leaving Ellie behind.

Ellie and every hope for his future.

A sudden idea sent a chill through him. What if she went with him? He could buy another car. She and the children could come with him to Mexico. They could start a new life there and never have to worry about Kavanaugh again.

Partner turned into his lane and stopped at the barn door, but Bram didn't move. He had to follow this thought through....

If Ellie came with him, they'd have each other. He'd take care of them. They'd have a ranch down there, and Johnny would love being a cowboy.

Partner tossed his head, pulling on the reins in Bram's hands. They were home.

But as Bram climbed out of the buggy and opened the barn door, he knew it was useless. He couldn't uproot Ellie from the only home she had ever known. If she came with him to Mexico, they'd have to leave more than just her family. Everything she knew and loved was here. Her home, her family, her faith, her heritage.

He knew now what he hadn't known twelve years ago—his own identity was defined here, among the Amish. His heritage. He might be able to survive away from it, but he could never ask Ellie and the children to bear that burden with him.

But could he bear leaving without her?

Bram unhitched Partner and took his harness off. The horse was warm but not too hot. The time in the shady grass at Ellie's house and then the slow walk home had been good for him. Bram got the currycomb and brush and began giving him a good grooming.

Bram tried to let his mind go blank as he concentrated on the familiar task, but the thoughts kept swirling.

"God, what should I do?" he prayed out loud, leaning on Partner's back.

The idea came so suddenly, so clearly, Bram knew it couldn't be anything but the answer to his prayer. His search for Kavanaugh had been fruitless so far—but he had been an Amishman hunting for an *Englischer*. To find an *Englischer,* he needed to be one. To find a gangster...

*Ja,* if he went deeper undercover, inserted himself into the seamier side of these towns surrounding him, he could track down that snake in the sewers where he lived, places no Amishman would go. He would need to use every skill he had honed during those years in Chicago. It would be dangerous, but there was no other way to find Kavanaugh.

And once Kavanaugh was arrested, he'd have no reason to leave.

# Chapter Fifteen

Sunday's weather was pleasant, and after the meeting at Deacon Beachey's home, the men moved church benches into the shady backyard for the fellowship meal and visiting afterward.

Ellie sat with Annie Beachey watching the children play while Annie tried to calm her new baby, Micah. Ellie took the crying baby when his mother offered him to her.

"See if you can help him. After trying to keep him quiet all through the meeting, I'm exhausted."

"Oh, I'm sure you are." Ellie held the wee bundle in her arms and rocked him. "It's been so hot. Could it be heat rash?"

"*Ja,* he has heat rash and a terrible diaper rash. I just can't seem to get rid of it."

"Has he been eating well?"

"*Ja,* and your *mam* told me to give him some water, too, since it's been so hot." Annie stroked the baby's head.

Ellie turned the baby so his stomach was pressed against her hand. He gave a loud belch.

"Do you think that's what was wrong with him?"

Ellie smiled at her friend as the baby's cries subsided. "*Ja,* I think so."

She continued rocking little Micah. *Ach,* holding a baby was a sweet joy.

"I haven't seen much of Bram lately," Annie said. "Have you been able to talk with him often?"

Ellie looked across the shady yard at Bram, conversing with *Dat* and Matthew. She knew what Annie was really asking, but what could she say? Bram had become so important to her, but didn't he still belong to his *Englisch* past? Did she have any right to think of him as more than a friend?

"*Ne,* I haven't seen him for a week or so."

"*Ja,* well, he must be busy with his work."

"*Ja,* probably." She didn't tell Annie about the fears that kept her awake at night, the fears of a strange *Englischer* coming in search of Bram.

"*Ach,* Annie. There's Miriam. I want to see how she's doing."

Ellie and Annie made their way to the bench where Miriam was sitting on the shady side of the house.

"I'm so glad you were able to come to church this morning," Ellie said, rocking Micah back and forth.

"*Ja,* me, too," Miriam said. "The rheumatism keeps Hezekiah in his chair so much that we don't get out often anymore. Some days, he doesn't even get out of bed."

"I didn't know it was so bad," Ellie said.

"*Ach,* he didn't want to burden others with our troubles, but I tell him it's time. He can't do everything on his own anymore."

And if Daniel had lived, he wouldn't have to. The thought made Ellie hot with shame. They shouldn't have to ask for help; she should have offered sooner. But when would she have time to work on their farm?

"What can I do to help?"

"You don't need to worry about us. Mr. Brenneman helps when he can."

Just as Daniel would have.

"But when Mr. Brenneman finds another job, he won't have the time."

Miriam patted her hand. "The good Lord will take care of us. Hezekiah will find another neighbor to hire."

Verna Bontrager, one of Miriam's longtime friends, joined them on the bench. As the two older women visited, Ellie thought about Miriam's words.

She should have seen this earlier. Hezekiah's arthritis was worse every month, and yet it hadn't occurred to her that he couldn't do his work. Daniel planned that his farm and Hezekiah's would be joined together, with the older couple's small house as a *Dawdi Haus,* while Daniel and his children farmed the land. But none of them had foreseen Hezekiah's advancing arthritis or Daniel's death.

But what could she do? She had no money to pay for a hired hand and neither did Hezekiah. And yet if he didn't hire someone, the crops would be ruined.

The strawberries should have brought her some security by next year, but now there were barely a dozen plants in each row that were surviving. It would be at least two more years before she could count on income from that source, and that was only if she could afford to buy new plants next spring.

She rubbed the line between her eyebrows. Her headache was coming back.

Gott, *what am I to do?*

* * *

"So you're getting used to having a new baby in the house?" John Stoltzfus winked at Bram as he asked Matthew the question. Bram grinned back at him. Matthew hadn't been able to talk about anything else all day.

"*Ja,* I am. I've gotten used to the night feedings, even. I've been able to get plenty of sleep." Matthew's face was serious as he started another lengthy discussion about his new son's eating habits. John listened patiently, but Bram's mind wandered to Ellie.

He had the perfect vantage point under this tree. He watched Ellie and Annie join some older women, Ellie holding Matthew's new son, his nephew. The sight made his throat tight. What would it be like to see her holding his baby one day?

He shook his head and shut that thought behind a door. Not yet.

*Can't think about that now, not until Kavanaugh is taken care of.*

He glanced her way again. She looked *wonderful-gut* in her new dress. She was visiting with Annie and an older woman he had never seen before, but that worry line was back again. Something was bothering her. Was one of the children ill?

He scanned the crowd from his spot under an oak tree. Johnny and Susan were playing a game of tag with some other children. It took a while to find Danny, but Bram finally spotted him on Sally Yoder's lap as she sat with Elizabeth Stoltzfus. He let out a sigh of relief. Everything seemed all right, but something had caused that crease to appear again.

Bram made his way through the maze of benches until he stood next to her. She looked perfect, graceful, feminine. He ached at the sight of her.

"Ellie, would you like to take a walk with me?"

He spoke softly, but Ellie had heard him. The older woman next to her looked on with interest.

"*Ja,* I would like that." She turned to give the baby to Annie, and then the older woman grasped Ellie's hand for a moment. A silent message of some kind. The two exchanged a smile. He would never understand women.

He took Ellie up the lane that passed by the barn and went toward a farm pond. It would give them a nice walk, not too far, and they would remain within sight of the rest of the congregation.

"Is something wrong?" he asked.

She looked at him, surprise on her face.

"*Ne.*" She looked away. "Well, *ja,* but it's nothing you need to worry about."

What a stubborn woman—didn't she know he would worry about anything that affected her?

"Tell me."

She walked in silence until they reached the pond. A frog jumped into the water as they approached the edge. They stopped, and Bram watched the ripples from the frog's splash until they disappeared on the opposite side of the small pond.

"It's Miriam and Hezekiah Miller."

"Who?"

"Daniel's aunt and uncle. They're the only family he had, and they had no other children."

"Hezekiah Miller?" Bram searched his memory of the names he knew. "The man with the cane?"

"*Ja,* that's him. His arthritis is getting worse, and without Daniel to help them…" She stopped as if she was staggering under a load too heavy for her to bear.

"Won't the church step in?"

"*Ach, ja,* with the heavy work. But it's the day-to-day chores that are hard for him, too."

Bram understood. In any other family the older folks would retire to their *Dawdi Haus,* helping with the chores they were able to do and enjoying the quieter days with their children nearby. But with no family, Hezekiah didn't have that option, even as frail as he seemed.

"I'm the only family they have left, but I don't know what I can do to help them right now. Maybe in a year or two I'll be able to hire some help for them, until Johnny's old enough."

She was counting on the strawberries.

"I told you I'm here for you, Ellie."

"But this isn't your responsibility. It's mine."

"I want to bear this burden with you, if you'll let me." He would bear all of her burdens if she'd let him.

She shook her head, looking at her feet. She chewed on her bottom lip, but that worry line was easing. Good. At least she was thinking about it.

"What could you do?"

"My farmwork is caught up, thanks to the church, and I don't have a family to take care of. I could drive over to help out." It would add some hours to his day, but he could still continue canvassing the area towns in his search for Kavanaugh.

"They live over by Topeka. That's at least four miles."

"Well, I won't be able to go every day, but often enough to help ease the work. Maybe some of the younger single men could do the same thing. There are enough of us that it wouldn't be too great a burden for anyone, and yet Hezekiah would have someone to help every day."

Bram was rewarded with a grateful look.

"Thank you. I never thought of anything like that."

He reached up and rubbed away the last of the crease between her eyes, letting his finger fall to caress her cheek.

"I told you, I can help you bear your burdens. All you have to do is ask. I'll talk to your *dat,* and between us we'll take care of it."

If only all *his* problems could be solved so easily.

A week later, Bram left home at dawn for his second turn at Hezekiah's farm. The older man appreciated the help, and Bram had found him to be cheerful the week before, in spite of his crippling disease. A morning spent working with him had flown by, and during the dinner with Miriam afterward, he had come to know Ellie through their eyes. She was as dear to them as any daughter could be.

The rest of his week hadn't been as pleasant as he became Dutch Sutter again, complete with *Englisch* clothes, and worked on sounding out contacts in Goshen, the most likely place to find any sign of Kavanaugh.

The suit he bought for the job was uncomfortable, although it was almost identical to the one he had worn in Chicago just a few months ago. When he put it on, it was as if Bram Lapp had disappeared. Daily shaving had completed the image, erasing the Amish look altogether.

He never thought going undercover could be this complicated, but it was effective. He had found just enough information to narrow Kavanaugh's activity to somewhere around Elkhart or South Bend, although he still had no idea where the prey was holed up or how many men he had working for him. Even so, it was time to find a phone and call in.

Partner's hooves clip-clopped on the cement road that took him through downtown Topeka. When Bram caught a whiff of bacon frying, his growling stomach reminded him he hadn't taken time for anything more than a cup of coffee before he'd left home. He took a deep breath of the mingled odors from the café. He'd have to stop in for some eggs and bacon before going on to Hezekiah's. He took another deep breath. *Ja,* and a few doughnuts.

Coming out of the café with a bag of doughnuts twenty minutes later, Bram noticed the telephone exchange office was open. This would be a good time to call Peters.

He stepped into the office and closed himself in a public booth. He picked up the receiver and watched the bored-looking operator through the glass until she answered.

"Number, please."

"I'd like to place a long-distance call to Elwood Peters, FBI, Chicago Division."

He wasn't surprised to hear her gasp on the other end, but he hoped she wasn't the kind to listen in on calls.

Ellie lifted one foot to rub it over a new mosquito bite on her other leg. Sunburn, mosquito bites and twenty quarts of strawberries from the Mennonite neighbors down the road, all before eight on a Thursday morning.

"Don't forget to keep stirring the jam, Mandy," *Mam* said as she set the last jar in the large pot to sterilize. She turned back to the table where Ellie was cleaning the final basket of this morning's picking of strawberries.

"Whew. Wouldn't it be nice if canning season was in the winter when a hot kitchen feels welcome?"

"*Ja, Mam,* you say that every year, but you're right. At least today is a little cooler than last week."

*Mam* nodded as she picked up her knife. Her fingers flew as she took the stem off each berry and sliced it.

The berries were small, making the work take even longer. A drought summer made even something as simple as strawberry jam more work.

"We're going to have strawberry shortcake for dinner, aren't we?" Mandy stood at the stove, as far away from the heat as she could and still stir the jam.

"Do you really feel like eating strawberries after spending the morning with them?" Ellie said, scratching a mosquito bite on her other leg.

"Well, maybe not the strawberries, but shortcake would be good."

By dinnertime three dozen jars of strawberry jam were cooling on the counter, and one of *Mam's* sweet, flaky shortcakes had just come out of the oven.

Johnny burst through the door, slamming the screen against the wall.

"*Memmi,* the cows are in the strawberry field!"

Ellie rushed to the back door to look. Her heart turned cold at the sight of the family's two milk cows and the yearling heifer in the field next to the *Dawdi Haus.* She grabbed *Mam*'s corn broom from the back porch and ran to the field. Johnny and Mandy were close behind her.

"You two go around them to the other side and get them to go toward the barn."

Ellie stayed near the gate and used the broom to guide the cows toward the hole in the fence on the other side. She groaned as the splayed hooves of the animals churned the dusty soil, uprooting row after row of plants. When Buttercup stopped to pull one of the remaining green survivors up with her teeth, Ellie swatted her bony rump with the broom.

"Get on there, you miserable cow! Get in your own pasture!"

Mabel, the heifer, was in no hurry to return to the shady grass. She danced around Johnny's and Mandy's efforts to get her to follow the others, scattering bits of strawberry leaves and roots with every jump. Ellie added the broom to their efforts to corral her, but it wasn't until Benjamin joined them that they were finally able to get all three cows through the hole in the fence.

Ellie turned to survey the damage. The field had looked pitiful before, but now it was gone. The money she had invested, the hours watering them, the worry... Any hope of seeing Daniel's dreams fulfilled lay trampled in the dust.

Ellie felt *Mam*'s comforting arms around her shoulders and wanted to bury her face against her and cry, just as if she was Susan's age, but she wasn't a four-year-old.

*Dat* and Reuben joined Benjamin in the task of mending the fence. They finished the quick patch, and then *Dat* joined Ellie.

"*Ach,* Ellie. This is too bad."

Rebecca stood at the gate with Susan and Danny, while the rest of the family gathered around Ellie. Whatever came of this, she wasn't going to have to bear it alone.

"What will you do?" Benjamin's voice was subdued. He had to be almost as disappointed as she was after all the work he had put into this project.

Ellie shook her head. "I don't know."

*Mam* squeezed her shoulders. "The Lord will provide. You'll see."

"*Ja,* I know."

But when? How would she ever pay Bram back now?

Bram spent Friday morning in Elkhart after taking the Interurban from Goshen. A larger town than the county seat, and closer to South Bend and Chicago, Elkhart had much more to offer someone like Kavanaugh. He had found some evidence of criminal activity—duly noted and passed on to the local police—but no sign of the gangster.

He changed his clothes in the public restroom in Goshen and turned Partner toward the Stoltzfus farm. It had been more than a week since he had seen Ellie. The desire to talk with her had grown into an aching need. How had he survived before he met her?

He had called Peters again before heading home from Elkhart, letting him know what he had found. The FBI agent would put his findings together with the information other agents had been able to gather on the Chicago end. They were closing in, squeezing a tight circle around South Bend. That had to be where Kavanaugh's new headquarters were. Peters told him the feds would be making their move soon, and then Bram's job would be over—as long as the cops were thorough this time and the gangster didn't slip through the cracks. Another day or two and he'd call Peters again, just to see what progress had been made.

Meanwhile… He smiled, enjoying the thought. *Ja,* meanwhile, once they got Kavanaugh out of the way, he could stay right here. No more FBI, no more Mexico on his horizon, no more running, just the sweet anticipation of courting the most beautiful woman he had ever met. He'd start by asking her to a picnic with the children at Emma Lake.

The first thing Bram saw when he turned Partner into the Stoltzfus barnyard was Reuben working in Ellie's strawberry field with a singletree plow. What happened to the strawberries?

Ellie came out of the *Dawdi Haus* to greet him as he tied his horse to the hitching rail.

"Good afternoon, Bram."

It was all he could do to keep from taking her in his arms, but he settled for a brief touch on her shoulder.

"What's Reuben doing with the plow?"

"*Ach,* the cows got into the field yesterday and ruined anything that was left."

Her voice was flat with discouragement.

"You're not planting more right away, are you?"

"*Ne.* I can't buy more plants now, even if I thought they might survive. *Dat*'s planting buckwheat."

Bram nodded. Buckwheat grew quickly, and they'd be able to harvest it before frost, even with this late planting. He glanced at the clear blue sky and amended his thought—they'd get a harvest if the rain came.

"The worst part…" Ellie lowered her voice as she walked with him into the shade of one of the maple trees. "The worst part is that I won't be able to pay you back as soon as I hoped."

"Don't worry about that."

"But I do. I hate being in debt. I have to save for next year's taxes, but I will pay you back."

"Ellie, I said don't worry about it. I'm not worried. Everything will work out."

"That's what *Mam* always says." Ellie looked away from him, watching the dust cloud behind Reuben's plow.

Bram reached up and turned her chin toward him. "Your mother is right, as usual."

Her expression was solemn. He longed to kiss her cheek. Maybe that would force her into a smile. He dropped his hand and cleared his throat.

"I came to ask if you'd like to have a picnic on Sunday—you and the children. We could drive over to the lake, and the children could go wading…" He stopped as she looked away from him again.

"I don't want the children to be a burden to you."

"Your children are never a burden." He waited until she looked at him again, then smiled and stroked the line of her jaw with his thumb. "I never regret any time I spend with you or the children. Being with the four of you for a day is the nicest thing I can think of." He took Ellie's hand in his and turned it over, stroking her palm with his finger. "I want to take you on this picnic. Please come."

She hesitated for a long minute. He enfolded her hand in his, longing to be able to pull her into his embrace. He stole a glance to her face. The worry line was there, her lips drawn into an expression of doubt. Confusion. Something still stood between them.

"I…I can't, Bram. It isn't fair to…" She stopped, biting her bottom lip between her teeth.

"It isn't fair to whom, Ellie?"

She whispered the answer. "To me. To the children. The more time we spend together, the more they like you, and the more they'll miss you when you're gone."

"What if I told you I wasn't going anywhere?"

"What?"

"My job is almost finished, and I thought maybe I'd stay on." He smiled, anticipating the pleased look of surprise he'd see in her eyes, but instead her worry line deepened farther.

"Stay on? Do you mean as part of the community?"

"*Ja,* sure."

"Become a member of the church?"

Bram shifted and looked away. He hadn't thought about joining the church since his brief conversation with Bishop Yoder. Was he ready to take that step?

"I…I don't know. Maybe."

Ellie pulled her hand out of his and took a step, putting distance between them.

"I've let myself become too close to you, Bram. I can't keep being friends with someone who's a non-member."

"And if I never joined the church?"

She lifted her eyes to his, her voice a whisper. "Then I can't see you anymore."

Bram swallowed and looked to the sky. How was he supposed to handle this?

"Give me some time, Ellie. I need to take care of this thing with Kavanaugh."

"And then what?" She gave him a trembling smile. "After you take care of this problem, what comes next? You look like you're Amish, Bram, but you've never left the *Englischer* behind. What if you're never ready to submit to the church?"

Bram tore his gaze away from her clear blue eyes. She was right. He felt like swearing, but could only accept her words. If he couldn't submit to the church, everything he had come to treasure here would slip through his fingers. Even Ellie. Even the children.

But to join the church, to agree to live by the *Ordnung,* to give up his freedom, his independence…

Did she know what she was asking him to do?

"If it was Levi Zook standing between us, I'd fight for you. I wouldn't give up until you chose one of us, and then I'd abide by your decision. But this…Ellie… You're asking me to give up everything." He stopped and rubbed the back of his neck.

She looked at him, her eyes wet. "Sometimes *Gott* asks us to give up what we hold dear in order to give us the better thing He has for us."

Bram shook his head. "I don't know if I can believe that."

"You can trust *Gott*, Bram."

Could he trust God that far? He wasn't sure.

## *Chapter Sixteen*

Bram left the house the next morning with a check of the clear blue sky. Another day with no rain meant the crops would continue to suffer. He glanced at the cornfield on his way to the barn, but there was little change. The seeds had sprouted, but by now the plants should be almost a foot high, with bright green leaves reaching upward. Here it was nearly the Fourth of July, and the plants were barely six inches high, dull leaves hanging from the fragile stalks.

He harnessed Partner and hitched him up to head to the telephone exchange in Topeka. He was itching to find out if Kavanaugh was in custody. If the gangster was out of the way, he'd be able to settle into his life here—but what kind of life would it be?

Little spurts of dust rose with Partner's hoofbeats in the empty road as the relentless question echoed in his mind. Ellie was right—if he stayed here, he'd have to make a decision to either join the Amish church or leave it. How could he make a decision like that?

At the corner ahead, a buggy turned onto his road, trotting fast. As it drew closer, Bram saw that Matthew was driving. He pulled Partner to a halt when the two buggies met.

Bram's gut wrenched when he saw Matthew's haggard face. Something was wrong. Terribly wrong.

Ellie…

"Matthew, what's happened?"

"It's Hezekiah Miller. He's missing."

"What do you mean, he's missing?" Elderly Amishmen didn't just disappear.

"Amos Troyer went this morning to help out and found Miriam beside herself. Hezekiah never came in from doing his chores last night."

"I'm on my way over there. Where's Ellie?"

"She and Elizabeth went to Hezekiah's as soon as they got the news. I've got more families to tell, and then I'll be down there."

Bram gave a brief nod goodbye in return to Matthew's and then slapped the reins on Partner's back. The gelding set off at a fast trot.

Taking a deep breath to steady himself, Bram thought of all the possible reasons for Hezekiah's disappearance. If it was any of the other farmers, he might have thought the old man had decided to take a walk around one of the fence lines in the evening, but as crippled as Hezekiah was, he wouldn't go farther than the barn itself. Not alone. Not willingly.

He chirruped to Partner again, even though the horse was keeping up his steady, fast pace. Where had they looked already? Bram went over the farm in his mind, glad he had been there often enough in the past two weeks that it was familiar. It was only ten acres, not so large that Hezekiah could get disoriented and lost. The creek had steep banks—could he have slipped down them? He'd make sure someone looked there.

The woodlot wasn't big, but it was dense with undergrowth. Another place to make sure of. The barn itself? It was fairly small, but there were still places to look.

Bram pulled into the small farmyard, glad to see it crowded with buggies. The people had come together in this crisis, as they always did.

A couple boys had been given the job of seeing to the horses. Bram handed Partner's reins to one of them, then strode to the house, where he saw the men and older boys gathering around the back porch.

John Stoltzfus nodded as Bram joined the group, his mouth set in a firm line. Almost every man from the church was here. Bram nodded to Jim Brenneman, Ellie's *Englisch* tenant, while John organized the searchers.

"Amos already searched the barn and farmyard this morning, before sending for help. We'll divide the rest of the farm between us. Look in all the fencerows, ditches, anywhere he may be lying hurt."

John sent a grim look around the circle of faces and then nodded to Bishop Yoder, who stood at the edge of the circle. The old bishop lifted his hands, shaking with palsy, to bless the men as he prayed. The rhythm of the *Deitsch* words flowed over Bram, giving him strength and confidence. With God's help, they were sure to find Hezekiah.

Before joining John and his boys as they headed to the east fence line, Bram glanced toward the house. Ellie stood in the doorway, holding on to the frame as if it were her lifeline. He caught her eye and nodded, giving her a smile that he hoped would be reassuring. She returned his smile with a worried one of her own and disappeared into the kitchen.

* * *

Ellie turned back to the kitchen and joined *Mam* at the counter, where she prepared chicken casseroles for the men who would be hungry at dinnertime. Ellie prayed it would be a celebration dinner as she chopped stalks of celery for the casseroles.

Miriam stood at the counter next to her sink, where she could watch the fields through the window while she kneaded bread dough. She seemed calm, but her movements lacked the smooth efficiency that was normal for the older woman.

Ellie remembered her own panic when Daniel was lying in bed, hurt, while she sat helpless at his side, waiting through that long day only to face his death at the end. Miriam must be feeling the same thickening of her throat, the same telescoping of sight to that last glimpse of her husband, and yet she continued to knead the dough until it was nearly overworked.

Ellie's eyes blurred as she concentrated on the knife and the celery. What would any of them do without Hezekiah?

*Mam* put two large casseroles into the oven and went over to Miriam while Ellie washed up at the sink.

"Come, Miriam, the bread has been kneaded enough. Let it rest now."

*Mam* took Miriam's hands in her own and handed her to Ellie. The older woman's eyes stayed fixed out the window, but she was as compliant as Susan when Ellie washed her floury hands at the sink while *Mam* covered the dough with a damp towel.

"Let's have another cup of coffee while the dough rises." *Mam* got three cups from the cupboard. "Ellie, can you pour us all a cup?"

Ellie led Miriam to a chair at the kitchen table. She

had seen *Mam* do this same thing many times during a crisis. Keep things as normal as possible. Keep the conversation going. Anything to keep Miriam's mind off what the men were doing, what they might find or if they never found anything.

"I won't be able to go on without him." Miriam's voice was edged with tears, and Ellie stifled a sudden sob. The last time she had heard Miriam's voice like that had been the evening of Daniel's death, when the waiting at his bedside finally ended. Ellie's heart chilled at the thought of the lonely night vigil Miriam had just spent waiting for her husband to walk through the door, a vigil that had only ended with Amos's arrival in the morning.

"*Ja,* you will. *Gott* will give you strength." *Mam*'s words were solid ground in this miserable morning.

"They're sure to find him soon, with all those men searching." Ellie tried to sound hopeful, but Miriam didn't seem to notice she had spoken.

"*Ja,* Ellie's right. They're sure to find him soon."

Miriam got up from the table to look out the window over the sink again. "*Ach,* if only I could help them."

Whatever happened with Hezekiah, Ellie knew she couldn't let Miriam stay on the farm without some help. The men of the church had been faithful in coming to help with the work, but even that hadn't prevented this accident.

Ellie looked at Miriam over her coffee cup as the older woman stood at the window watching the searchers for the first sign that her husband had been found. She rose to stand next to her, a woman as dear to her as her own *mam.* She put her arm around Miriam's shoulders and supported her as the elderly woman leaned into Ellie's strong embrace. They would share this vigil together.

\* \* \*

Bram made his way to the woodlot growing on either side of the fence that separated Hezekiah's farm from Ellie's, the farm the Brennemans were renting.

He eyed the brambles that grew at the sunny edge of the lot. Yellow jackets buzzed hungrily at the stunted black raspberries that covered them. It would take a determined man to break through that mess, and he would leave a trail. Hezekiah certainly didn't have the strength to do it.

Bram followed a path through the grass as it skirted the brambles and then stopped where it disappeared in a narrow tunnel leading into the trees. Could Hezekiah have gone in there?

Looking around, Bram spotted Benjamin ten yards behind him.

"Ben, over here."

"What did you find?"

"Look here," he said as Benjamin leaned down to look through the narrow opening. "Could he have followed a cow through there?"

"*Ja,* I think so." Benjamin pointed to a deep, cleft-hooved print in the long grass just outside the opening. "That's not a deer print. If he was following a stray cow, he might have tried it."

Benjamin ducked and started down the narrow tunnel. Bram waited, listening to the sounds of the other searchers, praying they would find Hezekiah alive.

"Here! Bram, in here. Hurry!"

Bram echoed Benjamin's shout to the other searchers, then followed the trail into the woods, ignoring the brambles that snagged at his clothes. He paused just inside the shadowed cover of the trees, letting his eyes adjust. The close, humid air pressed against him and hummed with mosquitoes.

"Bram, he's over here. I found him."

Benjamin knelt next to Hezekiah's prostrate form; the old man's body slumped over a fallen log. Adrenaline shot through Bram when he saw blood-matted hair on Hezekiah's face. Kneeling next to him, Bram checked for a pulse. He thanked God it was there, faint but steady.

"Is he…"

"He's still alive."

"We need to get him to the house."

"Not yet. We need to see where he's hurt first."

The thick air of the woodlot filled with voices as the other searchers joined them. One by one, the men fell silent as Bram checked Hezekiah's arms and legs. The old man groaned when Bram turned his head to find the source of the bleeding. A cold shock went through him when he found the wound. That ugly bruise didn't come from a fall—he had been hit by something hard.

Bram spoke to John hovering at his shoulder.

"We can move him, but we need to make a litter out of a blanket or something."

Two of the boys left the group. They would take the news to the house and fetch the blanket.

"Will he be all right?" John's voice was raspy as he looked down at his longtime friend.

"I don't know. It looks like he has a concussion, and spending the night on the ground hasn't done him any good. He's been eaten up by mosquitoes." Bram looked at John. "He'll need the doctor. Can someone fetch him?"

"I will." Mr. Brenneman spoke up. "I'll take my car."

Bram supervised as Hezekiah was moved onto a

blanket, but he stayed behind as the group took the elderly man into the house. There had to be clues to tell him what had happened here last night.

He looked around to get his bearings. The fallen tree was in a low spot, near a ditch that might be a small stream in a rainy year. Bram walked around the log, outside the perimeter of where the group of men had been standing. He found the cow's prints in the soft ground of the ditch and the print of Hezekiah's work boot.

Following the ditch farther along, Bram found what he dreaded. There had been two men in the woodlot, and judging from the footprint in a muddy spot at the bottom of the ditch, they weren't Amish. That print had been made by someone wearing shoes, not work boots. Bram slipped his hand inside his pocket and grasped the reassuring handle of his pistol.

Following the faint signs on the disturbed floor of dead leaves, Bram arrived at the edge of the woodlot about fifty feet from the trail. Here he found a cleared space littered with discarded cigarettes and a couple of empty bottles that told him one or two men had spent several hours here—maybe even several days. A short log had been stood on its end. From the number of cigarette butts on the ground around it, it looked as if someone had used it as a seat for a long time. Why?

Bram sat on the stump. What he saw made his stomach clench. An opening had been cleared in the brambles, just big enough to give him a perfect view of the barn, house and fields. Someone had sat here watching the farm.

Hezekiah must have found them, surprising them as he followed that stupid cow. Bram could see how the scene played out: two gangsters overpowering the old man, cracking his skull with a gun butt and then leaving him for dead.

He leaned down and picked up an empty cigarette packet, not wanting to believe what he saw. They were Jose L. Piedra cigarettes from Cuba, Kavanaugh's favorite. The only reason for Kavanaugh being here was that they had somehow tracked him down. Bram's mouth went dry. He never thought his efforts to help out would put the old man in danger, but if Kavanaugh had found him here, at Hezekiah's farm, who else had he unwittingly set up as a target?

Turning slowly, his eyes pierced the shadowy depths of the woodlot. Surely with the crowd of searchers that had been on the farm that morning, the gangsters would have cleared out, but there was still a chance they could be hiding in the underbrush, waiting. Hand on his gun, Bram made his way to the path through the bushes and headed to the house, the spot between his shoulder blades itching the whole time.

Ellie stood with Miriam and *Mam* at Hezekiah's bedside, listening to the doctor's advice.

"He has a concussion, which can be dangerous." The *Englisch* doctor pulled the light summer quilt up to Hezekiah's shoulders as he rose to his feet and gave Miriam's hand a reassuring squeeze.

"Keep him warm and quiet, and I wouldn't let him get out of bed for a couple days. If there are any changes, or if he falls asleep and you're not able to wake him, send for me right away."

Miriam nodded as the doctor snapped his black bag shut and followed *Dat* out of the room.

"I'll stay with you tonight, Miriam," *Mam* said. "I

know I can count on Ellie and the girls to take care of things at home for a day or two."

"*Ja,* of course," Ellie said. She helped Miriam to her small rocking chair next to the bed and then stepped out of the room and headed to the quiet front porch. The creak of the front screen door as she pushed it open was a comforting reassurance that everything was going to be all right, in spite of the day's turmoil.

Her stomach did a flip when she saw Bram sitting on the porch swing. If yesterday's conversation had never happened, she could have found some comfort in his presence. As it was, she folded her arms in front of her and stood in the gap between the front door and the swing. How could she mend this rift between them?

"I thought everyone had gone home," she said.

Bram's face was set in a worried frown, but why? Hezekiah was going to be fine.

"Not yet," he said. "I want to make sure everything is going to be okay."

"You heard the doctor. Hezekiah has a concussion, but he'll recover." Thanks to Bram.

He didn't answer, just looked toward the barn. His hands gripped the edge of the porch swing. Something more than Hezekiah was worrying him.

"Bram, what's wrong?"

He slid over to make room for her next to him on the swing. Ellie sat, waiting for his answer.

"Hezekiah's injury wasn't an accident."

"What do you mean?"

"He came across that man I told you about—Kavanaugh." Bram swallowed, his Adam's apple bobbing in his throat.

"But how would he? I mean, what does that man have to do with Hezekiah?"

He turned to her, his eyes dark. "Me. He must have tracked me here one day and then waited for me to come back. He's been hiding in the woodlot, and Hezekiah must have surprised him last night."

"Where is he now?"

Bram shook his head, his face stony. "I have no idea." He sighed, looking toward the barn and the fields beyond it once more.

Ellie felt the thrill of fear that tales of wolves had given her when she was a little girl. She would look into the trees and imagine them lurking there, waiting to pounce when she wasn't looking. But this fear had a name. This wolf was real.

Bram took her hand, running his thumb across the back of it, and then with a sudden groan, he gathered her to him. Ellie clung close, pressing her ear against his chest, his steady heartbeat reassuring her of his strength. He would protect her, if he could.

He pressed her closer to him and kissed the top of her head. "Ellie," he whispered, "I couldn't bear it if he hurt you."

"He won't, Bram." She tried to smile as he released her enough to lift her chin and look into her face. "Between you, *Dat* and my brothers, I'm very well protected."

"I'd like to believe that." He stroked her cheek with his thumb. "I'm sorry about what I said yesterday. I've been miserable ever since then, knowing we disagree."

She nodded. That same disagreement still hung between them.

"I won't rest until I find Kavanaugh. You know that."

A cold screw twisted her heart.

"That isn't our way, Bram. Vengeance belongs to the Lord."

"This isn't vengeance, Ellie. This is my job." His hand lingered on her cheek, and then he rose so abruptly he sent the swing rocking. "I'll see you tomorrow?"

Ellie nodded, regretting the rift that widened between them.

"*Ja,* tomorrow at church."

Bram drummed his fingers on the desk in the telephone booth at the exchange as he waited for the operator to make the connection.

"Peters here."

"It's Dutch."

"Dutch, are you all right?"

"Yes, I'm fine, but I'm worried about Kavanaugh. Do you have any news?"

"The information you gave us so far was right on the mark. Kavanaugh has been expanding operations into South Bend, Fort Wayne, Toledo and Detroit. We were able to track down one of his boys in South Bend, and the thug sang like a canary."

Bram wiped his face with his handkerchief and propped the door of the telephone booth open to let in some air. If Peters had done his job, then who had attacked Hezekiah?

"So you got Kavanaugh?"

"That's just it. We rounded up a dozen of his men, but he was nowhere to be found."

Bram rubbed his palm on his pant leg. So he was right about Kavanaugh hunting for him. The gangster was getting desperate.

Peters went on. "That stool pigeon told us Kavanaugh went out west. That he is working in Los Angeles now."

Bram's mouth was dry. "He's not in California—he's

here. He almost killed an old man last night, a man who owns a farm I've been working on."

There was silence on the other end, and then Peters cleared his throat.

"It looks like your cover is gone, Dutch. You need to get out of there."

Bram leaned his head against the wooden side of the telephone booth. Peters was right. *"Ja, es richtig...."*

"Dutch? Are you still there?"

"Yes, I'm here. I said you're right. I'll call if I need anything, but I hope you don't hear from me."

"Right. And, Dutch, take care of yourself."

Bram hung up the telephone. The tables were turned again, and he was no longer the hunter. As long as the snake was still around, he couldn't risk staying here.

He sighed and slumped against the side of the telephone booth. Just when he had begun to hope...but no. Home and family? They weren't for him. He was a fool to think his life could be anything more than hunting down men like Kavanaugh. Ellie deserved more than that, much more.

But there was one thing he could do for her. He could draw Kavanaugh away from here, away from Ellie and this community. Once he drew him far enough away, he'd make sure the gangster never got a chance to come back.

Bram rubbed the back of his neck, suddenly aware of how long this day had been. And it had been the last day. He had no illusions about what could happen when he offered himself as bait, but he couldn't hope to get rid of that snake without sacrificing himself.

There was one last risk he would take, though. If

Kavanaugh hadn't found him by morning, he'd attend the Sunday meeting. He couldn't bear to leave without seeing Ellie one more time.

## Chapter Seventeen

Mornings on church Sundays usually started early, but this one was even earlier for Ellie. Since *Mam* had stayed with the Millers last night, Ellie took on the task of getting the entire family ready for Sunday meeting. She was thankful for the long ride in the buggy to Amos Troyer's. The children rode quietly, making up for their lost sleep after an early breakfast.

Watching the passing fields, Ellie tried to quell the sinking feeling in her stomach. What would she say when she saw Bram? Was he still set on taking revenge for Hezekiah's wound? He had said it wasn't vengeance—but could it really be anything else?

"We have much to be thankful for today, knowing Hezekiah is safe," *Dat* said. He seldom spoke on the drive to meeting, using the time to pray about what he would say if he were asked to give the sermon.

"*Ja,* we do, but I can't help worrying about them. How will they live on their farm?"

*Dat* reached over and laid his hand on hers. "*Gott* knows their needs. Reuben is going to live with them for the rest of the summer and into the fall, and after that, we'll see what *Gott* has planned. Keep trusting Him."

* * *

Caution still dogged Bram as he tended to his few chores before church. If Kavanaugh knew where he was, what was keeping him from showing his face? Driving through the still, morning air, he kept his eyes and ears open, but there was no sign of the Packard.

Bram set a mask over his frayed nerves as he drove into the Troyers' crowded farmyard. No one could suspect this would be his last time with them.

As he drove past the congregation lined up outside the barn, he caught sight of Ellie greeting another woman. She glanced toward him and gave him a smile, making his heart soar in spite of the thoughts of Kavanaugh hovering on all sides.

He joined the line of men just as the congregation started into the barn, and he chose a seat where he wouldn't be tempted to glance at Ellie during the service. She was by far the most beautiful woman there, but Bram grew cold every time he thought of what could happen if Kavanaugh knew about her. His gut twisted as he remembered the bloody gash on Hezekiah's head, but instead of the old man's matted gray hair, he saw Ellie's fine brown hair and *kapp*.

As Bishop Yoder and the ministers rose to go to an upstairs room for prayer, one of the older men started the first phrase of *Das Loblied,* and Bram joined in the familiar hymn with the congregation, his mind still on the gangster. If Kavanaugh was looking for him, wouldn't it be smart for him to lie low? But then how long would it take for him to stop feeling as if danger was stalking him? He would never get there. He'd always be looking over his shoulder. How long could he live that way?

Then, as he looked up between hymns, Bram saw

Ellie lean forward slightly, right into his field of vision. Her lips were parted in a smile as she whispered something to Susan, and her face held a look Bram hadn't seen before—joy, contentment. He couldn't stop staring at her. Longing for her filled his heart.

Bram knew what he had to do, in spite of the ache in his chest. Or because of it. As soon as Sunday meeting was over, he would leave. He'd leave Partner and the buggy at Matthew's, along with what was left of the cash he had. He could leave a note telling Matthew to give everything to Ellie. From there it wouldn't take long to walk to the highway, and then he could hitch a ride somewhere. Anywhere but Chicago. Anywhere but here.

Kavanaugh would follow him, with any luck—he'd leave a big enough trail—and it really didn't matter where the gangster caught up with him, as long as Ellie was safe.

He forced his eyes away from Ellie and her family. He was aware of the service continuing as one of the ministers prayed, but his mind was occupied in a war. He knew what he should do, but could he do it? He had never met a woman like Ellie. The thought of leaving her, of never seeing her again, pulled his heart in one direction, and then the knowledge of what could happen if Kavanaugh knew how much he cared about her sent cold fingers yanking him in another.

Bram forced his hands to unclench, willing himself to relax. He had to remember where he was. Matthew was sitting in front of him; Reuben and Benjamin Stoltzfus were to his right. Welcome Yoder was two benches in front of him, sitting next to Eli Schrock. These men had accepted him into their community, helped him on his farm and given him their time and advice. Could he turn his back on them? In the past few weeks he had gotten a taste of what the church could be, what his heritage could give him, and all he planned to do was use them and throw them away.

As soon as the service ended, Bram made his way through the men to the side of the barn. He glanced behind him as he slipped out the door, but the milling crowd cheated him out of one last look at Ellie. He closed the door, ignoring the sinking feeling in his belly.

*She's just a woman.*

Who was he kidding? There wasn't another woman like her.

He rounded the corner of the barn, heading toward the parked buggies, but stopped short when he saw John Stoltzfus waiting for him.

"Good morning, Bram."

"Good morning, John."

"I was hoping to talk to you."

Bram quelled the retort that came to his lips—words from his own anxiety. He couldn't speak to this man like that. Now that John had stopped him, he wouldn't be able to make his quick escape anyway. He mentally closed the door on his plans and forced himself to turn his attention to the older man.

"I was watching you during the meeting." John paused, pretending to study the buggies lined up in the field.

Bram waited. He knew John well enough to know that he would get to his point sooner if he let him do it in his own time, no matter how anxious he was to get going.

"Is something bothering you? You seemed distracted."

Bram almost choked. *Ja,* he was certainly distracted,

but he thought he was better at hiding it than that. One thing Bram had learned over the past several weeks was just how deep John's perception of people went.

"*Ja,* I've been worried about Hezekiah, just like everyone else. It kept me from paying attention to the meeting as I should have." If he gave John a partial explanation, maybe he would leave it at that. Once Bram was out of the area, Kavanaugh would be old news.

John turned to look at him.

"You've been on my mind a lot lately. Your name keeps coming to me at odd moments, and I always pray for you when it does." Bram didn't know what to say. Had anyone ever prayed for him before? "It can't be easy leaving your old life behind."

*He doesn't know the half of it,* Bram thought, but without the bitterness of a couple months ago. He felt an urge to confide in John—to warn him about Kavanaugh, about his part in the gang and the danger he had brought to this community—but the calm acceptance in John's eyes stopped him before he even started. He couldn't talk about the sordid things he was involved in. Not here, not now, not among these people. Once he left, it would all be over for them anyway.

"*Ne,* it isn't," Bram said. "I lived that way for many years, and old habits are hard to get rid of."

John nodded, waiting for him to go on. How much could he confess? John deserved to know.

"I've seen an old acquaintance around."

"Someone from Chicago." John's words were a statement, not a question. "Someone you don't want to run into again."

"I did some things there that…well, that I'm not proud of." Bram swallowed. He had already said more than he should, but he felt that silken coil again, urging him on. "I want to just leave them behind me, along with the people I knew there."

John's eyes were piercing. Could he see the details Bram was leaving out? Bram wasn't sure how much this man had already guessed.

"If you left any unfinished business, you should resolve that before trying to move on. Otherwise, you'll never be free of your past."

Bram rubbed the back of his neck as John paused.

"I heard an automobile go by our farm last night. A big, powerful one. No one around here owns a machine like that." John looked at him again. "It went by twice."

Bram's hand automatically went to the pocket where he carried his gun. He closed his cold fingers around the grip.

"You don't need your gun."

He shot a glance at the older man. How…

"*Ach, ja,* I've known about it for a long time."

Bram dropped his pretense. It looked as if John knew everything.

"John, this guy is dangerous. I need my gun."

"We are a people of peace, Bram. Guns have no place in our lives."

Bram looked away, anywhere but into the older man's face. John had no idea how violent life could be outside this community. Violence had to be dealt with or else innocent people would be hurt, people like Hezekiah.

"I need to protect myself. I need to protect the people around me."

"Do you believe *Gott* can protect you?"

Did he believe that? *Ja,* up to a point…but at what cost?

"I don't know," he answered John truthfully. "I'm not convinced that *Gott*'s protection works against bullets."

"Perhaps bullets aren't what you need to worry about." Not worry about bullets? What could be worse? What was he talking about? "Put your trust in Him, Bram." John paused until Bram looked at him. "Your very soul is in danger, and, more important, the soul of the other man. If he commits a heinous sin because of your actions…" John shook his head at his own words. "There are things more important than our lives."

Bram looked away again. He wished he could have that confidence, but he knew too much. He had seen too much.

"I have to go."

"Bram." John stopped him with a hand on his arm. "I'll still be praying for you."

Bram nodded his thanks and then continued to his buggy.

By the time Bram was within sight of his farm, his plan was set. He had to protect Ellie at all costs. If he survived somehow, could he come back eventually? And see Ellie married to another man? Someone like Levi Zook? The thought made his hands clench. No, he had to leave for good.

As he turned the horse into the barnyard, he saw it. The maroon Packard sat along the side of his barn, out of sight until he turned into the drive. The knot that had been growing in his stomach all morning exploded.

He sawed on Partner's reins, trying to get the horse to turn, but it was too late. Kavanaugh sauntered out of the barn, followed by Charlie Harris's lumbering form. Kavanaugh's face was stony, but Charlie's grin turned Bram's feet to ice. Running was out of the question. Bram couldn't pray. He put all his strength into keeping his voice steady.

"Hello, Kavanaugh. I didn't expect to see you around here."

The gangster's thin face twisted into a sneer as he gave Bram a cold smile. "I was surprised—but very happy—to see you while I was doing some business in Goshen a couple weeks ago."

Bram put an amazed look on his face. "I didn't see you there, but then, I've been busy."

"I can't help being curious to know—" Kavanaugh took a drag from his cigarette, measuring his words "—what you would be doing in that hick town, dressed like some—" he gestured with his cigarette toward Bram, the buggy, his Plain clothes "—like some *farmer*." He emphasized the last word with derision and then took another drag. Bram waited. Kavanaugh's right hand was tucked under his suit jacket, where he would have quick access to his gun.

"And then when I happened to see you at that old man's farm—" the cigarette smoke plumed from Kavanaugh's mouth and nose as he spoke "—I couldn't believe my luck."

He pulled another lungful of smoke from the cigarette.

"I didn't like it when you slipped away from us last night, you and that buggy." He exhaled the smoke. "I'm glad we finally tracked you down." The gangster paused and tapped some ash off the cigarette with a flick of his finger. "What happened to the Studebaker, Dutch?"

Bram was silent. He knew better than to respond when Kavanaugh was trying to bait him. Charlie, off to Bram's left, still grinned and flexed his hands.

"You left Chicago in a hurry and didn't tell anyone where you were going, and around that same time some G-men showed up, knocking on our door. That makes me wonder what you're up to. I wasn't sure where to even begin looking for you until I saw you on that farm wagon a few weeks ago."

Bram still didn't answer. Anything he said to Kavanaugh now would only make things worse for him.

Kavanaugh stood at the horse's side, eyes even more narrow than usual, staring at Bram. He threw his cigarette butt on the ground and twisted it into the dust with his heel. Without taking his eyes off Bram, he beckoned to Charlie.

"Get him down."

Charlie wasn't the type to be gentle at his work. He reached up and grabbed the front of Bram's coat, then pulled him off the seat as easily as a kitten. Charlie held him up; his feet brushed the dirt of the drive.

"Shall we go into the barn?" Kavanaugh's polite words mocked the desperate situation Bram was in. Unless a miracle happened, he was a goner.

Without waiting for an answer, Kavanaugh turned and led the way as Charlie dragged Bram after him. Dust motes swirled in the sunbeams, throwing bars across the shaded interior. Charlie backed Bram into the support beam with a shove, holding him with his arm across Bram's chest. Cigarette butts littered the dirt floor. They must have been waiting for him all morning.

Bram looked toward the roof as Kavanaugh closed the barn door. Thank *Gott* he had been able to see Ellie one last time.

Charlie patted him down, finding his gun. The thug stuck it in the waistband of his pants. When Bram eyed it, Charlie saw the direction of his gaze and slammed an elbow into his ribs.

"I wouldn't have taken you for a churchgoing chump," Kavanaugh began, lighting another cigarette. After tak-

ing a puff, he turned the burning end around, staring at
it as if he had never seen the glowing tip before. "We
don't like stool pigeons, Dutch. You know that. You betrayed me, and no one gets away with that. Want to tell
us what you told the feds?"

Ellie watched *Dat* closely. Ever since the meeting
ended and the women started preparing dinner, he'd
paced at the edges of the crowd. When she glanced
his way, he was often looking toward the road, where
Bram's buggy had disappeared.

She hadn't noticed Bram leaving until he was already on the road, his horse trotting away at a fast pace.
She couldn't remember the last time someone had left
Sunday meeting early, before the meal and fellowship
afterward. But if something had been wrong, wouldn't
he tell her?

Not long after the meal ended, *Dat* found Ellie as she
talked to yet another concerned woman about Hezekiah
and Miriam. "It's time to go." His voice was gruff, short,
and Ellie knew she shouldn't delay. *Dat* was never in a
hurry without a reason.

By the time Ellie had gathered her children, *Dat* was
waiting with the buggy. Mandy and Rebecca followed.

"But why can't we stay and come home with Reuben?" Rebecca asked as they climbed into the buggy.

Ellie turned to help Susan settle in the backseat between the girls. "Because the boys aren't coming home
until late, after the singing."

Even as Ellie spoke, she gave *Dat* a questioning
glance. Why the hurry?

*Dat* didn't speak, but started the horse off at a quick
trot. When he reached the end of the lane, he turned
west, instead of east toward home. *Now what?*

*"Dat,"* said Ellie, leaning close so the children in the back didn't hear, "is something bothering you?"

"I had a conversation with Bram earlier. I'm a bit worried about him, and I thought we'd drive past his place on the way home, just to check if things are all right."

Ellie felt a cold chill, even though *Dat*'s voice was calm. She trusted her father's judgment. He was able to read people so well, some thought he had a gift. If he felt this concerned after talking with Bram...

Had Bram found that man he was looking for? Fear wrapped its icy fingers around her heart. Bram was in danger.

The girls hadn't caught *Dat*'s tension. They chattered like birds as they played a game with Susan and Johnny in the backseat, Rebecca holding Danny on her lap.

Did that man, Kavanaugh, have something to do with why Bram had left church so early? In fact, he hadn't even looked at her all through the service. Ellie worried the inside of her lip. It wasn't like him to ignore her completely.

When *Dat* turned onto Bram's road, Ellie saw Partner in the lane between the gravel road and Bram's barn, but why wasn't he tied? For some reason Bram had just left the horse unattended, and Partner had pulled the buggy partway into the grass. As she watched, Partner took another step toward the long grass at the edge of the cornfield and the buggy tilted, along with her stomach. Where was Bram?

*Dat* pulled to a stop at the end of Bram's lane and handed the reins to Ellie. "You take the children home. I'm going to check on Bram."

"I'm coming with you."

*Dat* looked at her, weighing his decision. Finally he

nodded. "Mandy, you drive the buggy on home and look after the children."

Mandy gave Ellie a mystified look as she obediently climbed into *Dat*'s place and took the reins.

"We won't be long." Ellie smiled at her little sister as she climbed down. "It will be fine."

*Dat* waited until Mandy had driven off before turning to Ellie.

"There's something going on, and Bram may need help. I'm going to check the barn."

Ellie followed *Dat* as he walked toward the barn, glancing into Bram's buggy as he went.

Ellie crossed the lane to the other side, where she'd have a clearer view of the barn door, and stopped short. There was an automobile parked alongside the barn, out of sight until she'd seen it from this angle. What was going on here? Her mind flashed back to Bram's face when he had first told her about this man, this Kavanaugh. Could the automobile belong to him?

*Dat* reached the barn and paused, leaning against the wall next to the door as if he was listening to something. What? Was there someone inside with Bram? Ellie's stomach clenched.

She could hear indistinct sounds from inside the barn. Men's voices. She had to hear what they were saying.

She slipped up next to *Dat,* and they both listened to the men inside the barn.

"You're tougher than I thought." Ellie didn't recognize the voice, but she didn't want to meet the man it belonged to.

"It's no use, Kavanaugh. Peters knows where you are." Bram sounded weary but not afraid. "I talked to him yesterday. He's on his way here right now."

"Charlie, stand him up again."

There was a scuffling noise as Charlie obeyed the first voice.

So there were at least two men in the barn with Bram.

"Work him over some more. I have to know how much he told the feds."

A sickening sound filtered through the barn wall—the sound of something hard hitting flesh. Ellie's head pounded, and the icy fingers tightened around her heart. That was the sound of Bram being beaten. *Dat* knew it, too. He gave Ellie a hard look that ordered her to stay back and then rammed his shoulder against the barn doors, forcing them open with a crash of splintered wood.

The two men looked up, surprise and anger twisting both of their faces. Ellie took in the whole scene in one glance through the open door. Bram was pinned against a beam by a huge man, his face bloody and raw. He looked straight at Ellie, and fear filled his eyes when he recognized her. *Dat* walked into the barn, his hands outstretched in an effort to calm the situation, watching the big man.

Then Ellie saw the smaller man, his clean, tailored suit a stark contrast to Bram's torn and bloody clothes. His eyes on *Dat,* he threw a cigarette down and in one fluid motion pulled a pistol from beneath his suit jacket.

Ellie's feet were lead. She must keep that man from using his gun. She ran forward and grasped the cloth of his sleeve. He spun around, swinging the gun toward her face, his eyes sharp with evil intentions. The blow caught Ellie on the side of her head as she turned away from him, then he had no more regard for her than a fly he had just swatted away.

As she fell to the floor, Ellie was horrified to see him raise his gun again, pointing it toward *Dat*.

# Chapter Eighteen

The crash of the barn door brought Bram to his senses. Was he dreaming? No, the sharp pain in his ribs was all too real. John strode into the barn between Kavanaugh and Charlie, holding out a hand toward each, a gentle smile on his face. Bram sent a quick prayer for *Gott* to protect this brave, foolish man. Charlie froze, his suspicious eyes on John.

"Surely, brother, we can talk about our differences without resorting to violence," John said, his voice calm in the charged air.

Bram looked past him to Ellie standing in the barn door, and the fog cleared out of his mind with a rush.

*No, she can't be here!*

Charlie turned toward John, readying a ham-size fist at shoulder level. Without the thug's hand pinning him against the supporting beam, Bram swayed. The air around him turned black. Staggering, he shook his head, trying to clear his sight. When he looked up again, the first thing he saw was Kavanaugh backhanding Ellie. He gathered what strength he had to go to her aid, but when Kavanaugh's hand lifted, the snub nose of the pistol pointing straight at John, Bram changed direction and sprang to his left, shoving John over just as Kavanaugh's finger squeezed the trigger of the gun.

He and John skidded to the floor as Kavanaugh's gun roared in the small barn. Bram rolled to his knees—Ellie was still in danger—and stopped as he faced Charlie's prostrate form on the dirt floor beside him, a bloom of red blood soaking his shirt's shoulder. Bram's pistol was still tucked in Charlie's waistband, right in front of his eyes. He grabbed it and turned to face Kavanaugh, every nerve focused on his target.

The gangster's face was calm, his eyes like steel. Bram had seen that look before—the man was determined to kill. Deliberately, Bram raised the gun in his hand to meet Kavanaugh's stare.

"Drop your gun." His voice croaked, but he was able to force the words out. Blood ran into his mouth from a split lip, and he spit it out.

Kavanaugh's lip curled in the sneer that was his trademark. "No cop is going to take me."

The snub nose of Kavanaugh's gun steadied as the gangster's finger tightened on the trigger. Bram shot at the same time. His body jerked as Kavanaugh's bullet hit his chest, and he fell into blackness.

The small man fell to the ground, but Ellie didn't look at him as she flew to Bram. *Dat* reached him first, turning him on his back. The wound was just a blackened hole in Bram's shirt, but as Ellie watched, blood began spurting out of it.

"Good," *Dat* said as he propped up Bram's head. "He's still alive."

Stars whirled around Ellie, the icy grip on her heart squeezing mercilessly. *Dat* gripped her arm, covering it with Bram's blood.

"I need your help, Ellie. We need to get him to a doctor."

Ellie swallowed. Bram's face was pale, and blood was everywhere. Just like Daniel.

"What do I need to do?" Her voice cracked in a whisper of breath.

*Dat* removed his jacket and tore off his shirt. Wadding it up, he pressed against the wound.

"Keep pressure on this."

Ellie pressed her hand against *Dat's* shirt, Bram's warm blood pulsing against her cold fingers.

"We need to get him to town. We'll take that automobile outside."

"The automobile?"

*Dat* looked at Ellie, his eyes grave. "This is a matter of life or death. It's here, so we'll use it."

Ellie kept pressure on Bram's wounds, walking beside *Dat* as he carried him to the big maroon machine. She sat on the backseat with Bram's head in her lap as *Dat* returned to the barn and carried the small gangster to the automobile. The man was barely conscious as *Dat* set him in the front seat, and he slumped against the door.

*Dat* sat in the driver's seat, pausing to study the controls.

"Can you make it work?"

*Dat* gave her a grim smile as he turned on the motor. "*Ja,* I drove an ambulance during the war, remember? It wasn't too much different from this."

"What about the other man?" Ellie tried to remember if he was dead or only hurt.

"He'll be all right. I tied him to the barn post, and I'll send someone to get him when we get to the hospital."

Once *Dat* figured out the controls of the automobile,

the trip into Goshen was faster than Ellie had ever experienced. *Dat* knew more about driving than Ellie imagined, but the machine still bucked and stuttered as he tried to make it speed along the dusty road.

Bram lay deathly still for the entire trip, his head resting in her lap. Ellie watched his pale face as she leaned over him, keeping her fingers pressed against the makeshift bandages. She tried to pray, but the words didn't survive the icy grip on her heart. Memories of Daniel flooded her mind. Once again she was helpless, hopeless, watching the man she loved as he lay dying. With every breath that made his chest rise beneath her fingers, she took a breath herself. Which one would be his last?

Ellie blinked back tears, watching Bram's face. She loved him. Her mind embraced what she had feared all along. Could she love him? Love meant risking her heart, risking loss again. Could she bear that?

As *Dat* pulled up to the hospital, the car's engine sputtered and died. Ellie stayed with Bram as *Dat* ran into the building, her numb hands pressed against Bram's wounds. The automobile's door swung open, and a man in white looked in.

"We'll take it from here, ma'am."

As they took Bram and put him on a wheeled cot, Ellie's hands fell uselessly into her lap. She watched the small man, Kavanaugh, being wheeled into the hospital behind Bram. What could she do now?

*Dat* opened the door next to her.

"Come, daughter. We'll wait for news inside."

Ellie looked down at her bloody hands and dress. *Dat*'s Sunday coat was just as bad.

"Like this?"

*Dat* smiled at her, but the smile didn't change the worried look in his eyes.

"*Ja.* This is a hospital. They're used to these things here."

Ellie let *Dat* help her into one of the chairs lining the hall just inside the door of the hospital. *Englischers* were everywhere, even on a Sunday afternoon. *Dat* went to the desk to use the telephone while she sat. Her hands shook as she stared at the blood that covered them. Bram's blood.

She barely noticed when *Dat* took the seat next to her.

"I called the Wrights," he said. "They'll take the news to Eli's, and it will be passed on from there."

As the afternoon wore on, people started showing up at the hospital. Annie and Matthew Beachey were among the first, and Annie had brought some fresh clothes for them both.

By the time Ellie changed her dress, the corridor was filled with Amish. Friends and family surrounded them. She numbly returned to her seat and heard *Dat* relating the news to some recent arrivals.

"The doctor said they would have to operate. He said it didn't look like the bullet had hit his lung, but it broke his shoulder blade. He wasn't sure what other damage had been done."

*Dat*'s words sank in slowly. Was Bram still alive?

*Mam* sat down, and Ellie found herself clinging to her. She gave way to the tears that she had dammed up. Her failed promises to Daniel, her doubts about Bram, her own miserable pride all caught up in tears that flowed like a spring flood.

Bram gunned the engine, Kavanaugh's breath hot on the back of his neck.

"Go, go, go!" The gangster cursed at him, and Bram put all his weight on the accelerator, but his foot couldn't reach the floor—the Packard didn't move. Bram risked a look over his shoulder. Kavanaugh's face disappeared in an explosive flash.

Bram's eyes shot open. Ellie was in danger. He struggled to sit up, fighting against the pain that seared across his shoulder and down his back.

Ellie's face came into view.

"Bram, don't try to move."

But Kavanaugh would kill her; he had to move. He fought against the black fog in his mind.

"Bram, it's all right. You're in the hospital."

Ellie's voice pierced the thick layer. The hospital? Pieces of the events in the barn fell into place in his mind like shattered glass shards, arranging themselves into bits of memory. He lay still, watching her face. Her blue eyes were red-rimmed and wet, as if she had been crying. A tear made its way down her cheek, and he tried to lift his hand to brush it away, but the only thing that moved was his index finger. His right arm, shoulder and chest were covered in bandages. Kavanaugh… Where was he?

His eyes sought Ellie's again. "Wh…wh…"

"Shh. Don't try to talk."

Ellie moved away as a nurse bustled in. Quiet shoes whispered on the wooden floors.

"Lie still, young man." The middle-aged nurse spoke in a no-nonsense tone, and he couldn't fight her. His chest felt as if a heavy weight held it down. The nurse gave him a sip of water after checking his pulse and temperature.

"He's doing fine so far." The nurse shook the thermometer and placed it in her pocket. "You may stay only a few more minutes. He needs to get his rest."

The nurse left the room as Ellie came into view again. Behind her were John and Elizabeth.

"Tell me what happened to Kavanaugh." His voice was stronger. The water had helped.

Ellie glanced at John. The older man looked down at his feet, then back at Bram. "You shot him."

"Is he dead?"

John shook his head. "*Ne,* praise *Gott.*"

"Where is he? You can't let him get away."

"He's here in the hospital, along with that other man."

Bram closed his eyes, exhausted. He had to let Peters know where to find them, but not now.

"We'd better go."

Bram forced his eyes open to see John ushering Elizabeth out of the room. Ellie stood by his feet.

"I need to go, too."

"*Ne,* wait."

She moved to his side and rested her hand on his as it lay outside the covers. Her mouth quivered as she looked at him.

"If you and your father hadn't come... I still don't know how you got there."

"*Dat* had a feeling there was something wrong."

"*Ja,* he was right." Bram closed his eyes, but he opened them again as he heard Ellie start to move away. "Don't go."

Ellie shook her head. "I need to. The nurses won't let me stay." Her hands shook, as if she was trying to bear up under a great strain.

"I'm not going to die, Ellie. I'm here for you."

Ellie smiled at him, a quick, tearful smile, and then

turned and followed her parents out the door as the nurse came in again.

"Now, no arguing. You need your sleep." The nurse adjusted his pillows, checked his IV and took his pulse again. Her eyebrows rose as she looked at him. "Your pulse is up a bit."

"I need you to do something for me."

The nurse didn't answer until he had swallowed the pills she gave him.

"Will it help you rest?"

"*Ja*...I mean yes. I need to make a phone call."

"No phone calls for you, young man." She moved to the end of his bed to adjust the sheets.

"Is there someone who could send a wire for me?"

"I can send a telegram for you, but you have to promise to go to sleep then. All right?"

Bram nodded, and the movement made his head ring. He gave the nurse Peters's information.

"Tell him where I am and that I have some of his friends." He moved his head toward her too quickly and winced from the pain.

"None of that. I'll send your message."

"One more thing. I have to talk to the police." His voice was getting weaker. Making an effort to rally his strength just made him sink further. Whatever drug she had given him was taking effect.

"Sure. They'll be here first thing in the morning to talk to you if you're feeling up to it. They always do for a shooting." She unfolded a blanket over his legs. "Although what Amish folk are doing involved in a shooting..." Her voice faded.

"Those other men..." But she was already out the door, beyond hearing. He was helpless against the sleep that claimed him.

\* \* \*

Ellie sat alone in the back of the buggy while *Dat* drove home. Brownie's hooves kept up their tireless cadence on the road while lightning bugs hovered above the fields in the growing darkness, floating in the hot breezes that carried the scent of acres of cornfields.

Exhaustion made her head thick, numb, so much like the days after Daniel's death....

But Bram wasn't dead. Ellie choked back a sob before *Mam* could hear it. This was what she had been afraid of, wasn't it? That if she let herself care for another man...

Bram wasn't dead, but that didn't mean he felt anything for her. That man in the barn... Ellie shuddered as she remembered his cold eyes, the blow that had sent her reeling to the ground. This was Bram's world—violence, blood, death. Did *Gott* have any place in a world like that?

*Mam* turned in her seat and reached back, resting her hand on Ellie's knee. "Bram seems to be doing well after his surgery, doesn't he?"

Ellie nodded, not trusting her voice.

"Annie said they would move him into their house after he's released from the hospital. We'll have to be sure to get the women together to can her garden, since she certainly won't have time." *Mam* paused, looking carefully at Ellie's face in the growing darkness. "It will be all right, daughter. Bram will come back to us."

"It doesn't matter, though, does it?" The words came before Ellie could stop them, strident in the night air. "He's never been one of us. He's *Englisch,* and he'll be going back to his *Englisch* world now that he's caught those two criminals." She ended with a choked sob.

*Mam* glanced at *Dat* and then turned around to face

the front again. Ellie's face burned. Her words and her tone had both been hateful.

"I'm sorry *Mam, Dat*. I shouldn't have said that."

"We don't know Bram well." *Dat*'s voice was soft, tender, almost sad. The things he had seen today had shaken him, too. "But I do know this, Ellie. He's an honorable man, but his past followed him here. We'll have to wait and see how today's events will affect him."

"*Ja,* you're right."

*Mam* and *Dat* lapsed into silence, and Ellie let the swaying motion of the buggy calm her. Could Bram ever come back and be one of them? His words as he had spoken to that man in the barn had been as cold as death, and the determined look on his face as he had fired his gun haunted her memory. She saw no reluctance to use violence in his actions, only the same set look she had seen on *Dat*'s face when he killed a snake. But this Kavanaugh wasn't a snake; he was a man, and violence against another man was against the *Ordnung*. Against the Bible. How could Bishop accept him into the church after this?

Bram woke with every temperature and pulse check through the night. If these nurses were so concerned about him sleeping, why didn't they leave him alone so he could do it?

Dawn brought a shift change with a visitor. Elwood Peters walked into his room as soon as the nurse had finished with the temperature check.

"I'm glad to see you're still with us." The older man's clothes were rumpled, his face gray and unshaven.

"You look worse than I feel." As he tried to smile, Bram concentrated on keeping his body still. Every movement sent a shot of pain through his chest.

Peters pulled a chair over to Bram's bedside and sat heavily on it, tossing his hat onto the blanket covering Bram's legs.

"Yeah, sleeping on a train will do that to you."

He reached into his pocket for his pack of cigarettes, tossed one out into his waiting hand and then stopped with a mild curse.

"I forgot. No cigarettes in here." He gestured his hand toward the oxygen tank sitting next to Bram's bed.

Bram found himself cringing at Peters's language. When had cursing become offensive? It hadn't been that long since he had talked the same way.

"What about Kavanaugh?" Bram had to know.

"Kavanaugh is still here, just a couple doors down the hall. He's in worse shape than you are. His goon—"

"Charlie Harris."

"Yeah, Charlie. He had a flesh wound in his shoulder, and he's in the city jail this morning."

Bram's muscles released their tension with Peters's words. He sank into the softness of the hospital bed. Ellie was safe. How soon would he see her again?

"With those two in custody, Kavanaugh's gang is finished." Peters leaned back in his chair, tapping his cigarette against his knee. "It's a good feeling, Dutch, and we couldn't have done it without you and your work."

"Yeah, well, just keep that part to yourself."

"Are you sure? There's a reward. It would set you up for life."

"I don't want money for this. Give it to the policemen's fund or something."

Peters tapped his cigarette against his knee and stared out the window. He had something on his mind.

"Now that this business is over, we could use you back. The gangs are all moving out west. California,

Nevada. We made Chicago too hot for them. You could work for us out there. Become an agent, not just an informant." He shifted his eyes to Bram's. "You show real promise. You have a gift for this kind of work."

Bram couldn't look at Peters. He moved his gaze toward the window. No clouds. They sure could use some rain.

What Peters was offering…wasn't that what he had always wanted? He knew he would be a good agent. It would be a hard life and probably a short one—agents didn't have a very long life expectancy. But the thrill of getting his man! He had felt something like it when he had faced Kavanaugh in the barn. How many crooks could he get off the streets? How many innocent lives could he protect in that kind of work?

The hollow clip-clop of an Amish buggy on the street outside drifted up to his open window. The measured beats of the horse's hooves slowed his thoughts, brought them back to Ellie, the children, his farm, the church. He felt that fluid, silken movement again, caressing his mind.

That unseen presence had never left him since he'd first felt it—since he'd first come back. Would it be with him if he took Peters up on his offer? Even if it was, his heart would be here.

The sounds of the buggy faded off into the distance. He knew where he belonged.

# Chapter Nineteen

After three weeks of lying in a hospital bed, Bram was anxious to get out of there, although he'd hate giving up the electric fan that cooled the ward. The end of July could be stiflingly hot in northern Indiana, but this year the temperatures felt like a blast furnace, and still no rain in sight.

He leafed through a copy of *Look* magazine. The headlines spoke of the coming Olympic Games in Berlin, a civil war in Spain, the heat wave two weeks ago that had claimed nearly five thousand lives across the nation. And Adolph Hitler's picture was everywhere.

Bram let the magazine fall closed and pushed it away, along with the news. He was so weary of the world and its problems. Was John right when he said believers were to keep themselves separate from the world? John was confident in his belief in *Gott* and the brotherhood of the believers—but where did his confidence come from? The older man centered his world on his church and his family, not the cares of the world.

Not that he wasn't concerned about the people in the world—Bram had heard the killing heat and the violence in Spain mentioned in his prayers—but they weren't his utmost concern. John's greatest desire, he had said, was to see his children and grandchildren close around the family table, in fellowship and love.

A fitful breeze fluttered in the leaves of the maple tree outside the window, catching Bram's eye, and he watched them turn one way and then the other, limp and ragged in the dry heat. "Blown by the cares of the world," John had said once.

John's words described Bram perfectly. Tossed and turned by events and ideas that had no place in the Amish life, but where did they fit into his life? What was his greatest desire?

Memories of the day he and Ellie had taken the children to LaGrange came to his mind. Family. Home. The bright laughter in Johnny's eyes, Susan's shy smile, Danny's downy-soft hair. And Ellie.

Could he be to them what John was to his family? Could he be the one to pray for them, discipline them, lead them to a life of obedience and joy?

The window disappeared as his eyes grew wet. Could this be why *Gott* had brought him home to Indiana?

The large ward was quiet in the afternoon heat, with most of the men dozing or reading. Sitting up slowly, Bram waited for the gray fog in his head to clear. He had been given bathroom privileges just yesterday, but he was still too weak to walk down the hall alone. The young, pretty nurse who worked the day shift glanced up from her charts and walked toward his bed.

"Now, Mr. Lapp, you aren't going to try anything dangerous on your own, are you?" Her voice was light, but the set of her mouth told him she still wouldn't put up with his efforts to take care of himself.

"I just wanted to go down the hall for a bit." The gray was clearing, and he tried a smile. It worked.

The pretty nurse smiled back at him and felt his forehead in a way that was half professional check, half a caress. "I'll get a wheelchair and take you myself."

He eased into the chair she brought, glad he had the use of one hand to help steady himself. As soon as he was settled, the nurse wheeled him toward the hallway.

"I hear you're going home today," she said as the cumbersome chair rolled along the narrow hall. Bram searched through his mind for her name but came up empty.

"That's right. The doctor's letting me go to my sister's house. She'll take good care of me."

"We'll certainly miss you here." She gave him another smile as she opened the door of the bathroom for him and helped him to his feet. "You'll be all right on your own?"

Bram steadied his shaking knees. He hated being so weak, but there was no chance he was letting the nurse help him in the bathroom. "Sure, I'll be fine."

Once he finished, he was glad to sink into the wheelchair again. Who knew a man could lose his strength so quickly?

As the nurse started wheeling him back to the ward, he kept his gaze on the door at the far end of the hall. He'd be going through that door soon, free to get his life started again. Free to see Ellie again. As if his thoughts had beckoned her, the door opened and Ellie walked into the hallway, followed by her father.

At the sight of her slim form with her black bonnet and a lightweight black shawl covering the blue dress, Bram's eyes grew moist again. He leaned toward her. Couldn't this chair go any faster?

"It looks like you have visitors," the nurse said.

John stepped forward. "We're here to take Bram home, if he's ready to go."

Home. Bram sought Ellie's eyes. She glanced at him once with a tentative smile and then looked at the floor.

"The forms still need to be signed by the doctor," the nurse said. "But you can wait on the sunporch until they're ready."

"I'll wait with them," Bram said, watching Ellie. He hadn't seen her since he had woken up after his surgery—he hadn't seen anyone except John. The older man had stopped in to visit a couple times a week, taking the time to talk with Bram about nothing in particular, and always giving Bram guidance, sharing his faith and answering his questions.

After the nurse wheeled Bram to the screened-in porch that overlooked the street outside, she disappeared to find his doctor. Ellie sat in a chair near Bram, still silent, while John walked to the screened window and looked out.

"Well," he said, clearing his throat, "I think I'll go find a drink of water."

The wink he gave Bram as he left the room made Bram smile, in spite of Ellie's silence. John would be gone for a while, giving them a chance to talk.

Ellie sat with her hands folded in her lap, her eyes on the trees outside the window. Bram reached his left hand out to touch her, brushing her arm with his fingers. At his touch, she turned to him.

"I've missed you," he whispered.

Her gaze pierced him. "Are you all right?" she asked and then caught her bottom lip between her teeth.

"*Ja,* I'm feeling better every day."

"*Dat* said you were on the mend."

*"Ja."* He had to ask her. "Ellie, your *dat* came to see me often. Why didn't you come with him?"

She looked away. "I wasn't sure you wanted me to."

Didn't want her to?

"Why would you think that?" His voice rose louder than he meant, and Ellie jumped at the sound.

"I'm sorry." Bram dropped his voice. "I only meant that I wanted to see you. You could have come. I…I need you."

Ellie scooted her chair closer to his and laid her hand on his arm as it rested on the wheelchair. He pulled her hand into his lap and held it.

"Now that you've found that man, you'll be leaving, won't you?"

Bram's hand stroked her fingers one by one. *"Ne,* I won't be going back. I have a few loose ends to tie up in Chicago, but then I'll be here to stay."

Ellie turned her head away, pulling her hand from his. Chicago? Once he left, he would never come back.

"You believe me, don't you, Ellie?"

She hesitated. She had trusted him once, but now? Before she could answer, the nurse swept into the room, followed by an orderly.

"Here we are, Mr. Lapp. The forms are all signed. Mr. Stoltzfus has paid your bill, so everything is taken care of."

A week later, Bram couldn't wait any longer. He was going to see Ellie if it killed him, and if Matthew hadn't helped him harness Partner and hitch up the buggy, it just might have. He drove slowly, easing the horse around the rougher sections of the road, and made it to the Stoltzfus farm without too much pain.

As he drove up the lane, Ellie waved to him from the middle of the garden. He pulled Partner to a halt by the trough and eased down from the buggy. Ellie met him at the edge of the grass, lugging a bushel basket full of tomatoes. He started to reach out to take the basket from her, but the pain in his shoulder reminded him he was still too weak.

Ellie set the basket in the grass and gave him a smile.

"You must be feeling better, to make the trip over here." She shaded her eyes with her hand, her tanned face and sun-bleached hair telling him how many days she had worked out here in the garden.

"*Ja,* I am." Bram stepped closer to her and wiped a smudge of dirt from her cheek. "Why don't you have any help today?"

Ellie shrugged. "Benjamin is working in the fields, and *Mam* and *Dat* took the children to Lovina's. These tomatoes need to be picked, whether I do them alone or with help. It isn't hard work, but I'm ready for a rest. Would you like some tea?"

"*Ja,* that sounds good."

Bram walked with her to the *Dawdi Haus,* listening to her talk about the children, the garden, the weather… It all went over his head as he watched her expression change with each new subject. She was more beautiful than he had remembered.

He let himself down into the seat of the glider with careful movements while Ellie went into the house to fetch the tea. The walk had exhausted him. He leaned his head back and started the glider moving with his foot. Insects hummed in the sultry air, and a slight breeze played with the leaves above his head. How many nights had he lain awake in the hospital thinking about sitting on this glider with Ellie?

By the time she brought his tea to him, Bram had gotten his breath back and took the glass from her with a smile.

*"Denki."* The first swallow was as delicious as the feeling that went through him when she sat next to him.

Silence hung between them. There were so many things he wanted to say to her. He had practiced them in the buggy all the way here, but now his tongue clung to the roof of his mouth. He took another swallow of tea.

"We haven't had a chance to talk." He stopped as he felt Ellie stiffen next to him. She moved slightly so that their arms no longer touched.

"You're going to Chicago."

*"Ja.* I have to, or else Kavanaugh will go free."

"I understand that, but…" She stopped.

He turned to look at her, shifting his weight as he moved to ease the pain in his shoulder. Her eyes were wet as she steadily looked toward the barley field, the barn, the fence. Anywhere but at him.

"Ellie, what's wrong?"

"I know you miss your life in Chicago. You were only here to do your job, and you never wanted to come back to the Amish life. Once you're gone, I'll never see you again."

How could she think that?

"After I give my deposition, I'll be back."

"Your deposition? Do you mean a court trial?"

*"Ne,* not quite. The lawyers wanted me to testify against Kavanaugh for his attack on Hezekiah and for shooting me, but the Amish don't bring lawsuits against people. John helped me understand that."

Ellie looked at him. *"Dat?"*

*"Ja.* He helped me sort through how I can keep my commitments to my job and still stay faithful to

the church. Bishop approved the deposition, since I wouldn't be appearing in court to do it."

"And since you haven't taken the vows of baptism." She turned her head away from him again.

"*Ne,* not yet, but I will when I get back. Once all the ties to my past life are cut, I'll be free to commit to the church and to you."

She shook her head. "Don't lie to me again, Bram."

"I'm not lying. I never did lie to you, Ellie."

Then she looked at him, the pain in her eyes unbearable. When had she stopped trusting him?

"How can I believe you? I want to, but I can't."

Bram rubbed his forehead. This wasn't the way he wanted this conversation to go.

"What can I do to make you believe me?"

Ellie's voice was soft, strained through tears. "I don't know."

Bram reached out his hand to touch her cheek, feeling its soft warmth. He ran his finger along her jawline and caught the stray hair in his fingers. That stubborn lock of hair that never stayed in its place. Stubborn like her. He twisted it softly around one finger and then moved his hand to the back of her neck, drawing her to him. He held his lips on her cheek, breathing in her scent, and then released her.

"When I get home from Chicago, then you'll know I'm here to stay. I'll never leave you, Ellie."

## Chapter Twenty

❧

"*Memmi,* look! Look!"

Ellie turned from the sink full of dishes to see Susan holding Danny's hands as he walked from the front room into the kitchen.

"Danny's walking!"

"*Ja,* almost." A walking Danny would be twice as much work to keep track of, but she had known this day was coming. Time never stood still.

Susan let go of one of Danny's hands to brush some stray hair out of her face, and the baby plopped down on the floor.

"He'll need a bit more practice before he's ready to take off on his own."

"Can I take him outside?" Susan helped Danny stand again.

"*Ja,* but stay in the grass."

"Can we go to *Grossmutti*'s house?"

"*Ja,* sure. I'll be coming soon. Walk at the edge of the garden so Danny will have a soft place to land when he falls."

Danny crawled after Susan to the door and scooted down the porch steps. Ellie watched as Susan helped him to a standing position, and they started the tedious journey to the big house. Back at the sink she could see their entire route through the window while she finished washing the breakfast dishes. They were both growing up too quickly.

As thoughts of Bram crowded into her mind again, she scrubbed at a spot of dried egg yolk on a plate. Why couldn't she stop thinking about him? He had left for Chicago more than a week ago, and she needed to put him out of her mind. She had feared losing him to death, but losing him to the world wasn't any less painful.

The dishes done, Ellie took one last glance out the kitchen window. *Mam* had seen Susan and Danny coming and was holding the door open for them as Danny climbed up the back-porch steps toward her. She had probably already finished one canner full of tomatoes this morning, and it was time to get over there to help.

Ellie rubbed the crease between her eyebrows, easing her headache a bit. A buggy coming up the lane to the big house caught her eye and she paused. Who would be visiting this early in the morning? Matthew Beachey got down from the buggy, and then he went around to the other side to help someone else out. Had Annie come for a visit? *Ne,* it was a man.

*Dat* came out from the barn to meet them, Johnny running behind. When the man stepped forward to shake *Dat*'s hand, Ellie saw he was wearing *Englisch* clothes.

Bram. He was here.

Johnny stopped in front of him. She could almost see the shy hesitation on his face before Bram bent down to gather the boy to him with one arm. Johnny flung his arms around Bram's neck.

The sight of Bram and Johnny's reunion held her captive at the window. Why hadn't she seen how completely Bram filled the empty place in Johnny's heart? Her son didn't just need a father; he needed Bram.

She needed Bram.

Ellie wiped tears from her cheeks with quick motions. If he meant to stay, then why was he back to wearing his *Englisch* clothes? He had to be here to say goodbye.

How could she bear that?

"Bram, I missed you."

The boy's words, whispered in his ear, brought tears to Bram's eyes.

Ignoring the ever-present pain in his shoulder, Bram held Johnny to himself for a moment with his good arm and then pulled back far enough to look into his face.

"Have you been taking good care of your *memmi?*"

Johnny nodded, his eyes shining. "*Ja,* Bram. I always take good care of her."

"And your sister? And Danny?"

"*Ja,* Bram."

"That's my boy." Bram half choked on the words.

Would Johnny be his boy? He hoped so. It was what he had been praying for.

Before he could stand again, Susan appeared at his side. Her shy smile told him just how much she had missed him, too. He wrapped his arm around her small frame and held her close, her little-girl body as fragile as a newborn chick. He wished he could lift her up in both arms, but that would have to wait until he had healed more.

He stood to greet Elizabeth as she came out of the house carrying Danny, but he couldn't help glancing beyond her through the screen door. Where was Ellie?

"Come up to the porch," John said, ushering them all toward the shaded front of the house. "We have some tea, don't we, Elizabeth?"

"For sure we do. I'll bring it out."

As Bram hesitated, John turned to him with a smile. "We'll wait for you on the porch, Bram. Why don't you go to the *Dawdi Haus* and tell Ellie you're here?"

Bram grinned at John, thankful the older man understood. He wished he was strong enough to run along the lane, but he had to content himself with a slow walk.

At the edge of the garden, Bram paused to straighten his jacket. The *Englisch* suit was uncomfortable, but he had insisted that Matthew bring him straight to the Stoltzfuses' from the train station. He had to see Ellie.

Movement at the *Dawdi Haus* kitchen window told him she knew he was there, but he still hesitated. What could he say to her? Just blurt out how much he loved her? That he wanted to marry her?

*Ne,* he had to take it slow, win back her trust. He took a deep breath and whooshed it out.

Even when he'd faced Kavanaugh straight on, he hadn't been this scared. The worst Kavanaugh could do was shoot him.

Ellie could sentence him to life without her.

Swallowing hard, Bram adjusted his hat. The distance to the back porch wasn't long, but before he reached it, the kitchen door opened. Ellie. She stood in the doorway watching him, her face unreadable.

"Good morning, Ellie."

"Hello, Bram." Her voice was cool.

His mouth was as dry as cotton.

"I've missed you." He tried smiling at her, but his face refused to obey. "Will you come sit on the glider with me?"

"*Ja,* I will."

Bram brushed a couple fallen leaves off the glider as they sat. Ellie gripped the edge of the seat on either side of her skirt, betraying how nervous she was. Somehow the thought comforted him.

The summer locusts began their daily serenade in the trees at the edge of the field.

"Six weeks till frost." He felt like kicking himself. Where had that come from? He wasn't here to talk about insects.

"What?"

"Something my *mam* used to say when she heard the locusts in August. There's six weeks until frost."

"*Ja,* you're right. My *mam* says the same."

They fell into silence again. Bram moved the glider with his foot. Where should he start?

"I've been—"

"*Dat* says—"

They both stopped.

"You go on, Ellie. What were you going to say?"

"Just that *Dat* says your farm is doing well."

"*Ja.* I'm thankful John and the other men kept it going for me."

"With Partner over here, you had no animals for them to tend to, so it wasn't too much work."

More silence.

Bram pushed his foot against the ground, setting the glider into motion again.

"I have to tell you something."

She tensed, but didn't look at him.

"I've requested to be baptized." Her head shot toward him, her eyes round. "Bishop has been coming to Matthew's for my instruction, and I'm joining the community next Sunday."

\* \* \*

Ellie waited for his teasing grin. He wasn't serious, was he?

"You're joining the church?" she asked, watching his face.

Bram smiled, his eyes warm and sincere. "*Ja,* at the next Sunday meeting."

Ellie gripped the edge of the glider seat harder, willing her trembling hands to still. A thin shaft of light pierced her thoughts. He wasn't saying goodbye; he was staying.

"But I thought…well, your trip to Chicago, your *Englisch* clothes…"

Bram reached up, pulled off the necktie and stuffed it into his pocket.

"I didn't let Matthew take me home to change. I had to see you."

"Bishop is allowing you to join the church even though you shot a man?"

"I had to shoot him. He had hurt you, and he intended to kill all of us. It was my job to stop him, one way or another. He didn't leave me any choice."

"But won't you keep working for the FBI?"

Bram's left hand closed over hers, warm, strong and confident.

"Ellie, that life is behind me now. I've confessed everything to the Bishop and your father. What's more important is that *Gott* knows everything. When Kavanaugh found me, I was on my way to find him and have it out with him, once and for all." He squeezed her hand. "I knew I wasn't going to survive. I knew I'd never see you again. But I did survive. It's like I have a new life, and I don't want to waste a minute of it."

His clear, steady eyes told her more than his words, but she had to ask...

"If it happened again—if you run across someone from your past like that—would you do it again? Could you shoot a man?"

Bram looked at the ground, his grip on her hand tightening. "I can't say for sure unless I was in that situation again." He looked back at her, his eyes moist. "But I hope I would act as *Gott* desires, that He would give me the strength to do the right thing. I still believe I need to protect my family, my friends, but I hope I would be able to do it in a way that protects the other person also. That's all I can promise."

"And Bishop believes that's enough?"

"*Ja.* He says desiring to obey *Gott* and praying for His help is as much as any man can promise."

Bram leaned across her lap, taking her other hand from the edge of the glider. He cupped her two small hands in his large one. Ellie let them rest there, birds surrounded by a protecting hedge.

"I know this is where I belong, Ellie, with you and with this community."

The small shaft of light widened, plunging into her soul with the dawn of understanding.

"You're really staying?"

"*Ja,* Ellie." He rubbed his thumb along the side of her finger, his touch sending tingles up her arm. "I've done some terrible things, Ellie, but I've never lied to you."

She looked into his eyes, meeting the hope she saw there.

"I was wrong not to trust you, Bram." *Ja,* she should have known she could always trust him.

Bram raised his hand to her face, catching the stray lock of hair.

"Ellie, I couldn't bear to live without you." His voice was a whisper as he drew her close.

"You don't have to."

Bram's kiss was gentle, tentative. He brushed her lips with his and then drew her to him in a close embrace. Ellie lost herself as he held her with his good arm, pressing her ear against his chest to listen to the reassuring beat of his heart. She could rest here forever.

Two weeks later, Bram sighed as he pushed away his empty plate and leaned back in the chair. Miriam's sugar-cream pie was the best he had ever tasted.

"There's another piece left," Miriam said, pushing the dish toward Bram.

"*Ne, denki,* I couldn't eat another bite."

"I'll take it." Reuben reached for the dish and dug into the last piece as if he was starving. He shouldn't be. He had been living with Hezekiah and Miriam since the accident, and Miriam had doted on him with her cooking.

Hezekiah chuckled. "I sure like that young man's appetite."

As Miriam started clearing the table, Bram turned to the older man. "I've told you what I have in mind, and you've looked at the house plans." Miriam paused to listen to Bram, and he glanced up at her. "What do you think?"

"Well," Hezekiah said, reaching for Miriam's hand, "it was hard to hand the work over to Reuben this summer, but I have to admit the rest has done me good. I feel better than I have in a long time. I know Miriam has worried about what would become of us when I couldn't work anymore, especially after we lost Daniel." He looked at Bram, his eyes bright and sure. "We'll move in as soon as you're ready for us."

Miriam squeezed Hezekiah's shoulder. "*Ach,* and I have to thank you, Bram. To live so close to Ellie and the children…" She smiled as she busied herself with the dishes.

"Now, don't say anything to Ellie yet." Bram looked at Reuben. "She doesn't know anything about this, and I don't want her to until I get a chance to tell her."

Reuben grinned at him as he got up from the table to head back to his chores. "You had better let her in on the secret soon, then. I know my sister. If she hears a rumor about a new *Dawdi Haus* being built at your place, she'll ferret out the truth faster than anybody."

Bram went out to his buggy, leaving Miriam and Hezekiah to discuss their packing. He hoped to get the *Dawdi Haus* built before winter, but he had one more thing to do first. It was time to let Ellie in on his plans.

He couldn't believe he hadn't thought of this solution before. Having Hezekiah and Miriam close would help ease Ellie's mind, and he was looking forward to having the older man's help to build up his farmland. Hezekiah may not be able to walk behind a plow anymore, but his knowledge of farming would never go to waste.

Partner pranced and blew a couple times before he settled into his steady trot, enjoying the cooler fall weather as much as he did. Bram settled in for the drive to the Stoltzfus farm, watching the corn crops in the fields he passed.

It had been a long, hot, dry summer, but it looked as if the farmers would have enough of a harvest to survive. His own crop would give him enough to use for the winter and enough seed for next spring, but nothing extra to sell.

It didn't matter. Bram still couldn't shake the feeling that he had opened a door and discovered a wonderful new world. Now if he could only convince Ellie to share it with him.

He had spent nearly every evening with her since coming home from Chicago. He would meet her on her glider at dusk, after the children had gone to bed, and they'd sit for an hour or more.

Sometimes they talked. Bram thought they'd run out of things to talk about, but they never did. He grinned to himself. They wouldn't run out of things to talk about in a hundred years.

Other times they sat quietly, holding hands, or with Bram's arm around Ellie's shoulder, while he kept the glider swinging with one foot. He wouldn't get tired of that in a hundred years, either. He'd have to make sure he built a glider like that for their own place.

Their own place.

Bram chirruped at Partner, suddenly anxious to hear Ellie's answer to his question.

The tomato plants had started producing again with the onset of cooler weather. Ellie pushed aside the old, dry stems from the summer to find the tomatoes that grew amid the new, green leaves. A second chance at life brought new fruitfulness to the tomatoes.

Ellie glanced toward the glider at the side of the *Dawdi Haus*. The tomatoes weren't the only things with a second chance. She couldn't keep a smile off her face at the thought. How would she ever have known love could be so sweet a second time? She couldn't bear the thought of waiting until this evening to see Bram again.

"*Memmi,* help!" Susan's cry came to her ears yet again.

*Ach,* there was Danny, heading for the cow pen at the side of the barn. Ever since he had learned to walk, the cow pen was his favorite destination. Until school started last week, Susan had helped Mandy or Rebecca watch the toddler while Ellie did her chores, but now that Susan was on her own, Danny was proving to be a handful.

Ellie caught him just as he reached the fence and swung him up in her arms as he giggled. The little stinker! He liked being caught as much as he wanted to see the cows. She tickled his belly to hear him laugh again as she carried him back to the toys Susan had set up in the grassy yard.

"*Ach,* Danny, you play here with Susan for a little while longer while I pick the rest of the tomatoes."

"Won't he just run away again?" Susan tried to get Danny to play with a toy cow.

"*Ja,* probably. Just do like you've been doing. Call me when he does."

Buggy wheels in the lane caught her attention.

"*Memmi,* look. It's Bram." Susan ran to the hitching rail by the *Dawdi Haus* to wait for him.

Ellie forgot the tomatoes when she saw Bram. He glanced her way with his crooked grin as he pulled Partner to a stop, then turned his attention to Susan while he tied the horse.

"This is a nice surprise," Ellie greeted him as he held Susan up to give Partner a pat on the nose.

"I have another surprise for you," he murmured in her ear as he gave her cheek a kiss. "Do you think your *mam* can take care of Susan and Danny?"

Bram wouldn't wait for her to change out of her work

dress or even wash her hands. As soon as the children were taken care of, she was in his buggy and they were heading down the road.

Ellie sat close to him, her hand tucked in his arm.

"Where are we going?"

Bram leaned over and kissed her *kapp*.

"I have something to show you at the farm."

"Will I like it?"

"*Ja,* I think you will. But the more you pester me with questions, the longer it will take to get there."

Ellie laughed. "I think Partner could take us there himself, no matter how many questions I ask you."

Bram just grinned and slapped the reins on the horse's back.

Ellie hadn't been to Bram's farm since the shooting, but everything looked like a normal, quiet Amish farm as they drove up the short lane. She looked toward the house. Which stove had he ended up buying? And was the sitting room livable? It must be. Bram had been settled there for several weeks. She climbed down from the buggy and started toward the house.

"*Ne,* not that way. Come with me."

He took her hand and led her around the house and down a slope to a level spot near the creek.

"What do you think?"

Ellie looked around. The place was quiet and secluded, even though it was still close to the farmhouse. "It's nice, I guess. Why?"

He let go of her hand and paced along an imaginary line. "This is the front, and the door will be right here. The front porch will go around the corner—" he turned and paced along another line between her and the creek "—this way, so you can look out on the creek in the evening."

"You're building a house here? Why do you need another house?"

Bram acted as if she hadn't spoken. He turned another right angle and paced along a third side of the square.

"The back door will be here, with a walk going to the privy." He gestured toward the outhouse that sat at an equal distance between his imaginary house and the farmhouse up the slope. "And then on this side, there'll be space for a garden."

A garden? He was planning a house here, but that garden space looked too small for a family. "Bram, you already have a garden."

He walked back to her and took her hand again.

"*Ja,* I already have a garden, but Miriam likes to plant flowers, doesn't she?"

Ellie stopped, smiling at his sly grin. "Are you trying to tell me something?"

"I've already talked to Hezekiah and Miriam, and they're pleased about it."

"About what?"

"This." He swept his hand around them to take in the proposed house he had laid out for her. "This will be their *Dawdi Haus.* They're going to move in as soon as we can get it built."

Ellie's eyes blurred. He was doing this for a couple he wasn't related to? Why would he do that? But if they lived here, with Bram, she wouldn't have any more worries about them. They would be so close, only a couple miles away, and she'd be able to see them more often. Every day if she wanted to.

Bram's finger slipped under her chin and lifted it so she looked into his eyes. "Miriam can't wait to live next door to you and the children."

He moved his hand to the side of her face, and she felt him tuck the strand of hair behind her ear. Her breath caught as she realized what he had said. "What do you mean, next door?"

"Ellie," he said, his voice soft, intimate. He leaned closer to her. "I love you, and I want you to be my wife. Will you marry me?"

He smiled his crooked grin, but this time it was unsure, hopeful. She hadn't noticed the way his beard hid his dimple until now. He had stopped shaving again after the shooting, and his beard was getting so long he looked like a married man, but that dimple was still there. A secret they shared.

Just the first of all the secrets they would share. A wave swept over her, leaving her breathless. Bram wanted her to be his. How could she bear this joy?

"*Ja,* Bram, *ja.* I'll marry you."

He pulled her close to him, and she molded her body to his, pressing her ear against his chest to listen to his heartbeat.

Bram was kissing her forehead, her nose, nudging her face up with each kiss until he caught her lips with his. She lifted her hand to pull him closer as she let herself drown in his kiss. This was her Bram.

# Epilogue

"Are you nervous?" Mandy's question after the family's morning prayers were over made Ellie laugh.

"Why should I be nervous? This is my second wedding day."

"Ellie won't have to be worried about anything," *Mam* said as she finished washing the dishes. "Everything is ready, thanks to all the willing helpers we've had."

*Mam* dried her hands and started the day's work with her usual brisk enthusiasm.

"Rebecca, remember, you and your friends are in charge of the little ones today. And, Mandy, will you please keep an eye out to give them a hand if they need it?"

"*Ja, Mam,* you can count on it."

*Mam* smiled at both girls. "I know I can. Now, let's bring up the jars of chow-chow from the cellar and start the chicken frying...."

*Mam* shooed the girls down the cellar steps in front of her, but turned to Ellie before following them.

"I have prayed for this day, daughter. *Gott*'s blessings will go with you."

"I know, *Memmi*. He is blessing our family already."

Ellie was alone in the kitchen—alone for the last time before her sisters and aunts started arriving to help with the wedding dinner. She looked around the spacious room. More than anywhere else in the world, this kitchen meant home and family. She had missed the significance of the kitchen before her first wedding. Perhaps she had taken it for granted, but she never would again. It was the center of the home.

She smoothed her hand along the grain of the old table and then rested it on the back of *Dat*'s chair. *Dat* had made this chair a place of humility, mercy and grace. She had learned about *Gott* as she listened to *Dat* read from the Bible as he sat here, and as he read their morning and evening prayers while they each knelt at their chairs.

Her whole life had been bracketed by *Dat*'s prayers at the beginning and end of every day. Even when she and Daniel had been married, he had included their names in his prayers just as he included Zac, Lovina, Sally and their families as they married one by one. Tomorrow he would start including Bram and their family in those same prayers.

Bram had taken her with him last night as they moved her things into their new house. The new table in the kitchen was as big as this one. His grin when she had protested that the table was much too large for the five of them still made her smile. They both hoped it wouldn't be too large for long.

Tears of thanksgiving came to Ellie's eyes as she thought of Bram's chair at the head of that long table. He had built a shelf on the wall behind his chair and placed his Bible there, along with the copy of *Die Ernsthafte Christenpflicht*, the prayer book *Dat* had given him and the copy of the *Ausbund* hymnal that had been her gift to him. Bram was going to be a wonderful husband and father, leading his family as well as her *Dat* ever had.

Even as early as it was, the community would soon start arriving. First the women who would help prepare the huge amounts of food they would need to feed dinner and supper to two hundred people, and then the other families.

Then at nine o'clock the service would begin. She and Bram would miss the singing, as they would spend that time with Bishop Yoder, receiving the final counsel before taking their vows. Then the sermons would begin, the sermons that would lead the entire church in reflecting on the meaning of marriage and the solemnity and permanence of the vows she and Bram would soon take.

Ellie peeked in the doorway of the front room. All the walls had been pushed back to make room for the benches for the service, as if it were a Sunday meeting. She leaned her head on the door frame, her mind filling the benches with her family and loved ones of the community.

After the sermons, she and Bram would stand before the church with their witnesses—Matthew, Annie, Lovina and Noah—and then they would say their simple vows, promising to love and bear and be patient with each other until death.

Could she love Bram?

*Ach, ja.* She already loved him with all her heart.

Could she be patient with him?

*Ja.* Her love would provide the patience she would need.

Could she bear him? Bear his bad moods as well as

his good? Bear his sorrows as well as his joys? Bear his failures as well as his successes?

*Ja.* She could bear anything at Bram's side.

The back door opened with a sharp squeak of the hinges, and Ellie turned to see Bram filling the doorway. His face broke into a grin when he saw her. "I hoped I'd find you here."

"Couldn't you wait until the wedding?"

"*Ne,* not today. I wanted to be alone with you for just a minute, before everyone else gets here. You know we won't have a chance until late tonight."

"A chance for what?"

Bram's crooked grin twitched, and he crossed the room to her. "A chance for one more kiss before you become my wife."

Ellie rose on tiptoe to peck him on the cheek. "There you go."

Bram growled as he pulled her into his arms. "You know I want more of a kiss than that."

And then he kissed her with a passion she had never felt before.

*Ach, ja.* She could bear even this.

\* \* \* \* \*

*If you enjoyed this story by Jan Drexler,*
*be sure to check out the other books this month*
*from Love Inspired Historical!*

Dear Readers,

Thank you for choosing *The Prodigal Son Returns*. Ellie's story grew out of my grandmother's memories of raising her five children in northern Indiana during the Great Depression of the 1930s.

While not Amish, my grandparents were Plain people—Brethren—and lived in much the same way as Ellie's *Englisch* tenants, the Brennemans. My grandfather worked at whatever job he could find, from helping out on a neighbor's farm, to butchering, to working in the rubber factories in Goshen. My grandmother raised the children, planted gardens, preserved jars and jars of vegetables, fought to keep the family horses from eating the garden and fed her family from the leftovers my grandfather brought home from his butchering jobs. She also spent hours sewing—not only for her own family, but for families in need.

The 1930s were hard times, but also good times, as families relied on God and their neighbors to survive. May we learn to do the same in our own time.

I would love to hear from you. You can contact me on my website, www.JanDrexler.com, or on Facebook at Jan Drexler, Author.

Blessings to you and yours,

*Jan Drexler*

## Questions for Discussion

1. In the opening of the story, Bram has returned to his Amish roots. Have you ever tried to move back home after being away for several years? What changes did you see in your home? What changes had happened in your life during those years?

2. Ellie is reluctant to accept Bram into her life at first because he dresses and acts like an outsider. Was she right to keep her distance from him? How have you let first impressions determine how you treated a new acquaintance?

3. Bram grew up in an Amish family, but one that doesn't fit our modern stereotypes. What is your impression of the Amish? Do you assume every Amish family is the same?

4. Ellie tries to assuage the guilt she feels over her husband's death by doing the right thing—she obeys the church teachings, tries to be the perfect mother and daughter—but none of those things help ease her guilty conscience. Have you ever felt a similar way? What did you do about it?

5. Ellie's big step comes when she turns toward God in trust. Has something happened in your past that keeps you from trusting Him in some area of your life?

6. As Bram and Ellie grow closer, many barriers stand in their way, but the biggest is his reluctance to join

the church. Do you think it's important for couples to be united in their beliefs?

7. Bram fills a hole in the hearts of Ellie's children. If she hadn't met Bram, do you think Ellie could have provided everything her children needed without marrying again?

8. Levi Zook has tried to court Ellie, but she has turned him down because she doesn't love him. Was she right to wait for love, even when her family and church were urging her to marry for the sake of her children?

9. The growing romantic love between Ellie and Bram isn't the only kind of love in this story. What other kinds of love do you see displayed in Ellie's life?

10. Bram has had to give up many modern conveniences to go back to living the Amish life. Have you ever thought about what it would be like to live as an Amish person? What would be the hardest thing for you to give up?

11. When Bram faces the question of joining the church, his first reaction is that he doesn't want to give up his freedom and independence to become part of this close-knit community. But after John Stoltzfus visits him in the hospital, he changes his mind. Is there someone who has been a mentor for you? Is there someone you know who is looking for a mentor?

# REQUEST YOUR FREE BOOKS!

## 2 FREE INSPIRATIONAL NOVELS
## PLUS 2
## FREE
## MYSTERY GIFTS

*Love Inspired*
# HISTORICAL
### INSPIRATIONAL HISTORICAL ROMANCE

---

**YES!** Please send me 2 FREE Love Inspired® Historical novels and my 2 FREE mystery gifts (gifts are worth about $10). After receiving them, if I don't wish to receive any more books, I can return the shipping statement marked "cancel." If I don't cancel, I will receive 4 brand-new novels every month and be billed just $4.74 per book in the U.S. or $5.24 per book in Canada. That's a saving of at least 21% off the cover price. It's quite a bargain! Shipping and handling is just 50¢ per book in the U.S. and 75¢ per book in Canada.* I understand that accepting the 2 free books and gifts places me under no obligation to buy anything. I can always return a shipment and cancel at any time. Even if I never buy another book, the two free books and gifts are mine to keep forever.

102/302 IDN F5CN

| Name | (PLEASE PRINT) | |
|------|------|------|

| Address | | Apt. # |
|------|------|------|

| City | State/Prov. | Zip/Postal Code |
|------|------|------|

Signature (if under 18, a parent or guardian must sign)

### Mail to the Harlequin® Reader Service:
**IN U.S.A.:** P.O. Box 1867, Buffalo, NY 14240-1867
**IN CANADA:** P.O. Box 609, Fort Erie, Ontario L2A 5X3

**Want to try two free books from another series?**
**Call 1-800-873-8635 or visit www.ReaderService.com.**

\* Terms and prices subject to change without notice. Prices do not include applicable taxes. Sales tax applicable in N.Y. Canadian residents will be charged applicable taxes. Offer not valid in Quebec. This offer is limited to one order per household. Not valid for current subscribers to Love Inspired Historical books. All orders subject to credit approval. Credit or debit balances in a customer's account(s) may be offset by any other outstanding balance owed by or to the customer. Please allow 4 to 6 weeks for delivery. Offer available while quantities last.

**Your Privacy**—The Harlequin® Reader Service is committed to protecting your privacy. Our Privacy Policy is available online at www.ReaderService.com or upon request from the Harlequin Reader Service.

We make a portion of our mailing list available to reputable third parties that offer products we believe may interest you. If you prefer that we not exchange your name with third parties, or if you wish to clarify or modify your communication preferences, please visit us at www.ReaderService.com/consumerschoice or write to us at Harlequin Reader Service Preference Service, P.O. Box 9062, Buffalo, NY 14269. Include your complete name and address.

LIH13R

SPECIAL EXCERPT FROM

*Love Inspired* HISTORICAL

*Is Daisy's next-door neighbor more than she
bargained for?*

*Read on for a sneak peek at
THE BRIDE NEXT DOOR by Winnie Griggs,
available June 2013 from Love Inspired Historical.*

Daisy frowned as she heard her visitor leave. For all his
fine airs, Mr. Fulton could be mighty rude. He'd all but said
he didn't believe her to be a good cook and didn't think
she'd be able to open her own restaurant. And if that wasn't
bad enough, she'd seen the way he looked down his nose
at her.

Ah, well, Mr. Fulton didn't really know her yet. She
couldn't really blame him for being in a bad mood. And she
shouldn't forget that he *had* helped her out from under that
shelving, so she should be grateful.

She'd just have to prove to Mr. Fulton and the rest of the
townsfolk that she aimed to be a good citizen. Starting with
making this place clean and inviting. Too bad she didn't have
a broom and mop yet. For now she'd just make do as best she
could.

She grabbed her bedroll, but before she could get the
makeshift bed unrolled, her neighbor returned, a scowl on
his face.

"Mr. Fulton, I'm so sorry if I'm making too much noise
again. I–"

He shook his head impatiently. She noticed he was carrying
a broom and a cloth-wrapped bundle.

He set the broom against the wall. "I thought you might be

able to make use of this," he said. Then he thrust the parcel her way. "I also brought this for you."

His tone was short, gruff, as if he wasn't happy.

She unwrapped the parcel and was surprised to find an apple, a slab of cheese and a thick slice of bread inside. "Why, thank you. This is so kind of you."

He waved aside her thanks. "It's just a few bits left over from my dinner."

"Still, it's very neighborly."

But he still wore that impatient scowl. "Yes, well, I'll leave you to get settled in. See that you keep the noise down."

She smothered a sigh, wondering why he had to spoil his gesture with a grumpy attitude. "Good night."

"Good night."

As she watched him leave this time, her smile returned. Regardless of his sour expression, Mr. Fulton had been quite kind. Perhaps she'd already made her first friend.

*Will Daisy find a way to win the heart of Mr. Fulton?*

*Don't miss THE BRIDE NEXT DOOR by Winnie Griggs, on sale June 2013 wherever Love Inspired Historical books are sold!*